ISAAC BASHEVIS SINGER emigrated to the United States
from Warsaw in 1935. Winner of the 1978 Nobel Prize for
Literature, and the National Book Award, he died in 1991.
Among his great body of work are such masterpieces as *Satan
in Goray*; *The Magician of Lublin*; *The Spinoza of Market Street*;
The Slave; *Gimpel, the Fool*; and *Enemies: A Love Story* (Signet).
His *Death of Methusaleh and Other Stories, The King of the Fields*,
and *Scum* are available in Plume editions.

BOOKS BY ISAAC BASHEVIS SINGER

NOVELS
The Manor {I. The Manor   II. The Estate}
The Family Moskat · The Magician of Lublin
Satan in Goray · The Slave
Enemies, A Love Story · Shosha
The Penitent · The King of the Fields · Scum

STORIES
Gimpel the Fool · A Friend of Kafka · Short Friday
The Séance · The Spinoza of Market Street · Passions
A Crown of Feathers · Old Love · The Image
The Death of Methuselah

MEMOIRS
In My Father's Court

FOR CHILDREN
A Day of Pleasure · The Fools of Chelm
Mazel and Shlimazel or The Milk of a Lioness
When Shlemiel Went to Warsaw
A Tale of Three Wishes · Elijah the Slave
Joseph and Koza or The Sacrifice to the Vistula
Alone in the Wild Forest · The Wicked City
Naftali the Storyteller and His Horse, Sus
Why Noah Chose the Dove
The Power of Light
The Golem

COLLECTIONS
The Collected Stories
Stories for Children
An Isaac Bashevis Singer Reader

ISAAC BASHEVIS SINGER

THE

CERTIFICATE

TRANSLATED BY LEONARD WOLF

A PLUME BOOK

PLUME
Published by the Penguin Group
Penguin Books USA Inc., 375 Hudson Street, New York, New York 10014, U.S.A.
Penguin Books Ltd, 27 Wrights Lane, London W8 5TZ, England
Penguin Books Australia Ltd, Ringwood, Victoria, Australia
Penguin Books Canada Ltd, 10 Alcorn Avenue, Toronto, Canada M4V 3B2
Penguin Books (N.Z.) Ltd, 182-190 Wairau Road, Auckland 10, New Zealand

Penguin Books Ltd, Registered Offices: Harmondsworth, Middlesex, England

Published by Plume, an imprint of Dutton Signet, a division of Penguin Books
USA Inc. Published by arrangement with Farrar, Straus, & Giroux, Inc.

First Plume Printing, November, 1993
10 9 8 7 6 5 4 3 2 1

 REGISTERED TRADEMARK—MARCA REGISTRADA

LIBRARY OF CONGRESS CATALOGING-IN-PUBLICATION DATA
Singer, Isaac Bashevis, 1904–1991
    [Tsertifikat. English]
    The certificate / Isaac Bashevis Singer : translated by Leonard
Wolf.
        p.   cm.
    Previously published : New York : Farrar, Straus, Giroux, 1992.
    ISBN 0-452-27092-8
    I. Title.
    [PJ5129.S49T7513   1993]
    839'.0933—dc20   93-24023
                                                        CIP

Printed in the United States of America
Original hardcover designed by Fritz Metsch

PUBLISHER'S NOTE
This is a work of fiction. Names, characters, places, and incidents either are the
product of the author's imagination or are used fictitiously, and any resemblance
to actual persons, living or dead, events, or locales is entirely coincidental.

THE CERTIFICATE

I

"IT'S late—it's late for everything," I said to myself. In those days, I often spoke to myself. At eighteen and a half one is no longer a day student, and it's even too late to learn a trade. In a couple of years I'd be drafted. I'd lost the best years of my life reading books without much purpose, digging away at eternal questions, losing myself in sexual fantasies, and battling countless neuroses.

In my backpack—among several dirty shirts, handkerchiefs, and socks—there were a few manuscripts in Hebrew and Yiddish, an unfinished novel, an essay on Spinoza and the Cabala, and a miniature collection of what I called "poems in prose." I had already concluded that not one of my writings was publishable, having myself analyzed the faults of my belletristic productions. A writer as well known as Dr. Ashkenazi had told me that my essay was childish; a famous Hebrew poet had sharply criticized my Hebrew writings. They all had the same thing to say—I needed to perfect myself, I was not yet mature.

But mature or immature, I'd had nothing to eat all day. I also had to find someplace to spend the night. In addition to what was in my backpack, I carried two books, remnants from my father's bookshelves during the time we had lived in Warsaw, books that I meant to sell. Good Lord, how long ago that childhood in Warsaw seemed.

At eighteen and a half, I had already lived through entire epochs. I was born in the period of the Russo-Japanese War. Ten years later, the Great War broke out and the Germans entered

Warsaw. In less than nineteen years, I had lived through the February Revolution, the October Revolution, the Polish-Bolshevik War. I'd spent four years in that godforsaken small town Byaledrevne. Then I returned to Warsaw and studied in a normal school and had even been employed as a teacher of sorts in a town in Greater Poland. I had begun writing in Hebrew, then changed over to Yiddish. I'd been persecuted by Hasidim and been consoled by my readings in Spinoza's *Ethics*. I had even tasted the joys of love. Imagine—I was hardly nineteen years old. There were times when I thought of myself as an old man.

On this gloomy autumn day, there were gray and yellowish skies lowering over the rooftops of Warsaw. At intervals lights were being turned on in store windows. The sidewalks were still damp from the rain. Streetcars jangled by, and the wheels of droshkies, wagons, and trucks rattled over the cobbled streets. Throngs of people moved along the sidewalks carrying walking sticks, packages, umbrellas.

It appeared to be the same Warsaw that I remembered from 1917. But the five-year interval had brought about so many changes: there now were taxis in the streets; the German traffic director had disappeared, replaced by a Polish policeman; Russian signs had been repainted and were now in Polish. What else? Radio was new—if you put earpieces to your ears, you could hear music, speeches, all sorts of Polish dance melodies, and songs from the theater and operettas. In dance halls people were dancing the shimmy, the fox-trot, the Charleston. Women were wearing short dresses ending at their knees and hats that looked like overturned pots. The press was full of talk about the League of Nations and the terrible German inflation.

One had to have come from Warsaw to notice the changes. In my time in Warsaw there had been no Boy Scouts, no Jewish youths with the Star of David on their caps, no grown young women wearing socks. Students wore red-and-white hats instead of uniforms. Women were now studying at the university. The Russian flag had been replaced by the Polish, and the Russian eagle had become a Polish eagle. At the entrance to the Saxon Gardens there were no longer gendarmes to prevent caftan-clad Jews and Jewish women, wearing caps or wigs, from going in. Most visible of all the changes were the new hairdos of the young women which were now shorn *au garçon*, with their ears exposed. Polish officers with their square caps were continually buttoning their buttons as they exchanged salutes. Because of the rent control that had predominated since 1914, houses in Warsaw had become run down. Depending on how you looked at it, the city appeared either old or raggedly young. It was still hard to believe that Poland, after a hundred and fifty years of foreign domination, was an independent nation once more.

The Jews had received the Balfour Declaration from England, and the Jewish High Commissioner who ruled in the land of Israel was called upon to read the Torah on Saturdays. The Jewish streets of Warsaw swarmed with guardians, pioneers, and revisionists—as they called themselves. The strikers and revolutionaries of the 1905 Revolution were free again and openly carrying on propaganda. Thousands of young Jewish men and women had become Communists, and many of them were already behind bars in the "Arsenal" or in the Mokatower Jail.

Well, knowing all this did not make for a full belly. Pangs of hunger gnawed at me: I sniffed the aromas of coffee, fresh bagels, cheesecake, and a sort of *kichel* baked in oil, whose odor I remembered from the time I was a schoolboy. I did not have so much as a single pfennig (in Poland at this time, German money was still current). I carried two of my father's books: *The Responsa of Rabbi Akiva Eiger* and *The Shitah Mekubbetzot*, hoping to sell them.

That's how my circumstances (or moduses, as Spinoza calls them) were arranged: once again I had to leave the city to which I had struggled to return ever since I had failed so badly as a teacher of boys that the secretary of the Mizrachi had refused to give me a reference. My parents and my younger brother, Moishe, had settled in a tiny Polish town in Galicia. They had written to say that I would be welcome to visit only if I grew a beard and sidecurls. All the members of their community were followers of the Belzer rebbe, half of whom made a living as religious copyists. I knew, too, that my parents were oppressively poor.

Walking the streets, I fantasized a miracle: I meet a young woman in Warsaw who has her own room, comes from a rich family, is an orphan. I teach her Hebrew and Yiddish; she teaches me German, French, English. She inspires me to write a novel, which she translates, and I become famous. I am known as a second Knut Hamsun. I am ready to marry her, but she says, "What's the point? We can live together without all those ceremonies. What matters is that we love each other." She looks just like Lena, the watchmaker's daughter in Byaledrevne. We travel abroad together, visiting Berlin, Paris, London, even New York and Hollywood.

I knew that such fantasies could harm me and that, in my critical situation, I must be able to think clearly. But the truth is that I was a victim of compulsive thoughts. Within me there was a dybbuk speaking—or several dybbuks. I imagined I had discovered a nutriment which, on tasting it, renders one all-powerful and all-knowing. With no need for study, I would make one discovery after another, speak forgotten tongues, be able to pinpoint treasures buried on land or sunk in the sea, be able to read other people's thoughts and foretell the future. And why stop there? I would fly to the moon or to the planet Mars, where I would found a Jewish state. I would become king of the earth, of the entire solar system, and would live in a palace (suspended in midair) with my eighteen wives, beauties selected from all over the world. And Lena would be my queen.

"Hey!" I was nearly run down by a taxi. That's all I needed. The car came so close I could smell its gas. I must put an end to those fantasies. Pallot was right: such thoughts tend to inebriate the mind and to stupefy thought. Great men like Newton, Copernicus, Galileo, Einstein did not fantasize; they used their spiritual energies to discover important truths.

As I approached Nalewki Street, a young man stopped me and asked, "Do you want to exchange your currency?" He was a black marketeer who wanted dollars for Polish marks. I laughed inwardly and said, "I have no marks or dollars."

"What kinds of books are those?" he asked. I showed him the two volumes.

"Do you want to sell them?"

"Yes."

He leafed through the books. He nodded his head and stroked his small beard. "Whose owner's stamp is this?" he asked.

"It's my father's."

"Is that so? I know your father."

I felt myself getting unusually warm. "Yes?"

"He's still living?"

I could hardly repress my tears. "Yes, thank God. He's a rabbi somewhere in Galicia. How do you come to know him?"

"He once listened to me recite. Maier Yoel Shvartsshtayn used to give a watch to anyone who could learn fifty pages of Gemara by heart. One had to have letters from three rabbis."

A tremor raced up and down my spine. I thought my family had been entirely forgotten in Warsaw. Think how much had happened in the five years since we left—wars, epidemics, hunger—but here stood a young man who knew who I was! Perhaps he could help me. I could see that he was poor: his coat was so shabby that its coarse lining showed through, his boots were patched, his face was pale. He had a small blond beard at the tip of his chin, and his eyes, under his blond eyebrows, were close together and had a worried look. He asked, "Why are you selling the books? You won't get much for them."

"I need the money."

He blinked at me under contracted brows. "Yes, I remember you, a little boy with red sidecurls. You were running about in the studyhouse. Is your mother still living?"

"Yes, thank God."

"There were such dreadful illnesses then—people died like flies. Why aren't you with your father?"

"You can see for yourself that I'm not dressed like an Orthodox Jew."

"What are you, a student?"

"I want to be a writer."

"Where? For newspapers?"

"For journals and magazines."

"That's not good here; the Jew always gets it in the neck and he's robbed of every chance to make a living. I have a wife and children. The mark keeps falling, the dollar rising. What is it you write, pamphlets?"

"Stories."

"What does that mean?"

"Literature."

"Well, *where* is your real world?"

I made no reply, and the young man said, "You have to have luck to succeed. I was once a scholar who studied in Rebbe Krel's house. Maybe you know where that is—Number 3, Gnoya. Studying with me was a young man, Abrahm. After I got married we both took to dealing in foreign currency. He became a very rich man—money seemed to be drawn to him. He sits at home and everyone knows his address, while I have to stand out here in the street. Have you published anything?"

"Nothing."

"Who needs writers? The newspapers write lies. Judaism is laughed at. Books are filled with coarse stuff. What good can come of it, eh?"

2

NO, I was not about to leave this city. I'd spent enough time knocking about in the provinces. Everything I needed was right here—libraries, newspapers, publishing houses, lectures, even a Writers' Club. Here nobody else minded your business. After all, I had grown up in Warsaw, among the tramways, the droshkies, the newspaper kiosks, the theaters, the moviehouses, the billboards.

I stopped before a bookstore. Was there any subject that could not be found here?—physics, chemistry, geography, all sorts of travel experiences, the history of philosophy, all kinds of novels. A new psychologist had appeared, Dr. Freud, and I read the word "psychoanalysis" for the first time. For one zloty per month, one could join a neighborhood library and take out a different book each day. All I lacked was a place to sleep and a bit of bread. Could one imagine that in this huge town I'd not be able to find work to do? I was ready to do anything, even sweep the streets.

I thought of praying to God, but I remembered what Spinoza wrote: God is without emotion; He knows nothing about pity and works according to eternal laws. It made as much sense to pray to Him as to pray to a volcano, to a waterfall, or to a cliff.

As I stood before the window of the bookshop, I started searching in my breast pocket where I had stuffed all sorts of pieces of paper, including addresses. I even carried a small notebook. I had sold my two books to the black marketeer who remembered my father, and I had to make my mind up quickly whether to go to the train station to buy a ticket back to Byaledrevne or to try to find a place to spend the night in Warsaw.

I went into a pharmacy to make some phone calls. I had written down several numbers. Last summer I had spent a couple of weeks here and made a few acquaintances. I even had some distant relatives living here, of the sort that are called cousins, seven times removed. There was also a young woman named Sonya, whom I had actually kissed. She worked in a women's clothing shop and lived with her employers. From what she had told me, I knew that she also did their housework for additional money. She was not very pretty, and was some ten years older than I. Sonya had confided her entire life's story to me and we used the intimate pronoun *du* to each other. She might know someone who wanted to study Hebrew, or a family who would trade a room, or even a place to sleep, in exchange for lessons for their children. I had to do my best to stay in Warsaw. If I buried myself once more in Byaledrevne, I would be utterly lost.

Using the only phone in the store I called Sonya's number, but her line was busy. The moment I put the receiver down, a heavy woman beside me picked it up and got through. She cried "Momma!" joyfully and I could tell from the gleam in her eyes and the smile on her lips that she'd be talking for a long time. She'd been to a circumcision ceremony and described every detail: the circumciser, the man who presided over the ceremony, the godparents, the honey cake, the white bread, the soup, the meat, every detail of the clothing the women had worn.

I listened with a mixture of anger and envy. The woman seemed to be smacking her lips over every word. I suspected she was prolonging her conversation simply to irritate me. She repeated sentences, laughing at things that seemed humorless. "Aunt Raytse?" she said. "Well, she wore her *silk* dress!" and she began to giggle hoarsely. Dimples appeared in her fat cheeks, her double chin quivered, her teeth were huge.

Wild thoughts raced through my head as I stood there waiting. How did it happen that the modern Jew, who had managed to free himself from so many pious duties, continued to cling so stubbornly to the circumcision ceremony? Why did God require that generation after generation of Jews should snip off this particular bit of flesh? If I were to lie starving at her feet, this woman would not give me so much as a crust of bread. Then what made us both Jews? Was it religion—or community? And in what way are proletarians really bound to each other? I decided that none of these abstractions was worth a tinker's damn. Animals have the only true wisdom and *Homo sapiens* is an idiot.

When I left the pharmacy with my call uncompleted, I could feel my legs trembling. I must have something to eat. I started to hunt for a cheap restaurant or, better still, a snack shop. I had to guard every pfennig of the few marks I had received from the sale of my books. I noticed a small coffeehouse with a sign that showed a cow. Evidently they served dairy foods, and there were several empty tables. Even before I opened the glass door, I could smell coffee, fresh rolls, cocoa, cheesecake. "Even the dying don't want to be hungry," I said to myself, remembering that condemned criminals are given a last meal of their favorite foods before they go to the gallows. I opened the door and went in.

My shoes were down-at-the-heels and my cap was squashed— a couple of times recently I'd sat on it. My distraction was boundless. For example, I lost things for no apparent reason. Though my pockets had no holes in them, when I put a coin in my pocket it magically disappeared. If the tramway conductor gave me a ticket, I was utterly unable to find it when I was asked to show it. I'd put the few marks I'd gotten for the books into one of the back pockets of my pants and felt around several times to make sure that there was no hole in the back. I continued to thrust my hand in from time to time to make sure the money was still there—a gesture which by itself could finally create a hole.

I had developed a theory that what used to be called devils, trolls, gnomes, and imps now were called "nerves." Ancient evil spirits went by a new name. Nerves were not merely threads of tissue that sprouted downward from the brain into the spinal cord; they were superhuman forces possessed of strange powers. They could make bank notes disappear, snap buttons off clothes, untie shoelaces, twist a necktie awry ten times a day, pull a coat off its hanger. They did what in the old days was ascribed to demons. Wars, revolutions, crimes—all the evils that beset mankind—could be traced to them. It may be that they are the essential force in the universe. It was not unlikely that they were closely linked, or even identical, with the forces of gravity and of electromagnetism.

Why were all the diners looking at me? I had sat down at a table, and after ten minutes the waitress did not come. Had I become an invisible spirit? Did she suspect I had no money to pay the bill? On the chair beside me there was a newspaper in a wooden holder. I tried reading but couldn't get my eyes to focus. Golden and fiery webs appeared in the corners of my eyes. I was so hungry my mouth watered; my eyes drooped with fatigue. I had not slept in a bed the previous night, and instead had sat up all night in a chair in my brother's in-laws' home. I had reached their house late at night from the train station, absolutely penniless. I had lost all the money I had been paid when I was dismissed from my teaching job—that is, unless it had been stolen while my nose was in a book.

The waitress came over and I ordered rolls, two eggs, and coffee. I hankered after a bit of herring, but I could not risk ordering it lest I use up the money I needed to buy a ticket to Byaledrevne. I ate rolls and an omelette and washed them down with coffee. I dropped five cubes of sugar into my coffee glass. In my situation, every drop of energy counted. I swallowed every crumb.

While I was eating, I looked over the other customers. They were all Jews—intellectuals. One man was reading a Hebrew magazine and wore eyeglasses with thick lenses. He had a Van-dyke beard. Perhaps he could be useful to me, but I didn't dare approach him. I took a bank note from my pocket and paid the waitress. It seemed to me that she looked surprised.

I would dearly have liked to lay my head down on the table for a little doze, but I forced myself to resist the impulse.

By now, evening was coming on. The train to Byaledrevne would leave at eleven o'clock. I knew that the late trains were always crowded and to get a ticket one had to stand in line at the station. Taking up my backpack, I left the restaurant. The air outside was colder now and it seemed to me that I caught a whiff of snow in the air.

This time, to make my phone call, I went into a sausage shop. I rang and was connected. I heard Sonya's voice.

"*Prosze*, yes?"

"I don't know if you'll remember me," I said. "We met last summer in Swider. My name is David."

"David!" Of course she remembered me and was glad to hear from me. She used the intimate *du* we had adopted. "God in heaven, where are you?"

"God may be in heaven, but I'm in a sausage shop." I hadn't thought I was capable of joking, but the meal must have restored my energy. Besides, when someone spoke to me, I was completely transformed. I heard Sonya asking, "Where are you? When did you get to Warsaw?"

"Eh? Yesterday."

"Weren't you teaching somewhere?"

"Not any longer."

"Are you staying in Warsaw?"

"I'm not sure."

Sonya laughed. "Who knows, if *you* don't? You're a funny fellow."

Even as I spoke I felt I was undermining my position with her. "I don't have any money for a room. I don't have anything at all."

Sonya's voice was altered now, more muted. "What do you plan to do?"

"If I can't find anything here, I've got to go back to Byaledrevne—this very night."

"Why didn't you finish out your teaching term?"

"They didn't want me. They gave me a couple of young peasants to teach who weren't interested in studying. All they wanted to do was to chase pigeons. Thank God, I was sent away."

"Why didn't you write? You never sent me so much as a postcard. Nothing came of any of your promises." Then she added, "A letter has come for you. It's been here for nearly six weeks."

"A letter, for me?" I asked, excited. Someone had written to me! But why had the letter been sent to Sonya? I didn't remember having given anyone her address.

"What's in the letter?"

"I don't know. I don't open other people's mail. You never even left me your address. What kind of a man are you?" Sonya uttered the word "man" in a tone that was mocking on the one hand and yet had a certain feminine tenderness. Strange, I had hesitated to phone her because I had been ashamed of my situation, yet a letter was waiting for me in her home!

"When can we see each other?" I asked.

"We close the store at seven. By the time they've come home and we've eaten and washed the dishes, it'll be nine o'clock. Tonight the old folks are going to the movies, so come at nine."

"If I come as late as nine, I'll have to spend the night in Warsaw."

"So what? You're not going to sleep in the street. Oh dear God, you're still a schoolboy."

3

MY situation and attitude had been altered in a single moment. Fate was dealing with me the way the de- mons dealt with the wicked in hell, tossing me from fire to snow and from snow back into fire. I had been utterly lost, and suddenly I found a woman who said *du* to me, who cared that I had not written to her, and who had a letter for me.

No matter how hard I put my mind to the task, I could not remember to whom I had given Sonya's address. Was it a mistake, or a misunderstanding of some sort? One thing was certain, I could not go to Sonya's house wearing down-at-the-heels shoes. I must find a shoemaker who would fix them on the spot, so I hurried off.

I made quick calculations. There no longer was enough money for a ticket to Byaledrevne, and if I was going to spend the night in Warsaw, I'd have to pay for some food and I might have to pay for a room. "Better to die with shoes that are not worn," I said to myself, fully aware that what I was saying made no sense. I started off toward Krochmalna Street, remembering an inexpensive shoemaker in my old neighborhood at whose shop in 1917 I had had my shoes resoled. Who knows, that shoemaker might still be living. Perhaps he was still sitting in his cellar pounding away. Poor people did not have money to pay for moving to new apartments.

I did not walk, I ran. In any case, I wanted to get a glimpse of the street on which I had spent my childhood. After I came out on Gnoya Street, I found myself on Krochmalna. Neither Gnoya nor Krochmalna, as far as I could see, had changed at all. Gnoya Street still smelled of oil, of horse droppings, soap and axle grease. One saw more Jewish hats and long coats than in the other streets. Krochmalna Street looked narrower and even more poverty-stricken than I remembered. I recognized every building, every gate. Smells whose memory had been hidden in the darkest recesses of my mind assailed my nostrils. Here was Yanashe's courtyard, there was number 4 where I had once studied in the Shtibl of the Grodzisk Hasidim. It was said that the "Kiduchei Harim" had lived here about a hundred years ago. There was a *mikve*, a ritual bath. Was the Gradushisker studyhouse still here, and was Abba still the synagogue warden?

Number 6 was where the thieves and prostitutes used to hang out; next to it was Asher's milk shop. Then came Number 10 and there was our balcony. And finally Number 12, where we used to live until we left Warsaw. It would take days to make inquiries in all those places. I passed Rafal the shoemaker's, and it occurred to me that if he was still alive, he might recognize me. Looking up at his doorway, I saw the half-effaced picture of a boot on the familiar sign still hanging there.

As soon as I opened the door, I saw Rafal. His beard had turned gray, but he was still the same. Surrounded by apprentices, he sat at the same shoemaker's bench, pounding nails into a sole. I knew the scene I was about to play was both foolish and ridiculous, but I plucked up my courage to play it.

"Reb Rafal, you don't know me, but I know you." He let his hammer rest on the shoe sole and looked up. There was neither wonder nor recognition in his dark eyes as he regarded me.

"Who are you?" he asked in the hoarse voice that was so familiar to me.

"David, the rabbi's son. You often made shoes for me."

He looked more closely at me. He said, "Yes. It's really you."

We were both silent; then he asked, "And your father?"

"He's a rabbi in Galicia."

"Your mother?"

"Is with him."

"Your older brother, what was his name?"

"Aharon is in Russia."

"Ah. It seems to me you also had a sister."

"She's in London."

The apprentices had stopped their work. I said, "Reb Rafal, I've come to ask you for a favor, taking advantage of our former friendship. I need my shoes half-soled right away."

He cast a genial glance at one of his apprentices. There was a hint of both mockery and reproof in his look, as if he were mutely saying, "Some nerve!" Then he asked, "Who cut off your earlocks?"

"They were cut, that's all."

"Wait till my wife gets here—just think!"

"Reb Rafal, you can't turn me down," I said, astonished at

my tone. "It's terribly important to me." Language like this was not in my character at all.

Rafal wrinkled his forehead. "Well, if I can't, I can't. We're overwhelmed with work. Tell him, Khazkl."

"The boss is telling the truth," the apprentice said.

I promptly lost my optimism. "I'm sorry," I said, and turned.

"Wait, don't run off. How long has it been since you went away? The world's turned upside down and suddenly he's here again, grown up. He hasn't been forgotten, nor his father or mother. There's no rabbi in the street anymore. If one has to ask a question about ritual, one has to go to Rabbi Shakhna on Gnoya Street, or to Rabbi Mottl on Zhimne Street. Why doesn't your father come back?"

"Who can find an apartment in Warsaw?"

"Yes, it is hard. Let's take a look at your shoes."

Still standing, I took off my shoes. He gave them an appraising look and said, "Go on up to the gallery." How familiar this all was! I had often sat in that gallery.

As I went up the stairs, I philosophized to myself about Kant's *Prolegomena*. When I had studied it, very slowly, I used to intone the melody with which I had once studied Gemara. I was constantly engrossed by the problems of time, space, quality, and the other categories of reason.

What was time? According to Spinoza it was no more than a modus of thought, an attribute. Kant's idea was that time and space had the same aspect and the same substance or, from our point of view, the same forms of appearance. But then how could the years between 1917 and today be no more than forms of appearance? Could one say that the German occupation of Poland, the Russian Revolution, the Versailles Treaty, and so on did not exist in time? Here I was, seeing that Rafal was alive while Hershl, who had the milk shop, had died in 1919 from the epidemic. Rafal was still sitting at his workbench, while Hershl's body had rotted long ago and his wife, Raisele, already had another husband. Could one say that Hershl was still alive somewhere in the fourth dimension, pouring milk from canisters into the big metal basin from which he ladled quantities of milk into the pots and pitchers of his customers? If that were so, why then I was still a little schoolboy, or my mother was still a maiden to whom marriage to my father was being proposed. Something in me cried out, "Nonsense! Time is real. A philosophy is needed that is built on time and space. Time and space are both attributes of God."

I sat in a chair and watched Rafal working on my shoes. I suddenly remembered I had not asked him the price of the repairs. I breathed dust and the smell of leather. Then, since the reality of my situation could hardly be worse, my mind turned once again to philosophy.

In those years, I believed I was on the verge of a major discovery. A light would go on in my brain and all the world's riddles would be solved. One day I would become the most famous man in the world. Why couldn't that happen now? I had read somewhere that all the greatest discoveries had been made in the blink of an eye. One thing was clear: time could have neither beginning nor end, time and space were eternal. The problem was to define eternity. How could time have eternally existed; how could there be a space without bounds? Good Lord! I had thought these very same thoughts in Moishe Yitzhak's primary religious school at Number 5, Grzybowska Street. There never was a time when I had not ruminated on these questions.

Dust began to scratch at my throat and I started to cough. With old shoes lying about, scraps of leather, threads and rags, who could say how many microbes lived and multiplied here? Each rag harbored a world of these creatures. And each microbe was made up of atoms and molecules. Not long ago I had read that each atom was a sort of solar system. I, David, the rabbi's son, was sitting in the midst of eternity, turning with the earth on its axis, which in turn was circling the sun. I myself was an entire cosmos. Yet I also felt very fearful: I was a cosmos that had nowhere to spend the night.

Rafal's wife came in. When they told her who I was, she clapped her hands with glee. She brought me a glass of tea and said, "As I live and breathe, I was thinking of your mother just last week."

I thought, No, nothing is forgotten. To live is to remember. Perhaps the entire universe is no more than a tangle of memories.

Outside, night had fallen. The gas lamps were turned on (electricity had not yet been installed on Krochmalna Street). My eyelids closed and I dozed off. I began to dream and I made myself wake up. Then I fell sound asleep again. Someone was tugging at me, one of the apprentices. "Your shoes are done."

Drunk with fatigue, I stumbled down from the gallery and asked Rafal how much I owed. The price he asked was very low. "God forbid," he said. "I wouldn't have done it for anyone else."

Not having lost the habit of gratitude, I thanked him over and over again. I was already fantasizing how I would reward Rafal when I became the richest man on earth. My pocket watch showed that it was only six-twenty. I still had two hours and forty minutes before I was due at Sonya's. I bade them a kinsman's warm goodbye and went out into the street. The full soles and the repaired eyelets of my shoes filled me with courage. I walked taller and the ground I walked on seemed firmer.

Behind the gate at Number 10 it was as dark as it had always been. The steps leading to our old flat were as shrouded in gloom as they had been when I was a schoolboy. I stood before the gate awhile and looked into the courtyard, breathing in garbage and sewer odors and another indescribable smell. Many of the tenants in that building had died, but they had left their smells behind. I now understood how bloodhounds were able to follow criminals by their scent.

There was no gaslight in the apartments; only kerosene lamps glowed in the windows. I heard the tapping of the hammers in the shoemaker's shop, the humming of sewing machines, the crying of children, and the songs of weary mothers putting them to sleep. Nothing had changed; time had congealed here. It occurred to me that here in my old street I might discover the secret of time.

I started off toward Number 12, where the entrance to the three huge courtyards was as narrow as ever. I looked for Rifkele, who used to stand with hampers of bread, rolls, and Sabbath loaves. No doubt she was a mother of children by now.

There had been very few changes. I could smell again all the former odors I had known. This meant that time is change: where there is no change, there is no time. Evidently God had created time at the same instant He created the world.

I went up to the window of the flat where we had lived and looked in. Someone inside was looking out: a tall person wearing a cap pulled low over his eyes. There was a congealed darkness in the room. It would seem that the kerosene lamp had been turned off. We stared at each other. The look in his eyes seemed to be asking, "Why have you stopped here? What do you hope to find in my poverty?"

4

AT five minutes to nine, I started up the stairs to Sonya's apartment. There were electric lights burning at the entryway. The thickly muddied marble stairs and the brass mailboxes affixed to the wide doors had a settled look. I rang at the number I had been given, but there was no answer. Had I made a mistake in the address?

I heard footsteps and then Sonya opened the door without unhooking the chain, just enough to check me out. Yes, that was she, the dark-complected features, the prominent cheek-bones, the dark eyes. Once we had actually been close, about as intimate as a man and a woman can get, but this intimacy (the word would drive me mad) had ended long ago. Hesitating for a moment, Sonya unhooked the chain and I stepped into the corridor.

"Are you sick or anything?" she asked.

"Sick? No."

"You're as pale as death."

What she said frightened me. "I haven't slept all night. I've had all sorts of troubles," I said.

"Come on in. Don't stand at the door."

She walked before me, as if she were the woman of the house, and I followed, as if I were a guest. We came into a sort of salon, where everything in sight was old and soft—a mark of wealth. The huge chandelier was hung with a great many prisms. The light it shed was muted, dusty.

It was the same Sonya I had known. She had large earrings, a red coral necklace, and her hair was in two braids. She was not young, at least thirty years old. She had the serious look of someone who has lived through a great deal. Her tone as she spoke to me had the familiarity of a rather cooled friendship.

"What's the matter? You can't find anything to do?"

"I can't be a teacher."

"What can you be? Here's your letter."

I took the letter from her and held it in my hand. The pale blue envelope was wrinkled, and there was no indication of the sender's name. I expected to be disappointed, though the letter was now my only hope. I took out a sheet with a printed letterhead and read:

Dear Friend David,
The possibility about which you and I once talked has suddenly become a reality. If you still want to emigrate to Palestine, we can get you a certificate. Come to our office, and we'll talk the matter over.

Best wishes,
Dov Kalmenzohn

No, the letter did not disappoint me. On the contrary, it filled me with hope. I remembered Dov Kalmenzohn, an official in an organization of youthful Zionists whom I had met the previous summer and who had urged me to go to Palestine. I had met him at the beach at Swider, actually at the same place where I had met Sonya. He was a small fellow, deeply suntanned, with a little black beard and fiery dark eyes. He had done all sorts of stunts under the waterfall. He also taught girls to swim in the calm waters of the Swider River.

Kalmenzohn had spent several years in a colony in the land of Israel. We had had a chat—he, wearing a blue bathing suit, and I, a dark suit and a necktie—because I was too embarrassed to be seen undressed. He had urged me to go to Palestine. "What good is the Diaspora?" he asked. He noticed that I spoke Polish with an accent. I told him I couldn't do field work, and he replied, "Who among the colonists could, at the beginning? One learns how. Besides, we need teachers in Palestine. Even writers are useful." I wanted to ask him why such a fervent supporter of Israel as he was bathing in the Swider River and not in the Jordan? He seemed to guess my question and justified himself before I could utter it: "It had to do with personal matters," implying that he had a wife in Poland who was causing him problems.

On the whole, dedicated Zionists, party members, had shown very little interest in me. Sometimes they were openly scornful. I had not believed that Dov Kalmenzohn could get me a certificate. Since my plan had been to be a teacher in the provinces, and since I did not have a permanent address, I had given him my address in care of Sonya. I was certain he would forget all his promises the way all the officials of other organizations had, but he had not forgotten.

Sonya asked, "What's that letter about?"

"I've been offered a certificate that will help me get to Palestine."

"That would be really good luck," she said. "Take me with you."

"I'm not going yet."

"Oh, you'll go. I had a cousin who used to talk about emigrating to Australia. I always thought he was simply babbling, but suddenly he got up and went. Every time I get close to someone, off they go. That's the kind of luck I have."

"Can two people use the same certificate?"

"You mean a husband and wife. Yes, that's what they do. Marry me and we'll go to Palestine together. I'll work in the fields and you can write your stories."

"You mean it?"

"Why not? You're younger than I am, but I'm by no means old."

"Why would you want to go to Palestine? You won't have a nice place like this to live in."

"It's not my place. I work at the store all day long, and when I come home my employers go out and leave me here alone. What sort of life is that?"

It was true. Sonya was serious. She had made me a simple, straightforward proposal of marriage, and I thought, Anything's better than dying of hunger. But what I said was, "Well, there's nothing certain about any of this."

"Only death is certain," Sonya replied. "Come, let's eat. You look hungry."

"I've eaten," I lied.

"When? Don't be a yeshiva boy." She took me by the sleeve and led me into a huge kitchen with a stone floor and a table with chairs set around it. Sonya said, "I'm a sort of housemaid here, and housemaids get to entertain their boyfriends in the kitchen."

"I don't care which room I'm in."

"Why didn't you write? You practically swore that you would."

"I was so unhappy, I couldn't bring myself to write a letter."

"You should have left right away. We'd gotten so close there, at Swider Beach. Really close. And then you left, and I was sure that I'd have a letter from you in a couple of days. Instead, you disappeared. I thought you were a serious fellow," she said hesitantly.

"Only the Devil knows what I am."

"That night you talked so . . . I hardly know how to describe it . . . with such feeling."

I had spent the night with her in her employer's villa, while he and his wife had gone to the baths at Ciechocinek. I had sworn a solemn oath not to seduce her. She swore she was a virgin and didn't want to come to her husband as "damaged goods." That's how she expressed it. We had lain in the same bed for a whole night and she told me the story of her life.

Sonya was related to my brother's in-laws and came from a town in the province of Lublin. She had a father somewhere who had married again after the death of Sonya's mother. He had a half dozen children by his second wife, children Sonya did not know. Her father made a living as an elementary religious-school teacher.

Sonya liked to play Patience, dealing the cards out herself. She owned a book of dream interpretations. At the same time, she thought of herself as enlightened. She smoked cigarettes on the Sabbath and often went to the Yiddish theater. The Yiddish theater, the songs sung there, the comedies and tragedies performed, and the speeches the heroes spoke—this constituted all the culture Sonya had; it was the source of her education. In the Yiddish newspapers she read only the serialized novels.

She served me bread, butter, cheese, herring, and tea. I sat there chewing, with the painful feelings of a parasite and a deceiver. I had not the slightest intention of marrying this woman some ten or twelve years older than I. But I toyed with the idea of marriage because I thought I resembled those Gentile boys who came to eat in the kitchens of their girlfriend's employers. What difference did her age make, and why should I expect an educated woman? And then, if it came to that, what difference would an education make? If Goethe could live with a peasant woman, then I could marry Sonya. She was a hot-bodied woman.

When she kissed, she kissed soul kisses. She liked to tell frightful stories. She had already had several tragic love affairs. I recalled Esau's words "Behold, I am at the point of dying: and what shall this birthright profit me?"

Sonya said, "Where are you going to sleep?"

"With you, maybe?"

A light glowed in Sonya's gypsy eyes. "First, he's a shy yeshiva boy and then all at once he's a man-about-town. The old folks are at the movies. They'll be home at eleven o'clock."

"Oh?"

"Wait, I have an idea." Sonya laughed as she showed a gypsy's mouthful of white teeth. The house had two entrances. If I waited somewhere in the courtyard until midnight, then I could come back when the old couple were sound asleep and stay until morning. "If they catch us, we'll both be out in the street," she said.

"You can always find a job."

"True. Maybe I ought to lend you a couple of marks so you can go to a hotel."

"I don't have a passport."

"Not even a birth certificate?"

"Nothing."

"How can you move about Warsaw without documents? You're really a strange fellow, altogether peculiar."

I explained to her why I had no papers. The archives of the town in which I was born were destroyed by fire during the war. If I wanted my birth certificate, I'd have to travel to that town and get witnesses to prove that I came from there. To get a passport, I also needed a copy of my father's birth certificate, or something that was called an "extract from the permanent record." All this required both time and money.

Sonya said, "What will you do if they stop you in the street and ask for your passport? They may think that you're subject to the draft."

"That's true, yes."

"How old are you?"

"I'm in my nineteenth year."

"You're too young for me. What do I need a kid for? I prefer a mature man. If you want to go to Palestine, you'll need lots of documents."

"Yes, I know."

"You know everything, but you don't do a thing. A man ought to be—what's the word—energetic."

"I'll muddle through somehow."

"How? Eat your food. They don't want leftovers here anyway. You'll stay till a quarter to eleven. The lights over the stairs go out at eleven, but what difference does that make? You have no other option."

"That's true. Thanks."

"What a strange fellow you are—yes, downright funny."

5

SONYA woke me before dawn, as we lay pressed against each other in her narrow bed in the small alcove near the kitchen. She murmured, "You have to go now."

For a moment, I could not remember who I was, or where, or who was waking me, and suddenly I remembered everything. Sonya said, "You have to go now. It's six-thirty. The old man will be up in half an hour."

For a while we lay there, kissing. Then quietly I got dressed. Sonya did not want to turn on a light. We moved about in the dark like two ghosts. I felt the new soles of my shoes. Sonya said, "Don't leave anything behind."

What did I have that I could leave behind? Before I left, Sonya said, "Call me soon. Don't disappear again for months at a time." There was a hint of threat in her voice, of welcome feminine attachment. How could I have expected to spend the night with a woman? True, I had once again given her my word of honor that I would respect her. I had slept very little in the course of the night, a few hours at most. I had a bit of a headache and from time to time felt nausea rising in my throat.

At the door, Sonya handed me a packet of food she had apparently prepared the night before. Slowly I descended the dark stairs with the thoughtfulness of someone who takes up his yoke even before the day has dawned. "Is the gate open yet?" I asked myself. "The watchman must not see me." I went out through the main entrance and saw the watchman unlocking the gates. He moved heavily, solemnly, as if he were opening the gates of a prison. As soon as he returned to his hut, I slipped out into the street. It was still dark as night but, in a way, different. The lighted streetcars were crammed with passengers on their way to work. Here and there a grocery or dairy store was open. The driver of a steam-driven wagon was unloading warm loaves of bread fresh from the bakery. Some men were lifting down milk cans that had just come from the train station. The stars seemed to go out, and the light in the sky was a mixture of night and day interspersed with streaks of black and white, like ink on wallpaper. A trace of early-morning red showed on a fifth-floor windowpane. The world had completed one more turn on its axis. The daily routine was beginning once again.

"Where to now?" I wondered.

I'd been left with little money, but I still had enough for a cup of coffee. I passed a little coffeehouse and went in, but first I counted my change. What would happen if I didn't find Dov Kalmenzohn? What was I to do if he was out of town? A man like him traveled a good deal and he might be away at a conference or even abroad. This concern hovered over me, but I would not allow it to oppress me. "First let me drink a bit of coffee," I said to myself. "A transitory pleasure is still a pleasure. Some butterflies live no more than a day."

It's not considered proper in a restaurant to eat food you've brought in yourself, but I did it stealthily. When the waitress had her back turned, I took a roll out of my packet and bit into it. Sonya had also packed a couple of slices of bread, some white cheese, and an apple. I munched secretively, washing my food down with a swallow of coffee. Occasionally, I glanced at the entrance door.

It was now fully daylight, an overcast winter day. There was no snow, but balcony railings showed a thick frost. The morning papers had been delivered to the café, and the other customers —the affluent ones who ordered herring, rolls and butter, and omelettes—were reading them.

I sat for a while consoling myself inwardly. I had lived almost a full nineteen years on this earth, no one could take that away from me. So much was history, a portion of eternity. And I had spent a night with Sonya, a night of love. That too could not be taken from me. Clearly, one's first nineteen years were the best. Later, old age would come . . . But in any case, who knew whether Kalmenzohn was in Warsaw or whether the cosmos was not merely an accident? And if everything that was to be was already fated by higher powers, then somewhere they already knew what would happen to me. To them my future was an open book.

The waitress came by. "Do you want something more?"

"No, thank you."

Quickly she handed me my bill. I could see contempt and discontent in the look she gave me. Perhaps she had seen my packet of food. I couldn't stay here much longer.

I went out into the street and continued on my way. After all, animals lived out-of-doors naturally. Tiny birds spent frosty nights sleeping on rooftops and on branches. No doubt, primitive man had slept in the open.

Near a courtyard I saw a synagogue, and I went in to get warm. After all, I was still a Jew. I had ties to a synagogue. Suddenly I breathed an atmosphere of familiarity that made me feel I was not merely an eighteen-year-old youth but, rather, that I had the memories of a hundred-year-old man. Everything here seemed at once ancient and intimate: the Holy of Holies; the many books, including old books with torn spines; the bare tables; the people reciting their prayers or sitting at their studies; the smells of the lamp, of the stove, of bodies and sweat.

I carried my small backpack. There was a man with a yellow beard carrying a basket of hot beans covered with a cloth. There were porters sitting there who had ropes wrapped around their waists. It was as if I could deduce what they did from their clothes, their beards. The flour-dusted man with the two coats, one on top of the other, ran a grocery store. The tall man with the huge hands and square-cut fingernails was a carpenter; I recognized the colors of glue and varnish on his fingers. As the cantor was reciting the Eighteen Benedictions, one fellow was trying to sell a lottery ticket.

No, nothing had changed. The cantor recited, "Return in compassion to your holy city of Jerusalem as thou hast promised." How strange! Jews had been saying these same words for more than two thousand years, and now they were turning toward Jerusalem in earnest. I was waiting for a certificate. What a strange people, what a strange religion. What faith they put in words that had been written thousands of years ago.

Without thinking, I took a book from a shelf and sat down at a table, setting my backpack beside me on the bench. It was a volume of the Mishnah and in it I read, "One does not catch fish from a reservoir on a holiday and one does not feed them; but it is permitted to catch animals and birds and to feed them. Reb Shimon ben Gamliel says, 'Not all reservoirs are alike. The general rule is, if you have to catch them, then it is forbidden. If not, then it is permitted.' "

"Was this God's will?" I murmured to myself. "Is that why He created mammals, birds, and fish—so that people could catch and eat them? Could I possibly spend the rest of my life in this holy place? Or could I live somewhere on a kibbutz and be a goatherd or even a teacher of children?" I closed my eyes and heard the sounds of those praying around me, snatches of melodies from the Gemara, phrases of conversation from those who had interrupted their studies or their prayers.

From childhood on, I had sought for something to lean on, a

true, certain, and firm faith that was not to be denied, a clear goal. But everything had vanished, had dissolved, nothing was certain. Not God, not science, not the words of the ancient sages, nor the theories of the new ones. Once, in a coffeehouse, I'd picked up a newspaper in which I'd read an article about the situation in Europe: the Germans were rebelling against the Versailles Treaty, India was trying to break free of the British Empire, the Balkan peninsula was still the powder keg it had been in 1914, and Russia was threatened by famine. There was a government crisis imminent in Poland, and Jews were superfluous everywhere—even in the land of Israel. The Arabs were already warning that they would not tolerate an increased Jewish immigration.

"Is there no place in the world where one can have a little repose?" I asked. "Yes, in Switzerland. But they don't give visas to people like me. And it looks as if the gates of America are going to be locked."

The only true repose is in the grave. But who knows whether the corpse is really at rest? I leaned my head against the table and dozed. I could hear that they were reciting Kdusha, but I did not stand up. It may be that I was asleep and was thinking wakeful thoughts. "Holy, holy, holy." Why did He need so much praise? And why, if the earth was so full of His honor and His might, did He not bestir Himself to do something for suffering humanity?

I fell into a deep sleep and dreamed of the land of Israel, or perhaps Jerusalem. I was walking through a series of gates, one courtyard after another, that resembled those described in one of the tractates of the Gemara. Rooms, doors, stairways. Priests were immersing themselves in water. Levites arrived from somewhere, playing on lyres and trumpets, harps. It was the Passover season. Jews were going on pilgrimages.

"Where is this described?" I asked myself in my dream. "Has the Messiah come? If so, then what am I doing in Warsaw?" Everything I saw seemed strange—the sun had a holiday brightness; a gold coin I picked up had the words "God's punishment" inscribed in Yiddish. I stared at the coin, amazed—was Yiddish spoken in Jerusalem? And why should "God's punishment" be engraved on a coin? "It's too absurd," I said, and woke up.

I remembered the dream, even the gates, the corridors, the passages. I thought, That was not all merely fantasy. There was something real there, something I saw somewhere long ago. But that coin with the inscription is absurd. The Master of Dreams was giving me the finger.

I looked at the synagogue clock with its Hebrew letters standing for numbers. It was time to go to the Halutz office. It would be better to wait for Kalmenzohn than to risk losing track of him completely. Yes, everything now turned on whether Kalmenzohn was in town or not. If not, I had no other recourse but suicide.

I went into the street where, after the fetid air of the synagogue, I breathed in the fresh air gratefully. I thought, What if, when I put my hand in my pocket, I find a wallet filled with dollar bills? I'd rent a room in Warsaw, or perhaps go to Berlin or Paris. I would hire tutors with whom I would study mathematics, physics, languages. I would spend my mornings writing, my afternoons studying. In the evening I'd go to a coffeehouse or to the Kurfürstendamm or Montparnasse, and I'd take Lena with me. We would lie in bed together, listening to the sounds of Paris outside. In the morning we'd go to the window to look out at the Eiffel Tower.

Though I knew very well that there were no miracles, still I reached into my pocket. No, there was no wallet with dollar bills. I remembered Spinoza's remark about miracles: God and miracles are antitheses. God's laws and His being are one and the same. God had not the slightest pity for the sixty thousand Poles who died at Verdun. It all coincided perfectly with His Godlike nature, with His attributes.

I reached the address I'd been given and climbed the stairs. Even as I started up I could hear the sounds the Halutzim made.

I saw young men with disheveled hair and shirts of all colors and hairy-legged youths wearing shorts. Some wore shoes; others were barefooted. There were young women here too—female Halutzim, evidently. They were just as dark and disheveled as the young men, and had eyes that glowed from time to time with a land-of-Israel glow.

There was the sound of hammering and sawing. Chests and suitcases were being packed and tied with rope, and nails were being hammered. Everyone was in a hurry. I heard Hebrew, Polish, Yiddish spoken.

I tried to stop someone to ask about Dov Kalmenzohn, but before I could open my mouth, he or she was gone. I could simply not be heard in the tumult. I was finally able to stop a young woman and asked about Dov Kalmenzohn. She replied, "He doesn't come till eleven o'clock."

Thank God, Kalmenzohn was in town. But what would I do for the next couple of hours? I sat on a bench. Around me boxes were being packed to be sent to the Holy Land. Bedclothes, books, clothes, implements, and even dried sausages were being stuffed into chests and wicker trunks. Names of distant cities were called out. The young women smoked cigarettes and did the work of men. God's promise that He would return His wandering people to the land of their fathers was being fulfilled right before my eyes.

6

IT was after eleven when Dov Kalmenzohn arrived. I was afraid he would not recognize me and that he might have forgotten the whole matter, but he did remember and his greeting was friendly. He was still dark from his summer tan, and wore a short sheepskin coat and a shirt with an open collar. Youths and young women hurried to greet him, and formed a circle around him, each of them with one request or another, but he sent them off good-humoredly.

Kalmenzohn took me into a separate little room which was the editorial and administrative office of a Halutz journal. Here there were piles of newspapers, heaps of books, manuscripts, labels, rubber stamps, envelopes. The place smelled of wax and India ink. He cleared papers away from a couple of chairs and we sat down. He had lighted a cigarette and offered me one. Though usually I did not smoke, this time I took the cigarette. He said, "Where have you disappeared to? We gave that other certificate away to someone else, but if you want to emigrate, we can get you another. You're not married, are you?"

"Married? No."

"Don't blush, it happens. Listen, here's the thing. Each time England gives us a certificate, we try to cover as many emigrants with it as possible, because a certificate is valid for an entire family. It's better for us if a couple travels, but if two singles don't want to get married, we pull off a dirty trick. You marry the young woman and she travels with you as your wife—it's a fictive marriage. It happens sometimes that the fictive marriage turns into a real one, but that depends on the couple. They may want to separate when they reach the land of Israel, in which case the marriage is over. We know that it's not exactly right, but is it right for England to dictate to half the world and control the certificates that permit us to go back to our own land? Well, most of the men who get the certificates don't have money enough to make the trip, so the young women put up the money for them both. That money is, as it were, their dowry. I don't suppose you have the money for the trip."

"I don't have any money."

"Right. Now listen to me. I know a young woman who has to go to the land of Israel. She has a fiancé there. He went ahead of her. Now they want to get married. I know the family, good people. Her name is Minna. Her father is a Hasidic Jew, but you know how it is with us in Poland. She graduated from the

Gymnasium and has even studied in the university. She can only get to Israel on someone else's certificate, but she has a revulsion against a fictive marriage. The man might not release her and she's madly in love with her fiancé and she doesn't want to put up with any tricks. You seem to be a well-mannered fellow. I took one look at you back in Swider and I could tell at once what you were like. But more than that, you are several years younger than she is. And she is, as they say, a very reputable woman. In this matter, she is strangely reticent. I've already tried to find a young man for her, but each of them started acting up at once, and it drove her to absolute hysteria. I'll give her a phone call, but if I don't reach her by telephone, I'll give you a letter to her. What kinds of papers do you have?"

"I don't have any, but I can get them."

"You have to get your birth certificate and whatever else is needed just as soon as you can. If she agrees, then we'll get you a passport, and you can be off as soon as possible. The most important thing is, be careful how you behave. I don't think I have to explain that to you. You look like a tactful young fellow."

"I don't know how to thank you. You may rest assured that . . ."

"You seem a bit shy, but in this case, that's good. Her father was once a very rich man, but he's lost everything. The truth is, they're nearly bankrupt. I've known the family for years. I used to be her Hebrew teacher. They're true Jewish aristocrats. Wait one moment."

Dov Kalmenzohn lifted the telephone receiver and called a number. He asked for Miss Minna. He nodded his head, then hung up the phone. "She's not at home, but she'll be back for lunch. I'll give you a note. And I'll phone her, too. Wait just a moment, I'll be right back."

Dov Kalmenzohn went out into the large hall. I heard his voice. He was not only the secretary of the organization but its manager and perhaps the editor of the journal too. He grumbled in friendly fashion at the Halutzim, using the intimate *du* form for them all. He had told me to wait a moment, but in fact he was gone for nearly three-quarters of an hour.

I picked up one of the newspapers from the floor and read about a young man who, armed with a rifle, stood guard over a settlement on a rainy night when the wind whistled and jackals howled. The Arabs attacked him and shot him. Another young man, a rich young fellow who had gone off to the land of Israel to drain the swamps there by planting eucalyptus trees, had died of malaria. The article ended with the words "The Jewish people will never forget him."

I bent my head low. Who were "the Jewish people"? I had never so much as heard this man's name. Ah . . . everyone would be forgotten, even Goethe, if the earth should chance to collide with a comet. Everything would be turned to vapor, which would effectively wipe out all of history. On the other hand, Spinoza said that there was a trace of every soul in God. That is to say, the godhead was a sort of archive of humanity.

Dov Kalmenzohn came back carrying a sealed envelope. "Give this to Miss Minna. Her family name is Ahronson."

He gave me the address. Meir Ahronson lived on Leszno Street in a new house near Iron Street. Dov Kalmenzohn shook my hand firmly and asked me to keep in touch.

I left, astonished. "What a miracle it is that I'd had my shoes soled," I said to myself. I started to count the money in my pocket, because I had to get a shave. By now, the hair on my face was prickly. I could hardly go to the home of this aristocratic young woman with stubble on my face. But did I have enough money to pay the barber? And I was beginning to be hungry too.

I went into a barbershop. The barber was cutting some brag-gart's hair. The fellow was telling the story of a friend of his who had borrowed his apartment key and had brought a woman there. He demanded that she submit to him, otherwise he threatened to make a scandal and call the police. The story made me unhappy. I wanted to ask the man, "What's so clever about getting what you want by force?" But I kept still. The barber kept smacking his lips as he said, "Ah so. So."

"So that's the kind of fellow you are," I said to myself. "If I were the king of the world, I'd punish you so thoroughly that you'd be jailed into the tenth generation." He told the barber he wanted to be perfumed and powdered. He also asked for a shampoo and an electric massage. He had the neck and shoulders of a giant. How could one imagine that he was a descendant of Abraham, Isaac, and Jacob? Could he be called a Jew? "The whole essence of Jewishness has not been defined," I concluded.

As the man got up, the barber cleaned him with a brush. The young fellow looked into the mirror, trying to find something to complain to the barber about. Finally he left. When he had gone the barber said, "There's not a true word in anything he's said."

"Really?"

"All he knows is how to run after whores."

"So." I'd already condemned him to one hundred years in jail. The barber shaved me. Meanwhile, I worried about my collar, which I had put on clean yesterday. A spot on a collar can spoil a betrothal. After I was shaved, I asked how much it would cost. I was just able to pay what the barber asked and I was left without a pfennig.

I started toward Leszno Street. I still had a bit of the bread Sonya had given me. Now I took it out and gnawed on it as I went. It is not a good idea to meet a stranger while hungry. I knew that I would have to do everything I could to keep from being anxious or desperate. I must be ready for any eventuality. That was the secret of Napoleon, of the explorer Amundsen and other great achievers in the world: they were calm in the presence of the most dreadful dangers. Let me imagine that Leszno Street is a huge iceberg floating somewhere near the North Pole, sixty degrees below zero, and I'm completely out of provisions. A polar bear has stolen my sleeping bag . . .

Fantasizing and encouraging myself in this fashion, I arrived at the house. There was an elevator, but it was locked. The elevator was for tenants only, not for uninvited guests. As I climbed the stairs I wondered if I could handle the present situation calmly and tactfully—even a bit subserviently.

I had hardly touched the doorbell when I heard footsteps; then a servant opened the door to the length of the chain: a young Gentile woman with red cheeks and dark eyes. She wore a bonnet and a white skirt and looked more French than Polish. I told her I had a letter from Dov Kalmenzohn for Miss Minna Ahronson. She asked me to wait. I could smell borscht, forced meat, freshly baked cake. When the maid returned and unlatched the door, I went into a large corridor where paintings and etchings hung on the wall. The maid said, "The family is eating the midday meal. Will you be good enough to wait?"

"Of course."

"Here, please." And she indicated an upholstered chair beside a table on which there was a lamp and several magazines. "It seems that a rich man who's come down in the world is still a rich man," I said to myself. It struck me that I was probably the poorest man in Warsaw, without a groschen, without a bit of bread, without a place to spend the night. I owned nothing at all except the backpack that I'd put down beside the chair. I picked up one of the newspapers and read about an event in America. A millionaire had given a party for his daughter that had cost sixty thousand dollars. The flowers alone had cost five thousand, and the paper showed pictures of father and daughter. The millionaire had divorced his daughter's mother, and she, the ex-wife, had married an English lord. I turned the pages of the newspaper and yawned. "Baruch Spinoza, is all of this part of the godhead? Is all of this necessary and determined, a product of God's thought?"

I heard the muted sounds of dishes in another room. Someone spoke; someone laughed. All at once a small person with a diminutive gray beard and bags under his eyes, whose eyes seemed to be smiling, came into the room. Dov Kalmenzohn had said that Minna's father was a Hasidic Jew, but this man was wearing modern clothing. Not only that; he wore a square silk cap of the kind worn by Lithuanian Jews. There was an old-fashioned Jewish, genially paternal, and yet vague look on his face. The coat he wore was a bit too long, the cuffs of his trousers drooped over his shoes. There was a gold watch chain dangling across his vest. His open collar showed his neck, and he seemed to have lost weight. I got up as he approached me. Speaking with a Polish-accented Yiddish, he said, "You are Dovid Bendiger?"

"Yes."

"You're really a Bendiger?"

"Yes."

"Where are you from, eh?"

I told him that I'd been raised in Warsaw, and that I came from the Lublin district. He stroked his beard and said, "Why are you waiting in the hallway like a beggar at the door? Come in. We're eating our midday meal. You'll have a glass of tea with us."

"Thank you."

I followed after him. He led me into a brightly lighted dining room, where two women were sitting at the table: one with gray hair, the other light brown. The first woman raised a lorgnette through which she examined me; the other looked at me, half ironically and half contemptuously. I felt myself growing dizzy and I seemed to be seeing everything as through a fog. Was I going blind?

Meir Ahronson said to his wife, "Dvorah dear, this is the young man. His name is Bendiger, but he comes from the Lublin district. His father is a rabbi somewhere in Galicia. He says he was raised in Warsaw. This is my wife, and that's my daughter, Minna."

"Pleased to meet you," they said, speaking almost at precisely the same second.

"Sit here," said my host, pointing to a chair. "Dvorah dear, tell Tekla to bring in tea and something for him to eat."

"Why only tea and a snack?" his wife said melodically. "There's soup left, and some meat as well. Let the young man eat with us."

"Thank you, but I've eat . . ."

"Don't thank us. Eat," she said, interrupting me. "If you want to go to Palestine, you'll have to have energy."

7

LITTLE by little, the mist dissipated and I was able to see both women more clearly. It was evident that the mother had once been a beautiful woman. Her skin was now considerably flecked, her eyes were green, her nose short. She had a Slavic look. The daughter had her mother's eyes and nose, but she was the shorter of the two. Her brown hair had been cut short, so that her ears showed like a boy's. When she smiled, she displayed widely spaced teeth. There was a certain look of irony in her expression, a mixture of shyness and sarcasm.

The maid brought me a bowl of tomato soup and some bread. Meir Ahronson said, "You don't have to make an ablution, but you may want to make the blessing over the bread."

"Meir, let the young man be," Mrs. Ahronson said. "He's always trying to save someone for the World to Come."

"I'll be glad to make the blessing over the bread," I said, and murmured the prayer.

Meir Ahronson said, "What's he got to lose? Let him remember he's a Jew."

"They won't let one forget," his wife said.

I ate the soup, keeping in mind a rule I had read in some magazine—not to slurp it. I glanced frequently at Miss Minna. She drank her tea smiling into her glass. Her mother kept urging her to eat some of the *kichel* served with the tea, but Miss Minna did not bother to reply. I could tell she was spoiled, the only daughter. Even as she felt bound to her family, she felt a childish need to rebel. Miss Minna seemed young, but there was something in her manner that made it clear she was well into her twenties or perhaps thirties. I caught a hint of gray in her hair. Her lips were very thin, her chin angular. There was a scar from an operation under her right ear. Her neck was long and thin, and she wore a stiff collar, like a man's, over her blouse. Abruptly she stood up and, turning to me, said rather sternly, "When you've finished eating, come see me in my room."

I noticed that her dress hardly reached to her knees. She was wearing shoes with extraordinarily high heels. Her legs were graceful, but too thin. Her mother looked accusingly after her, though I had not observed in what way the daughter had offended. Mrs. Ahronson shook her head, as if prompted by some grief which could be neither expressed nor hidden.

Meir Ahronson said, "What will you do over there—in the land of Israel. Herd sheep?"

"They need all sorts of workers."

"For instance? Why didn't you become a rabbi, like your father?"

"I'm not that Orthodox."

"You've been to heaven and seen for yourself that God doesn't exist? Nonsense! Things are bad for Jews in Poland. But when was it ever good? So long as we clung to Judaism we could get on somehow. The present generation is neither one thing nor the other. They don't want to be Jews, and they aren't allowed to be Gentiles."

I said, "In Palestine they'll be allowed."

"Oh? So that's why you're going there? To become a Gentile? But they won't allow it there either."

Mrs. Ahronson raised her lorgnette. "Meir, you talk as if you yourself had been to heaven. Who needed this last war? And look at what's going on in Russia."

"Mankind has free will."

"You've got an answer for everything."

"Where do you live, young man?" she asked, turning to me.

"For the time being, nowhere."

"You're sleeping in the street?" Ahronson asked.

I told them the whole story of my experiences as a teacher.

Meir Ahronson smiled skeptically, as if to say, "An old story." He scratched his beard and murmured something, apparently reciting prayers. I gathered that he had had Hasidic origins but that because of his wealth he had been half transformed into a Maskil, an enlightened Jew.

Meir Ahronson had begun to yawn. Like many rich Warsaw Jews of his type, he had the habit of napping after the midday meal. He cast sleepy eyes toward the door to his bedroom.

Mrs. Ahronson lowered her lorgnette. "Go to my daughter," she said to me. "It's the first door to the right in the hallway."

I knocked at Miss Minna's door and entered a room whose walls were covered with yellowish tapestries and paintings in heavy gold frames, including a portrait of Miss Minna herself. The room contained a piano, some books bound in morocco and others with velvet and silken bindings and gold-leafed edges. There were also little pedestals on which stood porcelain and metal figures, an aquarium containing goldfish, lamps hung with prisms and crystals. There were small couches, a chaise longue, and two overstuffed chairs. Letters and clippings from newspapers and magazines were spread over the top of an elegant desk. This was not an ordinary room but rather the boudoir of a grande dame.

Miss Minna, her legs crossed, sat on a corner sofa. She was wearing brightly colored stockings and shoes of the same color. She made a gesture inviting me to come closer, but she did not ask me to sit down.

"Are you prepared to go to Palestine if you can get your passport and visa?"

"Yes, of course."

"Are your papers in order?"

"I haven't got them yet."

"How is your health?"

"I'm in good shape."

"Kalmenzohn says that you're a writer. What sort of writing do you do?"

"Actually I'm still a beginner."

"In what language do you write? I can see that you don't understand Polish."

"I used to write in Hebrew, but I've started to write in Yiddish."

"Jargon?"

"Call it what you like."

"It's not what I call it. Yiddish is a jargon—corrupted German with a mixture of Polish and Hebrew added. Hebrew has also become corrupted, and certainly Polish has. The language has neither grammar nor syntax. For whom do you write—the jargonist newspapers?"

"For no one. If I can find a publisher, I'll write a book, but I'm a long way from that."

"I've got to go to Palestine. I have a fiancé who is there. That's our situation. If two of us can travel on a single certificate, then you and I will have to go through a fictive marriage. Just as soon as we get to Palestine, you'll divorce me and go your own way."

"Yes, of course."

"You understand Hebrew?"

"I've written in Hebrew."

"I studied Hebrew once and Kalmenzohn was my teacher. But Hebrew is a difficult language. An entirely Asiatic tongue. I didn't make much progress in it, but I'm determined to master it. I don't want to lose another day. Can you teach me Hebrew?"

"If that's what you want."

"I want an hour each day. Grammar, reading, dictation, and conversation. I want to learn a minimum of twenty-five words a day. How much will you charge per hour?"

"Whatever you pay me will be enough."

"Oh, very well, then. What books will I need? I want to start tomorrow."

I told her what she needed—a *Hadibur Hebrei* by Krinski and a grammar book. She said, "I'll give you the money and you buy the books. Where do you live? Do you have a telephone?"

"For the time being, I don't live anywhere."

"What does that mean?"

I told Miss Minna what I had told her mother. She listened to me with a doubtful expression and some ill-concealed scorn. She said, "You can't live in the street. I'll advance you money for a week or two so you can find someplace to live. You have to be registered somewhere before you can get your documents. The matter has been delayed altogether too long because of my involvement with an ill-bred young man—in short, a fool. I hope you won't follow in his footsteps. Kalmenzohn praises you, and you seem to be a respectable fellow. Buy a newspaper and you'll find ads in it for rooms. I'll give you my telephone number. Call me back to let me know what's happened. You absolutely must have an address."

"Yes, I understand."

"Wait a moment." She went to her desk and opened a drawer from which she took a couple of bank notes. After consideration, she returned one of the notes. "This is for one week. You don't have to pay in advance, but they'll certainly want a deposit. If you don't find a room, where will you sleep tonight?"

"I have a place."

"Find a room as soon as you can. Be here tomorrow at twelve o'clock. That's the best time for me to have a lesson."

"All right, thank you."

"And this is for the *Hadibur Hebrei*. How much do you think it will cost? I think this should be enough."

"No, it won't cost this much."

"You can bring back the change. I think there's a Hebrew grammar lying among my books. I'll look around. Tomorrow it'll all be clear."

"Thanks so much."

I started toward the door. I had an impulse to look back, but I kept myself from doing so. I was astonished by the miracle that had happened to me. I had to thank God for His benevolence. I would have to thank Kalmenzohn, too.

I went out into the hall and took up my backpack. It felt lighter now, and I knew the reason. My legs felt strangely light. I now had some helpful connections in Warsaw, even if for only a little while. I left the house and bought newspapers and stopped on the sidewalk to read through the ads for vacant rooms. Standing there, I could not make head or tail of anything. I'd have to go somewhere for a cup of coffee. I got as far as a café at 38 Leszno Street and went in. I sat down at a table and, using a pencil, underlined several addresses. One of the ads interested me particularly. The room was not far away, and on the same street as Miss Minna's. It read:

> A small room without windows for a young man.
> Inexpensive.

That was all I needed. But there was still one worry; perhaps someone had already rented the room. The newspaper was printed early in the morning, before dawn, and I didn't dare lose a moment. I paid for my coffee and started back the way I'd come.

Though I had my doubts about all religious dogmas, still I retained the habit of prayer. I prayed now that the windowless little room had not been rented, remembering at the same time that the Gemara says he who prays to change an event that has already taken place makes a false prayer, because even God cannot make unhappen what has happened.

8

I ENTERED a small but clean asphalt-paved courtyard in whose midst there stood a single winter-bare tree. I asked someone for the location of the house number and was shown the correct entrance. It was still daylight, but it was already dusk on the stairs.

When I knocked at the door, I heard footsteps at once. Two women came to the door—one was tall, about thirty years old, and the other was shorter, in her twenties, or even younger. The older woman had a lean face, a long neck, and an aquiline nose. She had huge dark eyes and dark, disheveled curly hair, combed the way a man might comb it. Her ears, too, looked masculine. She had a cigarette butt between her lips and a genial look on her face. Instantly it occurred to me that she was a Communist—I don't know why.

The younger woman looked to me like a student. As I came closer, I saw that her nose, too, was not straight. But just as the other woman was bony and edgy, this one was well padded. Her bosom was high and she had reddish cheeks. She looked wonderfully healthy and alert, as if she had just returned from a dacha. Both women panted a little when they laughed, evidently having run to open the door, each trying to get there before the other.

Before I had a chance to open my mouth, the older one said, "You're here about the room, eh?"

"Yes."

"Come on in."

I turned hopeful at once. I was led down the dark hallway to a room in which a gas jet was burning.

It was a small place, more nearly an alcove than a room, with a bed, a small table, and a chair. There were books piled on three shelves, one on top of the other. The older woman said, "This is it. If you prefer to have sunbaths in your room, this isn't for you. But if you want a place to sleep, you can sleep here to your heart's content."

"I don't need sunbaths."

"You look as if you could use them. You're much too pale. But we can't help you with sunbaths." And the woman named a price that was ridiculously low.

I said, "I'll take the room."

"What, so quickly? Good. There was an engineer who lived here, a young man. He got a job in Danzig and left his books here, technical and math books. I don't understand a word of any of them. You're welcome to inherit them if you like. When would you like to move in?"

"Now."

"Ah, you do work quickly. We wanted to clean up a bit, but what is there to do? I'll change the bedding. Where are your things?"

I indicated my backpack. The shorter woman giggled. The older one said, "What are you, a poet?"

"I hope to be a writer."

"Many want to be."

"Would you like a deposit?"

"If you like, you can pay for half the month. Let that be your deposit." I counted out the money Miss Minna had given me. The older woman glanced at the money and handed it over to the younger one. "My name is Bella, or Bayla. Her name is Edusha, but her Yiddish name is Elke. I'm her aunt. She's one of my sister's daughters. My sister lives in London with her second husband, who is a rabbi. That's the whole story. What sort of work, besides poetry, do you do?"

"I'm getting ready to go to Palestine. I've got a certificate and . . ."

"In that case, how long are you planning to stay here?"

"Several months."

"Very well. Our renters don't stay here very long. They go

away and we have to start all over again. Since you have a certificate, isn't it true that you can take someone with you?"

"I've already made an arrangement with a young woman."

"He has an answer for everything! Are you a Zionist, eh?"

"I mean to go to Palestine."

"What are you going to do there? Eat St. John's bread along with the goats? England will never leave the place—not peacefully. What it takes it takes for itself, not for anyone else. They'll let a few Jews in and then they'll stir the Arabs up against them. That's England's eternal policy, divide and conquer. The Arabs have right on their side, too. It's their land, not yours. They've lived and fought there for two thousand years, and the only thing you have is a patent of nobility from God. God made a promise to Abraham. God has promised many things without keeping His word. It's amazing how foolish people can be."

"Bella, enough," said the niece.

"What harm am I doing him? I'm just saying what I think. You've been dazzled by false promises. You're a Pole, not a citizen of Israel. This is your country. Here's where society must be reorganized so that all people can live, not just a few pigs who grab everything for themselves while everyone else goes about with their tongues hanging out. You have to fight for a just society, you don't get it free."

"My aunt is a propagandist," Edusha said. "What's your name?"

"David Bendiger."

"Bendiger, eh? If you mean to go to Palestine, then go. It's the same world, wherever you go. There are workers there too. Jewish workers and Arab workers will have to unite. That's the direction history is taking."

"No one knows what direction history will take," I said.

"Oh yes, they do. It's known," Bella replied. "History is not some blind force. It has specific laws. So you're going to stay here. I have to change the bedding. Please, go into the living room and wait a bit. Edusha, show him where to go."

"Come with me."

Edusha opened a door and I went into a room that looked like a combination bedroom, dining room, and living room. It had a bed, a closet, a sofa, and a table with chairs. Everything looked old, run-down. The window looked out onto a dead wall.

"Sit down and make yourself at home," Edusha said. "In our house, everyone is like family. The engineer who lived here, Stanislas Kalbe, took his meals with us too. My aunt and I are good cooks. My mother went away, leaving me here, but I'm going to be married soon. My fiancé has to do some traveling, but when he gets back we're going to live together in an apartment somewhere. What are you planning to do in Palestine?"

"I don't know yet."

"The woman you're going with, is she your girlfriend, or is this one of those fictive marriages?"

"She has a fiancé there."

"Ah, I get it. Everything is fictive among the Zionists. The whole Zionist movement is a fiction and nothing more. But don't take it to heart. It's not your fault. You're a victim of circumstances. Capitalism has so warped everything that it'll need to be straightened out."

"Who's going to straighten whom—one hunchback straightening out the other?"

Edusha burst into clear, resounding laughter. "Well said, but you're not right. All of humanity isn't made up of hunchbacks. The masses are straight, though every effort is made to warp them with religion, with nationalism, and who knows what else. My mother is a pious Jewish woman who married a rabbi. My father died in the typhus epidemic. Our family is divided, half Orthodox, half modern. My grandfather is a very pious Jew—a scholar, a disciple of Alexandrov Hasidism. I mean my grandfather on my father's side. What do you write? Is it really poetry?"

"I'm trying to write short stories."

"Read me something. I love literature. One of my aunt's friends is a famous Yiddish poet. Maybe you've heard of him—Susskind Eikhl."

"No, I haven't heard of him."

"How come? Everyone knows who he is. He comes from Russia. He came here after the Polish-Bolshevist War. What do you write about? Shtetl life?"

"I'm still only a beginner."

"Everyone was a beginner at one time. What is it they say? —'Cracow wasn't built in a day.' Excuse me, there goes the telephone."

Edusha ran out into the hallway and I watched the movement of her hips. I noticed that the calves of her legs were thick, but her ankles were slim. "So," I said to myself, "a left-winger." I sat on the sofa, feeling amazed at everything. My own life seemed to me like a confused novel. I was neither from Warsaw nor from the provinces. In my eighteen and a half years I had been a wanderer, lived through wars, been a refugee—impediments to my education. In fact, I had lived my life in a perpetual state of crisis. Now I was ready to abandon everything and go to Palestine. I would have to write Hebrew, because no one needed Yiddish in Palestine. If the truth be told, who needed my Hebrew either? There every second Jew was a writer.

I was suddenly very tired. I leaned back and closed my eyes. Yes, everything is warped, I thought. And no one will straighten it out. I knew what had been done in Russia in the name of the revolution—millions of innocent people slaughtered, rabbis, merchants, and ordinary Jews shot. The Jewish Communists spat on Jewish history. For them, true Jewish history began in October 1917. The peasants starved. Russia put all of its hopes on a revolution in Germany. The motto for straightening anything out was "Off with his head."

Bella and Edusha came back together. "There's fresh linen on your bed," Bella said. "But you can stay here. Have you eaten?"

"Yes, I had lunch."

"You can eat if you want to. We won't charge you much. Tell us what you like and we'll make it for you. You can pay us later. That's the arrangement we had with Stanislas Kalbe, and we certainly didn't overcharge him. What sort of writing do you do?"

"Stories," Edusha interposed.

"I've written an essay, 'Spinoza and the Cabala.' "

Bella perked up. "You've studied philosophy?"

"I've done some reading."

"I tried reading Spinoza's *Ethics* once, but it's hard and I don't have that kind of patience. I'm interested only in whatever can help the masses directly."

"The masses care about knowledge too."

"Concrete knowledge, not Spinoza's inquiries. Above all, the masses need bread; and to get bread, they need power. If you don't have power, you lose your bread. Only when the masses acquire power will they have time to think about which came first, the chicken or the egg."

The telephone rang again and both women hurried toward it, jostling each other in the doorway. Bella cried, "Edusha, I'm going to break a leg because of you." Just then, the doorbell rang. Evidently someone else was coming to see the dark little room. I heard Edusha say, "Too late. Someone's already moved in."

II

IT was clear to me that I ought not to be in debt to these women, because I had not the slightest chance of repaying them. I had retired to my windowless room and fallen asleep. On the previous night with Sonya, I had not slept very well. We kept waking, and each time we woke, we embraced. Now that I was lying in a bed of my own, I fell into a deep sleep in which I dreamed that my father and I were studying the rules for salting meat in *Yoreh Deah*. In the introduction to the *Pri Megadim*, there is a reference to an opinion cited in the medieval book *Mordechai*. In my dream the "opinion" was transformed into a living person, who was explaining things and was somehow irritated with me. He was wearing a velvet gaberdine whose coattails dragged on the ground and a fur hat with a high crown. His yellow beard reached to his knees.

Edusha woke me. It seemed to me that she had changed her dress and looked flushed. I could hear the voice of a man outside, evidently a visitor. Edusha said, "If you sleep now, what will you do at night? Come join us. Supper's ready." She took it for granted that I belonged there.

I was shy about meeting the man who had come to visit. There was a twinkle in Edusha's eyes, and I could tell that in their living room—if that was the right name for it—I had been the subject of amused conversation. I had done a foolish thing: I should not have told them I was a writer.

I sat up feeling that inward—and outward—distress that comes from anxiety and from sleeping in one's clothes. My voice slightly hoarse, I thanked Edusha and promised to come soon.

"The groats are getting cold," she said, and left the room.

So then. They had cooked groats for supper. I smoothed out my necktie and tightened my loosened suspenders and patted down my red hair. There was a cracked little mirror hanging on the wall, showing a pale man wearing a wrinkled collar. I tried smoothing and adjusting my clothes. Then I went out into the hallway, where I heard the visitor laughing. It sounded like the artificial laughter of someone trying to be funny, who snorted through a single nostril. This kind of hilarity frightened me.

I opened the door and saw that the visitor was a young, curly-headed fellow who wore a black shirt with woven edges, in the revolutionary Russian manner. His face was girlishly pretty, with a sort of womanish frivolity in his look. He had a sly, scornful smile on his face as he took my measure.

Bella said, "This is Susskind Eikhl, and this is our new roomer. I've forgotten your name. Oh yes—Bendiger, David Bendiger."

"Bendiger, eh? Why not Kallisher. Or Berditshever," joked Susskind Eikhl. He offered me the tips of his fingers. His mien and his manners continually expressed his sense of himself as an important personage. His expression kept changing—irony, wit, envy. I had the feeling that he was imitating someone. He sat in an armchair at the head of the table. A cigarette between his girlish lips seemed to be emitting smoke of its own accord. At the other end of the table there was a plateful of groats, half a loaf of bread, butter, cheese, and a knife. It was my supper. I expressed my thanks and sat down.

It occurred to me that I ought to wash my hands. (My father used to say that in sleep a person was joined by Khetumah, an evil spirit, and that was why we should wash our hands after rising from sleep.) But I thought that the minute I turned my back on this fellow he would once again utter that laugh of his.

Bella said, "Comrade Bendiger . . . may I call you Comrade? . . . Susskind Eikhl is a famous poet. You can show him the things you've written. If they're good, he'll publish them."

Eikhl spat his cigarette away. "What are you writing, the memoirs of your future?" Both of the women laughed.

"There you go with your jokes. This is a serious young man. He's writing about Spinoza," Bella said.

"Really?"

"It's an essay, a beginning. It's not a matured work," I stammered.

"Why didn't you let it mature? An essay is like an apple. It mustn't be torn from the tree before it's ripe. If you do, it's sour. Or perhaps you're fond of sour essays."

"Eat, eat. He likes to mock, but he doesn't mean any harm," said Bella, excusing him. "At his age," she said, indicating me, "he can't produce mature work. But if I were the editor of a journal, I would print such things. What's fascinating is how the mind evolves. Take Byron's earliest poems, for example. They were hardly works of genius, they were a bit awkward. But you can feel in them the Byron-to-come, with all of his moods and caprices."

"You feel all that only because Byron became Byron, Bella. Ten thousand wretches wanted to be Byron and ended as wretches, still wanting. It may be better to wait awhile and see what emerges." Here Susskind Eikhl winked at Bella and took a drag on his cigarette. One of his eyes blinked as it seemed to be studying his own sculpted nose.

Though the groats had been well covered with gravy, I ate without tasting their flavor. Susskind Eikhl's sarcasm frightened me. I said, "I wouldn't want to publish something that was not mature."

"No? But what would happen if the people wanted it? What if the people should demand it? What if they shouted, 'We want Bendiger's essay. We won't leave until you show it to us in black and white.' What would you do then? There is a saying, 'The call of the people is like the call of God.' And I'm sure you haven't picked a quarrel with God."

"What topsy-turvy reasoning," Bella said. "You don't have to answer him. He gets crazy notions."

I could see that Susskind Eikhl was determined to make me look foolish before the women. I wanted to make a biting, witty reply, but I couldn't find the right words. I said, "There's no point to any of this. The possibility of anything like that happening is too remote."

"Ah, it could happen any day. Mankind needs an essay on Spinoza. Especially on Spinoza and the Cabala. As you see him, is Spinoza a Cabalist?"

"He was influenced by the Cabala."

"As far as I can tell, he was a rationalist and not a mystic."

"He believed in intuition."

"Intuition and mysticism are two entirely different things, Comrade . . . ah . . . uh . . . Bendiger. Great thinkers and great creators often make use of intuition. But a mystic hopes to seize God by the satin lapels of his coat, or he wants to make wine flow from a wall. I once looked into a book by Jacob Boehme and I concluded that his name was misprinted: it should have read Yankl Bahayme [Yankl Dummox]."

"I don't think even Lenin has a monopoly on truth," I said, astonished and a bit frightened by my own words.

Susskind Eikhl emitted a snort of laughter through a single nostril. There was a look of uncertain humor in his eyes. "Well then, you can write another essay entitled 'Lenin and the Cabala.' Point out to him how much he has been influenced by the Rebbe of Gur, or by some other mollycoddle. There's a black market for such wares. Even *The Protocols of the Elders of Zion* has a considerable readership."

"Come on, Susskind. Don't be so ill-humored," Bella said, wagging her finger at him. "When all is said and done, he's still just a lad. Almost a child."

"Denikin and his hordes of bandits were also almost children. If you really are a naïve child, then let me tell you something. There are only two places where a contemporary person can stand:

either on one side of the barricades or on the other. In our time, there is no such thing as neutrality. Or one's own country—or any other such invention. If you're not with Lenin, you're with Mussolini and Pilsudski. With Lloyd George, with MacDonald, and with all of the other Fascist garbage. And don't give me that business about those who have no involvement in the political arena. All those fine spirits are plate-lickers at the Fascist table. I have more in common with an open Fascist than I have with those holy artists bobbing about in the upper atmosphere who, poor things, have no idea of what's taking place here on this sinful earth."

"Bravo, Eikhl, now you're talking," Bella cried, clapping her hands.

"I don't consider my father to be a Fascist," I said. "And I don't believe your father is one either."

"I don't know who your father is. But my father is a deluded little man. A victim of a swinish system. Of course, he's not going to grab a gun and shoot workers, but that's because he's never held a gun in his hand and, poor fellow, has no idea how to shoot. If someone else were to do the shooting, my father would say, It is God's will—after which he'd stand by piously nodding his head."

"His father is a rabbi," Bella interjected.

"A rabbi, eh? I saw how the Yekaterinoslav rabbi carried bread and salt to Czar Nicholas. The rabbi bowed as low as if he were reciting the *Modim Anakhnu* prayer in the synagogue. Every Saturday they celebrated a *Mi She'beyrakh* in the synagogues, not only for the Czar but for his uncle, for his wife and all sorts of the Czar's relatives. They would have blessed Rasputin and paraded the Torah before him if they thought it would serve them."

"What about those who choose neither Lenin nor Mussolini? Should they all commit suicide?"

"They won't have to commit suicide."

"Three-quarters of the people in the world, then, will have to die because they don't believe in Lenin?"

"In the current conflict, everyone will have to find his place. When the revolution comes, the workers of Germany, France, China, and India will not crawl into holes. They won't write any essays about Spinoza and the Cabala." Susskind Eikhl again made that single-nostril snort.

"What will the Jews get out of the revolution?" I asked. "Most Jews are not workers. And we have no peasants among us at all. According to Lenin, we are all petit bourgeois or clerics who are simply rubbish to the revolution. Why should we fight if it only means that we'll achieve our own destruction?"

"Who is this 'we'? Jewish workers have the same interests as the masses everywhere. And those shopkeepers, smugglers, and bench pressers in the synagogues mean as little to me as last year's snow. If they can't find a way to be useful here on this earth, then let them go to God. He'll protect them. He's always protected them—the way he did against Chmielnitsky, against Petlyura. He's a good God, particularly to the pious little Jews."

Eikhl sucked on his cigarette, but it had gone out. He winked at Edusha with his left eye. Evidently he was irritated at himself for having gotten into a heated conversation with a provincial youth.

Bella said, "Eat, Comrade Bendiger. Don't take it to heart. You're still young. You'll have plenty of time to think these matters through. There are capitalists and workers in Palestine too. As far as I can tell, you're not going to be one of the capitalists."

"Nor a Communist either."

"Well, you'll certainly be something. History has its own surprises. But one thing is sure, warm groats are better than cold ones. Even a capitalist will agree that that's so."

2

OTHER guests were arriving and I went back to my room. I undressed and went to bed, but I was immediately bitten by bedbugs. I recalled an aphorism of Otto Vanninger's, "God did not create the bedbug." Well then, who did? And who created the cruel, the deluded, the maniacal? Who created Petlyura, Dzerzhinski, thieves, bandits, murderers?

I had turned out the gas jet and did not have a match with which to relight it. From the other room came the sound of voices and laughter. Evidently they were carrying on a literary discussion. I heard various names mentioned: Blok, Mayakovsky, Lunacharsky, Esenin. Susskind Eikhl must have recited one of his poems, because he received applause.

"Why don't they get rid of the bedbugs instead of providing the world with a revolution?" I asked myself. In 1917 I had been on the side of the revolution. I had been pleased that they had dethroned Czar Nicholas. They had driven off Puryshkevich and the Black Hundreds. But in 1920 when, for a few days, the Bolsheviks were in Byaledrevne I saw what they did. They shot several of the town's Jews. A street loafer became a commissar. Communist youths gathered in the Polish church and tore down various holy pictures and stirred the peasants to violence. My uncle Gabriel, the rabbi, just barely escaped being shot. They were so arrogant and committed so many atrocities that the town thanked God when the Polish soldiers returned—even though they, too, had tormented the Jews. Most of the Communists left with the Red Army, but some were sent to prison. One of them was hanged. A day or so later, his father died of a heart attack.

It was late at night when the visitors left, but Susskind Eikhl apparently stayed on. I heard them whispering in the other room, as well as Susskind's muted laughter. There was only a bed and a sofa in that room. Apparently Susskind Eikhl slept with Bella.

"Everything wants blood," I mused, "the bedbugs, the Communists, the Fascists. Every social reformer, every seeming idealist." I had recently become a pacifist. I had read Tolstoy, Ferster, Nogdehn. I had even toyed with the idea of becoming a vegetarian. Well, what was to be done about the bedbugs, fleas, lice? What would happen if wild beasts were to multiply, as they had in India, and tigers were to devour children? And what was to be done about nations that attacked their weaker neighbors?

My own life seemed dreary, personally and ideologically. I had quarreled with my parents and with my relatives.

I lay in bed and permitted the bedbugs to bite me. In my mind's eye, I could see Susskind Eikhl taking off his clothes in the next room and making love to Bella while her niece Edusah lay opposite them on the sofa. Who could tell, perhaps he was getting ready for an orgy with the two. I remembered how my father said, "Put on a necktie today, tomorrow you'll sin with a woman. Once you start imitating the Gentiles, it won't be long before you'll become like them."

I addressed him in my thoughts. "Yes, Father, from your point of view, you're right. But you build everything on the assumption that every word of the Torah, of the Gemara, of the Shulhan Arukh was handed down from Mt. Sinai. But if that turns out not to be true, then the whole structure of your thought collapses. And what is there for me to build on? On Spinoza's geometric method or on the Commentaries of Immanuel Kant? On the phrases of Nietzsche? Lord in heaven, I'm adrift on a bottomless sea, physically and spiritually."

I fell asleep and woke in a sweat early in the morning, with a heavy heart and a bedbug-tormented body. "There's no air here," I murmured. "I'm choking." I got up and opened the door to the hallway. From the living room snores could be heard. All three of them were snoring: Susskind Eikhl, Bella, Edusha. I stood there in the dark, wearing only my shirt, breathing the hallway air that smelled of gas and dirty laundry. There was not a window open anywhere. We were all breathing poison. I lay down again.

Edusha came to wake me later that morning. She knocked at the door, and before I had a chance to say a word, she came in and lighted the gas. She was wearing a bathrobe and slippers. I could see the hem of her nightgown. She looked as if she had slept well, and had a warm, desirable maiden freshness about her. She said, "I woke you!"

"No, I wasn't asleep."

"We have some breakfast for you. It's ten o'clock. How did you sleep?"

"Well."

"I have to tidy this place up a bit. When Stanislas Kalbe went away, he left things in a mess. Ah, men are such filthy creatures. If it weren't for us women, they couldn't cope at all."

"Does the poet live here?" I asked, hardly knowing what I said or why.

"Eikhl? What are you talking about? He went away last night. He was here until three o'clock. That's the way he is. He's an interesting fellow. Terribly talented. But it doesn't pay to argue with him. My aunt gets along with him, but I can't stand anyone who's so haughty. What if he *is* a poet? Poets are also made of flesh and blood, isn't that so?"

"Of course."

"You, on the other hand, are too withdrawn. As I see it, you live only once, and you should enjoy life all you can. What's the point of all those questions? It just means you lose another day."

"What kind of woman is your aunt?"

"Oh, she's an interesting case. She wants to triumph over everything and everyone. She had a husband, but she divorced him. He was a Hasid. A follower of . . . What's the rebbe's name? The Solokov rebbe. She longs for her child, who is with its father. Don't repeat a word of this. She'll tell you everything herself. But if I say anything about her she gets mad. She could have made a very advantageous marriage. Rich young men pursued her. But she treats money as if it were mud. The truth is, I'm the same way. If I like someone, it doesn't matter to me if he's a beggar."

"Is your fiancé a beggar?"

"Lipmann? It's just a way of talking. His parents are pious. He studied to become a lawyer, but he doesn't want to be one. Ah, it's a long story. It's supposed to be a secret and you won't tell anyone. He's going to the Soviet Union for a couple of months. We'll be married when he gets back. But you know, what does 'get married' mean? I don't need some rabbi's blessing, and he needs it even less. We'll take an apartment and live together."

"What's he going to do in the Soviet Union?"

"He's a well-educated man, a doer. He'll teach a course of some kind. He'll give lectures. I was going to go with him, but at the last moment his plans changed. And now I'm here alone. But never mind, it won't harm the revolution, as they say. And after all, how long is a few months? Winter will go by, and then, in spring, he'll come back. He'll be too busy over there to have time for other women. And if not, so what? A man is like a bee, always looking for honey in another flower. That's his nature. As for the flower, it gives its nectar to any bee that comes."

Edusha's eyes glowed with amusement. She said, "Go into the kitchen and wash up. Then come and eat. If you're going to live with us, you'll have to eat. We can't stand to let a young man go off to eat in a restaurant, where they'll charge him double for everything. And the food's not fresh there either." Then she asked, "Who's the woman who's going to travel with you on the certificate?"

"Her father was a rich man once. She has a fiancé in Palestine and she wants to go to him."

"I get it. You'll marry her and later you'll get a divorce."

"It's just a formality."

"Be careful. Many a young man has been trapped that way. What is she, an old maid?"

"She's not old."

"Why isn't her fiancé bringing her out?"

"I guess he can't."

"There's something wrong here, but it's none of my business. I'm not as involved in social questions as my aunt. But I keep my ears open and I know what's what. The whole Zionist thing is nothing but a swindle, a sterile fantasy. What will you do there? I had a girl friend who went there, a lovely woman. Rich too. She got it into her head that she wanted to help the Jewish people become productive, and so on. They set her to work in a field where it was so hot she practically burned her feet. And on top of that, she got malaria. And then one of the Halutzim or one of the *shomrim* latched on to her, and the next thing you know, he gives her a big belly. Then he disappears, who the hell knows where? She came home to Warsaw and left the child behind. And immediately she started longing for it. One evening she came to me and said, 'Edusha, braid me a couple of braids. I want to look nice tomorrow.' She hadn't cut her hair. It grew down to her waist. So I braided her a couple of braids. Then we talked for a while. Then we kissed and she went home. The next morning, the phone rang. Anna, a woman like a rose, had poisoned herself."

"People poison themselves in Russia too."

"Ah no. Life has some purpose there. Go wash yourself."

Edusha left the room. I was embarrassed to go into the kitchen because I didn't have any pajamas or bathrobe or slippers. One of the women might come in. Finally I hurried to the kitchen, where I washed in a great hurry. Then I got dressed and went into the middle room.

How strange! Both of the women were waiting for me to have breakfast. It made me uncomfortable. For one thing, I hadn't the least idea how I would repay them for my meals. Besides that, why should they wait for me to come to breakfast? As I sat down, it occurred to me that there was more than generosity at stake—there was an element of dependency here. These two women, it was apparent, could not stand being alone. Always —night and day—they needed someone else to be with them as well. It was all linked to the condition of contemporary mankind—to collectivism and the notion that people were mere cogs in a larger machine.

At the table, Bella and Edusha talked about all sorts of leftish encounters—of meetings, demonstrations, and marches. Evidently they read all the Warsaw papers, because they knew what every deputy to the parliament had said.

They talked about the theaters in Warsaw, about singers and speakers who had recently been on the radio. They talked about events in Berlin, Paris, London, Moscow—even Peking and Manchuria, as if the events had taken place nearby. The look in their eyes contained both pride and servility. When they uttered the words "Soviet Russia," their eyes glowed, as if it would be a sin to speak with anything but fervor.

Bella tasted a piece of bread, swallowed a mouthful of coffee, and smoked a cigarette. She blew three smoke rings and said, "Everything's going to turn topsy-turvy. The revolution will follow you to Palestine . . ."

3

SEVERAL days went by. I saw Sonya and told her about Miss Minna and the dark little room into which I had moved. On Saturdays, the shop where Sonya worked selling women's underclothing was closed and she could do what she wished. Since it was snowing, I went with her in the direction of the Praga Bridge. We went into a café and ordered coffee.

Sonya had serious complaints to make. Why hadn't I told her about the fictitious marriage? She would have gone to Palestine with me herself. How much longer was she expected to work as an employee in a store? All the customers were women. She had no opportunities to meet any men. In Palestine there were few women and it would be easy to get married there. Besides, she, Sonya, loved the outdoors: fields and woods and small villages. What was the good of walking the streets of Warsaw? You just got worn out, befuddled. "You wouldn't have had to keep me as your wife. I'd have given you your freedom," Sonya said.

"I can't make a fool of Miss Minna. Besides that, the man who got me the certificate was her teacher, and he got the certificate for her, not for me. If I go back on my word, that'll be the end of the certificate."

"What's to become of me, eh? I wake up in the middle of the night and can't get back to sleep. I think about my life—and how dismal it all is."

"I'll take you to Palestine."

"How? No, you'll forget me, you'll forget. You went away to become a teacher and you promised to write. But you were silent. When you get to Palestine you won't even remember that there is a Sonya anywhere." I wanted to pay for the coffee, but I found that all I had was a couple of worthless coins. I didn't even have enough money to take the streetcar. I felt the full weight of Sonya's accusations. I had, in a way, made use of her. She had helped me in my direst need. Even now, I'd be wandering around alone if it weren't for Sonya.

I remembered that Miss Minna had treated me the way a nobleman's wife used to treat a court Jew. I was teaching her Hebrew, but she mocked my Polish. She was preparing to marry me and had applied for papers, but she treated me with contempt. She was continually correcting my manners. How to sit; how to eat; how to greet people. On board ship we would be sharing a cabin, but Minna told me at once that I could not sleep in the cabin with her and would have to find a place somewhere else. Sometimes she spoke seriously with me, but then, as if she remembered who I was, abandoned her respectful tone.

It did not take me long to realize that I embarrassed Minna

with my appearance and with my behavior. I suffered from a cold and was constantly blowing my nose—and did not have enough handkerchiefs. I had bought a shaving kit with extra razor blades, but every time I shaved I cut my chin. I sent my shirts to a machine laundry, but I didn't have enough money to get them ironed. I turned my collar inside out.

Now here was Sonya, sitting angrily opposite me, with the look on her face of a woman who could not abide me but who could not make up her mind to leave. "Is this love?" I asked myself. And I replied, "No, it's loneliness."

For a while I sat there, with fantasies running through my head: of finding a treasure so that I could pay Sonya and everyone else who had ever done me a favor. I thought of the novel I would write about the situation in which I now found myself. But how could I get any writing done, since I lacked sleep and was oppressed by worries? I had no home; I lived in a cold house. There was no heater in my dark little room, and at night it was almost as cold as it was outside. I was already coughing a dry cough.

Suddenly my thoughts turned to suicide. I'd been thinking of this from the time I left home and felt I had no other option available to me. But what would my parents say when they got the news? Good Lord! I hadn't even written home. My mother, no doubt, was worrying herself sick. Every night I remembered that I hadn't written and made a solemn vow to write a letter or a postcard in the morning, but when morning came, I forgot to do it. In my mind I accused myself: "You're a murderer. A murderer."

Sonya said, "Would you like to go to the theater tonight? They're playing the operetta *The Princess Czardas*."

"No, Sonya."

"I'll buy you a ticket."

"No, I won't take it."

"We can't sit here all day. People are staring at us already."

It was true. The waitresses were giving us irritated looks. Sonya paid the bill and we went out.

How about hanging myself? But where? Should I drown myself in the Vistula? How strange, I feared death less than I did the cold water. Chills ran up and down my spine. At night I covered myself with two quilts, but I could never get warm enough. Poison? But what kind of poison? The best thing to do would be to jump into the sea from the boat that would take me to Palestine. The Mediterranean was a warm sea. And at sea there was little likelihood that anyone would come to my rescue.

Sonya put her arm through mine. "Don't be so sad. You know the saying, it's always darkest before dawn."

How could there be any dawn for me? I already knew the truth: I wasn't fit for anything in Palestine. When I visited the Halutzim Association, they regarded me with something like astonishment. They smiled, and every eye seemed to ask, "What's he doing here?" They wondered why Dov Kalmenzohn bothered with me. The same thing had happened to me a couple of years before in the rabbinical seminary, and before that in the study-house, and in cheder.

I went back with Sonya to the Jewish quarter. All at once she said, "Do you know what? I have the key to the store." It was a crazy idea to go to the store on a Saturday, in daylight, when all the Jewish businesses were closed. But we had no place else to go. When we got there, Sonya unlocked the door and we went inside. She arranged the outer gates so no one could come in. Inside, by a weak, glimmering light, we could see the shelves of boxes containing women's shirts, jackets, and stockings.

For a while, we sat on a couple of chairs and then we embraced. Sonya said, "If only the old man could see us now! He'd hang himself." She burst into laughter in the Sabbath dimness of the place. Occasionally she listened attentively, lest some relative of the owner passing by might notice that there was no lock on the front gate. It was even possible that a policeman could knock at the door, or some member of the Guardians of the Sabbath, checking to see that no merchant had violated the sanctity of the Sabbath.

Awkward as it was, where else could we have gone? We retained our provincial timidity: I didn't dare ask Sonya to come to my dark little room, and she wouldn't have wanted to come there either.

We kissed and hugged. Sonya paid no attention to my seductive whisperings and warned me all the while to be quiet and to moderate my wilder impulses. She intended to be a kosher bride on her wedding night, though it made no difference to her who her groom might be.

After an hour or so, Sonya let me out of the store first. Then after she had replaced the store's lock, she met me on the street corner and we resumed our stroll. We passed the house of the Halutzim and it occurred to me to pay them a visit with Sonya. It was unlikely that Dov Kalmenzohn would be there. Sonya hesitated awhile, but then she agreed to come with me.

Even as we were climbing the stairs, we heard the hubbub. Sabbath though it was, the electric lights were burning. The Halutzim were busy packing boxes, hammering nails, tying up chests, writing labels with thick pens and pencils. I read place-names like Constantsa, Jaffa, Haifa. A young giant with red hair, a summer-freckled face, and an unbuttoned shirt that revealed the red hair on his chest was closing a box with sealing wax. He smoked a cigarette as he worked. A young woman Halutz was pressing a blouse. Sonya looked on, amazed. Thank God that Kalmenzohn was away. I would have been embarrassed introducing Sonya to him.

A young man whom I had not seen before came up and asked, "When does your ship leave?"

"Not for a while yet. I don't have my passport."

"Maybe you need a fixer." He gave me the address of an administrator on Nowolipki Street who was able to supply a Halutz with everything he needed: a birth certificate, a passport, a draftee's booklet, a document indicating that one had given up one's Polish citizenship, and all sorts of other papers. Authentic as well as counterfeit documents. The youth was tall, erect, and had disheveled blond hair. I introduced him to Sonya. He asked, "Are the two of you traveling together?"

"Unfortunately no," Sonya replied. "Unfortunately" was a favorite word among small-town intellectuals.

"Why not? A man with a certificate can take a woman with him."

"He's already supplied himself with a woman."

"In that case . . . Here, sit down and make yourself at home. We never drive anyone away. I'm leaving this coming Wednesday."

"Are you also traveling with someone?"

"Come into the other room. It's quieter there."

We went into another room that appeared to be a library. The walls were crowded with bookshelves: Hebrew, Yiddish, Polish, German. There was no one in it now. We sat down, and the young man said, "I've got a girl back home. But the simple fact is that we didn't have the money for expenses. So I'm traveling with a fictive wife."

Sonya said, "You might fall in love with her."

The youth shook his head. "Never."

There was a pause, after which he asked me, "Do you smoke?"

"No thanks."

"What will you do in the Land? You don't look as if you could do physical labor."

"He's a writer," Sonya said, betraying me.

The youth became very serious. His eyebrows arched as he said, "We're going to need writers too. We are the People of the Book."

We sat for a while, the three of us, as twilight fell. As the youth smoked a cigarette, shadows fell across his face. At times when he took a drag on his cigarette, one caught a gleam of sorrow in his features. In his pale blue eyes, one saw tenacity, resolution.

I had given up believing in the sanctity of the Sabbath, but I was unable to forget what day of the week it was. Not far from where we were, Jews had eaten the three meals of the Sabbath and sung the B'nei Heichalah. In some little town in Galicia, my mother was murmuring the "God of Abraham" prayer. It seemed to me that I could see her darkened features and hear her heartfelt words inherited from grandmothers and great-grand-mothers.

God of Abraham, of Isaac and Jacob, protect your poor people of Israel. Your dear Sabbath is receding. May your dear week come to us, bringing health and prosperity, wealth and honor, wisdom and good deeds and rich rewards to all.

It was the prayer my mother uttered for me, her wandering son driven from his father's table, tossing about somewhere in a big city, sundered from Judaism but not yet lost to the Gentiles.

The People of the Book! What kinds of books could I write? What could I teach my people? To whom would my deeds provide a model of behavior?

Sonya seemed to have turned rigid. Her eyes, in the dark, protruded like those of some sort of night bird. I had the feeling that she had suddenly acquired the powers of a clairvoyant. Her eyes sparkled. In her own female fashion, she was taking leave of the Sabbath, which remained holy no matter how much it was violated. God's own day of rest, the Jew's day to take stock of his soul.

The Halutz took a long drag on his cigarette and then extinguished its stub on the edge of the table. "My last week in the Diaspora," he said.

4

THAT evening when Edusha called me to dinner, I found her fiancé, Hertz Lipmann, standing in the middle of the room. A man of middle height, broad-boned, with a sparse head of hair. His nose was somewhat fleshy, and he had thick lips and dense eyebrows, a square chin, a short neck. His head was set firmly on broad shoulders, he had large hands and short legs, and wore shoes with rounded tips. He made me think of those foot-weary soldiers who were home on leave. He had an air of strength, with the look of a man who was never frightened of hard labor. In his steely eyes there was a secret agent's look —the sort of suspicious gaze that one sometimes sees in their eyes.

Cheka! I thought the minute I saw him.

Edusha introduced me, but he did not put out his hand—he merely murmured something. He seated himself in the chair in which Bella usually sat and lighted a cigarette. Evidently he was determined not to talk about anything in my presence. He nodded his head or shook it to indicate yes or no. He gnawed at his thick lower lip or blew smoke in my direction. When he did utter a word or two, rarely, his voice was coarse and stern.

Edusha and Bella did what they could to get us two men to talk, but Hertz Lipmann refused to look my way. I thought he was hostile—first, because the women had rented their room to a man, and then, because I was going to go to Palestine, a non-kosher place in the eyes of a Jewish Communist.

I ate quickly and went back to my dark little room. It was only then that the conversation became lively in the middle room. The women were the chief speakers, and Lipmann's bass voice resounded like distant thunder. "What kinds of mothers have sons like him?" I asked myself. "How could two thousand years of exile produce such self-confidence?"

The existence of a Hertz Lipmann did not confirm my theory about Jews and Jewishness. I believed that the Jew was misplaced in the real world. Jews as a group (and I, as an individual) were a degenerated species, an anomaly among the nations—"a people that dwells alone." But apparently this stocky fellow was able to stand firmly with both feet on the ground.

A while later, Susskind Eikhl arrived and there was the din of conversation. Eikhl was contentious, shouted, and snorted laughter through a single nostril. Hertz Lipmann carried on about something in a lengthy monologue. Some hours later, I fell asleep. When I woke, I smelled coffee and heard footsteps in the kitchen and the hallway. It was Edusha coming to wake me, because in that dark little room there was no way to know whether it was day or night. She stood beside the door and spoke into the dark. "You're still asleep? It's nine o'clock."

"No, I'm not asleep. Thank you."

"Get dressed. We'll wait to have breakfast till you get there. How did you sleep, eh?"

I wanted to tell Edusha that the bedbugs had been at me all night long and that I had finally fallen asleep at dawn, but I said nothing. There was nothing I could do to change my situation. I already owed the women the price of many meals. I had not paid the rent for the second half of the month. No, they did not keep the apartment clean. I had noticed that Bella's bed linen was dirty, horsehair protruded from rents in the sofa, and the armchair, with a leg missing, had books under it to keep it steady. I had seen Bella, when she was about to fry meat, cutting it with a scissors instead of a knife.

I suffered every morning getting myself washed in the kitchen, since at any moment one of the women might appear. Besides that, the room was so cold that the water and the pipes were icy. The towel on which I tried to dry myself was invariably moist. I shaved with cold water and often cut myself. As I was standing before the sink, I heard Edusha singing a recently popular song. She had a melodic voice. Though she had no time for housecleaning, she often went to operettas and musicals and knew all the popular songs on the radio.

At breakfast that morning, Bella seemed unusually self-absorbed. She hardly spoke a word. She took a bite out of a roll, a drag on her cigarette. A while later, she got dressed and left the house. She looked like an elegant Amazon in her coat with its loop in the back and her hat like a helmet. Edusha ate her breakfast still wearing her bathrobe and her slippers.

When Bella had gone, Edusha and I chatted. She asked me about my certificate. What were the papers I still needed? She said, "Strange, I've been in Warsaw all my life, I was born here. But I have the feeling that I'm in a foreign city. As if I had just stopped here on my way somewhere."

"You too?"

"Ever since my mother went away, everything feels temporary. Hertz is leaving. And Bella won't be here for long. And you're going to go away too. One of these days, I'll end by being all alone."

"But your fiancé will return."

"I hope so, but . . . He has all sorts of plans. I oughtn't to tell you this, but in the Party one never knows where one is. If they decide to send him to Brazil or to Johannesburg, he has to pack his bags and go. It's like being in the army."

"He has something military about him."

"Yes, you're right. How is it that you noticed it so quickly? He has an iron will. His parents are poor—and pious as well. But he educated himself, staying up all night with his books. As disciplined as a soldier. Once he decides to do something, it becomes a holy purpose. Sadly enough, I'm completely the opposite."

"They say that opposites attract."

"Yes, but sometimes it's hard. What sort of person are you?"

"Entirely without a will of my own."

"Oh, don't say that. You have character on your side. Do you have a girlfriend? I mean a real one. Not the fictive one."

I told her about Lena, Yekutiel the watchmaker's daughter, in Byaledrevne. Edusha asked me, "You're certain she'll wait?"

"Nothing's certain."

"True. It's better to have no illusions at all. My philosophy is 'Spit on it all.' "

"It's easier to spit on someone else."

"On everything. Sometimes everything goes wrong. But when evening comes I get dressed and I go to the opera, where they let me in *na gape*. You know what that means? Sneaking in. I give the usher a couple of groschen. I may be terribly depressed, but when Digos or Gruschtshinski sings an aria, I forget all my troubles and I sing along with them. There's a whole bunch of us *na gapniks*. When one of us has a ticket, it's passed from hand to hand. We know all sorts of tricks for sneaking in. Sometimes I stand in the fourth gallery and look down into the loges. I know that the revolution will sweep all that capitalist garbage away, but it's interesting to look down at the beautiful women and their cavaliers. It's another sort of opera—pearls, diamonds, long necks, blond hairdos. The men are tall and erect, as if from some other world. I watch them nod their heads, bow, kiss the hands of the women, and I feel like laughing. It's as if grown children were at play. And then there's the opera itself: the executioner is ready to cut off the hero's head, and the hero, accompanied by the orchestra, sings an aria. Oh, I love the opera!"

"I've never been to one."

"Never? Ah, I'll have to take you with me one day. There is no opera in Palestine. Still, I'd like to go there just to see what it looks like. One day someone sang Arabic songs on the radio and I was instantly transported there among the tents and the camels in the desert. I was seized with a dreadful nostalgia, as if I had come from those regions myself."

"You and Hertz Lipmann don't really make a couple," I said, amazed by my own words.

Edusha was instantly attentive. The look she gave me was at once anxious and a bit sad. "Why do you say that?"

"Oh, he's entirely Reason and you're all Feeling."

"That's how it should be. You said it yourself earlier, that opposites attract. He has feelings too, but he controls himself. How can one play with feelings in a world like ours? At the pleasure of a couple of bourgeois we get a world war, in which twenty million people die. My own father died of typhus in that war. And why did it happen? Because England and Germany couldn't decide how to share oil. Now, is that right or not?"

"No, it's not right."

"Why not?"

"Because the oil was only an excuse. If they don't go to war over oil, they'll find some other reason."

"You're saying there is no hope for mankind."

"I'm afraid not."

"Is that your experience? If it is, then I pity you."

"The worst truth is better than the best self-deception," I replied, not knowing for certain whether I believed what I said or whether I was simply teasing Edusha. She stood, regarding me with a sad, questioning look.

The telephone rang and she ran into the hallway.

After a while I returned to my room. In the light of the yellow gas lamp there was neither day nor night. I chose a book at random from the shelf of books left behind by Stanislas Kalbe. As I was leafing through one of the mathematics books, the random thought came to me that Edusha and Kalbe had been lovers. After all, what could restrain a woman like her? Not fear of God and, in recent times, not even the fear of pregnancy. Sex had become a children's game for grownups. I myself had started something of a relationship with her just now. Why else would I have told her that she and Hertz Lipmann were not a couple?

I sat on the edge of my bed and thought about Lena.

On a muddy autumn evening, we had sworn to love each other forever. We had walked hand in hand in the dark all the way to the water mill. From time to time we stopped to kiss each other in the drizzle. It was a time in my life when I yearned night and day for the sight of her oval face, her dark eyes in which a maidenly gentleness and a child's naïveté glowed along with an anxiety as ancient as woman herself. When I took her in my arms, her whole being trembled like a fowl being readied for the Yom Kippur sacrifice. She used to say, "Tell me if you don't really mean it. I don't think love is a toy."

I gave her my most solemn word of honor that I loved her. That I would marry her. That I would be true to her till my last breath. But by now, I had even stopped writing to her. I had been seized by a paralyzing depression in the town where I had gone to be a teacher. Days went by in which I never left the house. I stopped speaking to the people in whose home I lived. I experienced a sort of sickly shyness, a need to hide away from everyone. I became so constipated that no amount of pills could loosen my bowels. I seemed to have become deaf and half blind. I was endlessly letting things fall out of my hands. When I wrote, I failed to complete certain letters and sometimes whole words. I had the painful feeling that I had ceased to be myself and was unable to become someone else.

III

I RANG the bell and the maid opened the door. "Miss Minna is not here," she said.

"Not here?"

"She had to go somewhere. She wants you to wait for her."

I seated myself in the chair in the hallway and started to leaf through the pages of the same magazine I had read the first time I came there, but Meir Ahronson, just as he had the last time, came out of his room wearing his cap and the coat that was too long for him. He said, "Come into my room. Minna will be back soon. Tekla, bring us a couple of glasses of tea."

I went into Meir Ahronson's study. There was an old rug on the floor, old books. The double windows were closed and the room smelled of dust and of the coal that had been freshly lighted in the stove. Meir Ahronson sat in an old armchair, a piece of furniture that dated back to the times of King Sobieski. It had a headrest and was studded with buttons made of bone. I sat on a leather-covered sofa that had rents in it. Tekla, the dark-eyed young Gentile woman with red cheeks, brought us tea and rock-hard *kichel*. I nearly cracked a tooth biting into it. Meir Ahronson took a swallow of tea and sighed. "Well then," he asked, "is she making any progress in Hebrew?"

"It's not easy. Especially the grammar."

"I studied grammar once. Do you think that today's grammar is grammar? It's all been shortened, simplified. My father was a Hasid but he wanted us to know the Scriptures just the same. He hired a Lithuanian to give us grammar lessons. The objective case, the subjective case. It all went in one ear and out the other. It was a different Warsaw. Jews were Jews then and not Gentiles. Money was easy to come by. The Russians built railroads and Jews grew rich. The Warsaw you now see was built by Jews. Nobody knew anything about taxes in those days. When the Czar needed money, he usually borrowed it from Rothschild or some banker. Now they flay you alive. I get called to the tax office every so often and show them my books. It doesn't help. The Gentiles say, 'You're lying, Jew. You're a swindler.' That's how they talk to Meir Ahronson in the new Poland. Their fathers were Sabbath servants, janitors. What's to become of us, eh? They want to pull us up by the roots."

"The Zionists are right," I said, merely to say something.

"Right about what? Nobody's going to give them Palestine. Nobody gets anything for nothing. Dreams, sterile fantasies. They've turned a Jew into a High Commissioner, but he does England's bidding, not what Nachum Sokolow wants. It's idiocy, stupidity. That Zbigniew Shapira, Minna's fiancé, has as much to do with Palestine as you have with Count Potocki. He's ruining himself. He went there to ruin himself. Minna told you about it, eh?"

"She hasn't told me anything."

"He's an engineer. He studied in Cracow and at the Sorbonne. In 1919, he enlisted in the Polish Army and was promoted eventually to the rank of major. They're in no hurry to turn a Jew into an officer, but he has a good head on his shoulders. He helped them to build bridges and who knows what all. His father is no longer living. His mother is old and partly lame. He's her only son—tall, good-looking, well educated, a real somebody. He knows very little about being a Jew, but that's the way of the present generation. They're afraid of the word 'Jew.' He met my Minna in Tsapat and they were betrothed at once. They had no need of a marriage broker. What does a father want? To derive a little pleasure from his children. I had another daughter, younger than Minna, but she's dead. She had an appendicitis attack and she died. It killed her mother. She's no longer the woman she was. Well, what's to be done? Everything's sent from above. With Minna, we thought things would run smoothly, but then Zbigniew did a really crazy thing. He stabbed himself with a knife to avoid being redrafted. He had to get out of Poland; otherwise he'd have gone to jail. He's in Palestine now, under an assumed name, and he won't stay there either. There you have it. She's studying Hebrew, but now Zbigniew wants to go to South Africa or to Brazil. He's a hothead. Every day a new project pops into his head."

"As an engineer, he can always earn a living, no matter where he goes."

"Ah, a living isn't good enough for him. He wants to be rich. He wants to be a millionaire—at once. He can't wait. He's clearly very smart. Something of a philosopher. And yet he does things as foolish as that. A healthy man to put himself into a sickbed of his own accord. His mother's been left alone. She can't walk, poor woman, she has swollen feet. She has to have things brought to her home, and she has no money to pay for anything. Any day now they'll throw her out of the apartment. Then where will she go? In a small town there's a poorhouse, but in Warsaw there's no such thing. Here you can die and no one will take the slightest notice. Troubles. People are their own worst enemies. I spoke frankly to my daughter: 'You marry a fellow like that and you put yourself at risk.' Who knows where he'll drag her? But she's in love. There's a new madness in the world. Love— they take one look at someone and get obsessed. Four weeks after the wedding, there's nothing but quarrels and blows. Well, what about you? Have you got your documents?"

"There's a fixer working on them, Barish Mendl."

"Yes, I know him. He manages a house for a friend of mine. He knows the nobility. He's got connections with everyone. Here in Poland bribes are the only way to get things done. Everyone puts his hand out, from cabinet ministers to loan underwriters. They all have outstretched hands and demanding mouths. Oh, there's the doorbell. It's probably Minna. Don't let on that I told you about Zbigniew. She thinks he can do no wrong. She believes in him as if he were a wonder rabbi."

"Shall I go to her?"

"Yes, if she finds you with me, she'll suspect I've been telling you things. In fact, everything I've said is an open secret."

I left behind a half glass of tea and a piece of *kichel* with a bite out of it and went into the hallway. The maid was opening the door for Minna, who was wearing a fur jacket and fur hat and carrying a fur-trimmed purse. She looked like a provincial noblewoman. The maid helped her take off her overshoes. Minna's face was reddened from the cold. Seeing me, her green eyes darkened and she grimaced, as if she had tasted something sour. "Why are you waiting out here? Go into my room."

I went into her room and waited a long while. I leafed through the books in her bookcase. There were dried flowers between the pages. Evidently she read a great deal of poetry. Occasionally verses had been underlined. Minna knew very well that I was a writer, but she had never talked with me about literature. What she usually talked about was Hebrew grammar or about the documents we needed. She was irritated each time she learned that there was more delay.

I stood there scanning lines of poetry, the opening phrases of short stories, aphorisms or excerpts from essays. There were various papers in the bookcase, as well as notebooks containing Minna's university lecture notes.

On a small table lay a huge album which I had not opened. I looked into it and my eye lighted at once upon Zbigniew Shapira's picture. A head taller than Minna, he stood with his arm around her. A dandy with a thin mustache, he carried a cane and wore a hard-visored cap. There was something deceitful and impatient about the smiling look in his eyes.

I heard Minna's step in the hallway and quickly closed the album. Minna came in. Angrily she asked, as she crossed the threshold, "What's holding up your documents? It can't be allowed to drag on like this."

"The fixer says he's doing all he can."

"We have to go through the ceremony no later than the beginning of next week."

"All right."

"I've decided to stop studying grammar. Just teach me vocabulary and pronunciation."

We spent about half an hour on vocabulary and pronunciation. Then curtly Minna asked, "Has Father been talking to you?"

"A little."

"What did he tell you?"

"Oh, he talked about the good old days."

"The good old days weren't as good as he likes to think. But try to persuade him otherwise. I used to think that people of his type and his age told the truth, but I've learned that they, too, tell lies. Today they tell you one thing, tomorrow they tell you something entirely different. And they also forget things. I was told that my grandfather Abraham Moishe was a magnate. Then it turned out that when he went to visit his rebbe, he went on foot because he couldn't afford the trip. How do you reconcile the two stories? I've made a solemn vow not to tell stories when I get old. And what about you? Your stories are also full of contradictions."

I was astonished at the way Minna spoke to me. Until now, she had avoided saying anything personal. I said, "My life is filled with contradictions."

"Why just yours? Really, what are you going to do in the Holy Land? I'm afraid that, from the minute we land, you'll have trouble earning a living."

"You needn't worry that I'll be a burden to anyone."

Minna was thoughtful for a bit. "That fellow, the Halutz— I've already forgotten his name—was too aggressive. You're quite the reverse. Someone like you is likely to lie down in the street and starve to death. I'm the same way. And what's worse, I was a student in a finishing school. One Jewish girl among fifty Gentiles. Most of the girls slept in a dormitory, but I insisted on having a room of my own. They were about to send me away, but finally they found me a room. In summer it was as hot as an oven, you could roast to death. In winter it was as cold as all outdoors. I lived for a year in that attic room, and I still don't know how I got out of there alive. But I never told my parents. The girls gradually stopped talking to me. To this day I don't know why. The teachers also avoided me. Not because I was Jewish. Another Jewish girl came there later. She was treated like a queen. I attended all my lectures and got the best grades. But I was made to feel that I didn't exist. Sometimes I myself doubted I existed. Since you're going to be a writer, all of this may be interesting to you. Back then, we read Slovatski's *Krul Dukh* and other mystical works—and I began to believe that I was a ghost no one could see. I've no idea why I'm telling you this. I want to learn fifty words a day.

"I have the impression that this fictive marriage of ours is like ghosts in a play. Sometimes I have the creepy feeling that you will never get your documents in order. That there are evil forces at work to frustrate my plans."

Minna spoke quickly even as she gave me a transfixing look. I grew warm and sensed that I was blushing. I said, "You can rest assured that I'm not in league with any evil spirits."

"Ah, I'm not so sure of that. Every time I wanted to accomplish anything in my life, some contrary force was directed against me and made it fail. If you're serious about being a writer, I could tell you stories about someone who was followed by a ghost."

"By all means, Miss Minna. Tell . . ."

"Not now. Maybe on board the ship, if we ever get on it. Sometimes I'm afraid that I'll never leave Warsaw. Something unexpected will happen and I'll be stuck here as in a trap."

2

IT all happened as if it were a real wedding. I was dressed in a white linen robe to remind me of the day of my death (as if I could forget it) and Minna was made to circle me seven times to fulfill the injunction *Ve nekeve t'sovev gever* [And the woman will turn around a man]. The rabbi, who had intelligent, worldly eyes and a long silver-white beard combed to form two points, recited the prayers and had us drink from a cup of wine. I had brought a little bottle of brandy and some *kichel* to give to the Jews who helped make up the prayer quorum.

Minna, as if she were proving some point, wore an old dress and had not bothered to comb her hair properly. At intervals she winked at me. We had become a little more friendly. She told me how Zbigniew Shapira fell in love with her and spoke of him with that look of adoration peculiar to women who are in love. She had never met a handsomer man, or one more intelligent. He had graduated from his high school with a gold medal. He had finally attained the rank of major in the Polish Army, but in fact carried out the duties of a general. When he took Minna to the theater, his criticisms of the plays were the same as those written later by professional critics. This was also true when he took her to a gallery opening at the Zacheta. He had been offered the position of docent at the University of Warsaw. Women were crazy about him—the most beautiful, the wealthiest women who belonged to the great families. But there was one thing about which Minna kept silent. She did not say what it was that had compelled him to leave Poland.

Now Minna stood under the wedding canopy, whose posts were being held by four Jewish passersby—two porters, a beggar, and a newspaper vendor. Her face expressed the sense of aloofness I had first seen in her father's face. She smiled a knowing, somewhat melancholy smile. She actually put out the tip of her tongue. I tried to smile back, but my face that day was curiously stiff. I knew I was deceiving not only England but God. The white garment I wore, the holy words that were being spoken, the candles the rabbi's wife had lighted in the silver candlesticks— all this gave me pause. What would my parents say if they knew?

The rabbi read out my father's name in the marriage contract in which I had inscribed, in Aramaic, a promise to pay the bride, Mindl, the daughter of Meir Elimelekh, two hundred gulden if I ever divorced her. My heirs were obligated to pay this sum in the event of my death. I undertook to support her, clothe her, and come unto her as a man to his wife.

Thank God, the ceremony was quickly over. The rabbi wished us *mazel tov*. The wedding canopy was dismantled. The men drank brandy and ate *kichel* and returned shortly after to the streets. The rabbi's wife wished us *mazel tov* and then blew out the candles. We walked out into the cold air.

Minna said, "Well, now what do we do?"

"We have to go to the fixer."

"Let's take a droshky."

The fixer, Barish Mendl, had acquired a number of documents for me, but he said more were required. The English consul was not easily fooled. The Polish government was in no hurry to issue an exit visa. Barish Mendl, a little fellow with a high forehead and a pale nose like a parrot's beak, requested money for official stamps, for official petitions, for documents that would help produce more documents. His costs were well beyond what had been anticipated. Time after time Minna had had to reach into her purse for more bank notes. She had already put down a deposit on a ship ticket for the two of us. Now we had to get the document that would officially make us husband and wife.

It seemed to me that not only I, but Minna too, was feeling a certain shyness now. She avoided looking into my eyes. When we walked, she kept herself apart from me. When we had to step down a curb, she refused to let me take her arm. And yet, as if it were done to spite each other, we had to spend the entire day together. We had an appointment with Dov Kalmenzohn in the offices of the Halutzim, and we had to go to a travel agency on Krulevski Street.

Now we went into a restaurant. The latest entry in my account book of humiliations was to have a woman paying for every droshky, for every glass of tea, for every tramway ticket. I choked on each mouthful. I was continually reassuring Minna that I was not hungry, not thirsty, that I preferred to walk.

I could see that my shabby clothes embarrassed her—my flattened cap, my overcoat with its two buttons missing, my old shoes, my stringy necktie. I shaved every day with razor blades that I whetted on the inside of a drinking glass, but later in the day I noticed that, having shaved in the dark, I had missed tufts of hair.

That evening, when I parted with Minna and started home to my dark and windowless room, I was too tired to indulge in my usual grand fantasies. I began by thinking of a half-ton diamond that I would find on the moon. Then the idea no longer warmed me. No, the wisest thing to do would be to end it all. But now I couldn't even do that with a clean conscience. Minna had spent a considerable sum of money on me and I could not die a swindler; I had to see to it that she finally joined Zbigniew Shapira.

I trod on the moist snow and felt myself sinking into Nirvana. It would seem that I was alive, but in fact I was really dead. I no longer had any needs or ambitions. I was what the materialists declared a human to be, an automaton. How strange! Ever since my childhood, I had wondered about my destined bride. That the woman who stood beside me under the marriage canopy was in love with another man, and that the marriage itself was a joke and a charade, intended to deceive others—this had never occurred to me.

I knocked and Edusha opened the door. Usually she met me with a smile. This time she seemed especially serious and a bit tearful. I knew why: I still hadn't paid for any of my meals.

I went to my little room and did not turn on the light. It was dark and stuffy. I felt my way around like a blind man and lay down on the bed. Usually there were voices, noise, and laughter to be heard coming from the living room, but tonight there was not a sound. I wasn't hungry, but I felt weak and hollow inside. I closed my eyes and lay there for a while, enfolded in darkness.

I had made myself dozens of promises to write to my parents, but some sort of contrary force kept me from doing it. I knew I should telephone Sonya, but I didn't make the call. I was suffering from a sort of spiritual paralysis.

I opened my eyes and asked aloud, "Is this darkness absolute? Has even the tiniest ray of light sneaked in? No, no light of any sort has penetrated here." Just the same, I had the feeling I was seeing some sort of reflection, a light, a color. Purple dots swam before my eyes and arranged themselves in all sorts of shifting patterns. A golden crown, brighter than anything I had ever seen, creating an otherworldly mixture of fire and gold, shone in the dark. Its outer edge was purple, but its center was black, like the pupil of an eye. "What is this?" I asked. "A dream? A vision? An optical illusion?"

I still hoped that Edusha would call me to dinner. I had eaten with Minna, but the cold had stimulated my appetite again. Perhaps this was a nervous hunger. I felt a twinge in the pit of my stomach. It seemed to me that I smelled groats and mushrooms cooking. Something within me laughed. A hungry groom on his wedding night, the bride gone home to her parents— what wild circumstances life could contrive!

The hallway usually had a small light burning in it, but tonight it was dark. Suddenly I heard footsteps. Edusha was coming to call me to dinner. I sat up and felt about for the matches on the bedside table. The door opened and Edusha asked, "Are you sleeping?"

"No, no."

"Why haven't you turned on the gas?"

"I like to sit in the dark."

"Why? I haven't made any supper tonight. Come into the living room. I have to talk with you."

I knew she wanted to talk about money and would be asking payment for my meals. She would tell me to vacate the room. Her voice had been muted, distant, and a bit mournful. Something was the matter.

I found matches, lighting one, and followed Edusha into the living room. There was a loaf of bread on the table. I'd never seen this room so dark, so empty. Somehow it reminded me of Tisha Bov. "Where's Bella?" I asked.

Edusha looked inquiringly at me and then, with a certain hesitation, she said, "There's no point in hiding it. Bella's been arrested."

"What!" I almost shouted. "How come? When did this happen?"

"I don't know. She didn't come home last night. Today they came to search the place. It's a good thing you weren't here. They burst in like bandits. She hadn't done anything wrong. The murderers, Fascist dogs!"

"Where is she?"

"I don't know. Usually they keep the prisoners first in the jail on Danilowiczalski Street. But I don't know for sure."

"They're likely to come again?" It was part question, part assertion.

"Yes, that's why I want to talk with you. They can pick on almost anyone. They wanted to arrest me. It was all I could do to talk them out of it."

"In that case, I ought to leave at once. At the moment, I can't pay my bill."

"I'm not asking you for money. I know what your situation is. It's impossible to live in the kind of system we have. The simple fact is, they choke you to death," Edusha said, putting her hand to her throat.

I knew very well what I ought to do—put on my coat, take up my backpack, and leave. But where would I go? If only I

hadn't lost contact with Sonya. There was no place I could go
—especially not to Minna, my fictive wife. I'd rather sleep in
the street than knock on her door and ask for shelter. I thought
awhile; then I said, "Do you object to my staying here?"

"Why would I object? If you're willing to risk it, that's your
business. But I think I ought to warn you—they've got a policeman stationed at the gate."

I hadn't noticed anyone at the gate, but plainclothes policemen
know how to disguise themselves. Minna's words about fate, and
about being caught as in a trap echoed in my ears now like a
prophecy. If I were arrested, that would be the end of everything—the exit visa, the certificate. Minna wouldn't even be
able to marry anyone because she was legally my wife.

In the midst of my predicament, I found myself amazed at
the trick fate had played on me, at the fiendishness with which
it had rearranged things. I promised myself that if I survived, I
would write a book about it one day. It occurred to me that a
writer, like Fate itself, had to create a design which on one hand
had the appearance of ordinary reality, and on the other hand
must imbue it with the discernment of the powers that controlled
the world.

I went to the window and looked out at the narrow bit of sky
visible above the blind wall across the courtyard. The moist
snowfall had changed into rain. The streak of sky, suffused with
moisture and cold, crouched over the rooftops. I turned to Edusha
and said, "Let them arrest me. I'm a lost soul anyway."

3

AFTER I decided to stay on, Edusha became more lively. Only then did it occur to me that we were alone in the house. She went to work getting my supper ready. We experienced the sort of exhilaration that mourners feel when a corpse has just been removed. Edusha brewed tea, putting herring roe, cheese, and butter on the table. As she served me she began a monologue.

"What do the damn Fascists want? How much longer will they continue to oppress the masses? The people are patient, too patient, but a day will come when the sufferings of the proletariat will become unbearable. Look what's happened in Russia. Nothing stopped the revolution: not the Denikins, not the Petlyuras, not the intervention of England, France, and the United States. It'll happen here too. It's just a matter of time.

"Bella knew very well what might happen to her," she went on. "But she's a great person. She couldn't abide that little Hasid of a husband of hers and look after children at a time when humanity was readying itself for a final battle. I'm much more egotistical than she is. I know I'm a bourgeois woman. I can be thrilled by an opera; I love to get dressed up; I adore fine painting, good furniture, and other such nonsense. But all the time I know the truth—none of this is worth a bean." Suddenly she remembered and asked, "What's the status of your certificate?"

"I went through with my fictive wedding today."

Edusha's face lighted up. "You got married? Where?"

"In a rabbi's house."

"Well then, you're entitled to a *mazel tov*."

"What ought I to reply? 'May it happen to you'? No, I wish you something better than that."

"Tell me everything that happened," Edusha said as she seated herself at the table.

I gave her every detail of the wedding. With Bella, I always felt embarrassed, but Edusha was my own age and we were alone. Susskind Eikhl and the other Communists would stay away from a compromised house; the first law of conspirators is: Avoid a tainted residence.

As we talked, we stopped once in a while and strained our ears to hear. At any moment, the police might come knocking at the door to arrest us both. For the time being we got on comfortably, like a couple.

She said, "Why don't you introduce me to your wife? It would be interesting."

"She's not my wife. She has a fiancé and she's in love with him."

"Ah, you never know. The whole business about a fiancé could be a lie. Women are very sly. No man can know just how sly they are."

"Why would she pay a poor young man's expenses?"

"People have their own reasons. This system's crazy anyway. Here we sit, and a couple of hours from now we could be taken away and charged with the most dreadful crimes. I want you to stay here, I'm afraid of being alone. But I'm terrified about what could happen to you if you're arrested. Just remember one thing: say as little as possible. You can tell them you're a boarder here and you don't know anything about our beliefs. And the fact that you've been given a certificate to go to Palestine ought to help you. Radical people don't get certificates—excuse me for being so frank. The fact is, you're also a victim of the capitalist system, which you don't understand. There are millions of people like you, and that's how Fascism succeeds. Drink your tea. A couple of days in the pokey never killed anyone. In one sense, a Fascist prison is the best kind of university."

"I don't need a university. But the truth is, I simply don't have anyplace else to go. Even jail would be better than freezing to death in the street."

"Don't take it so hard. It may be that they won't come at all. They got what they came for. And in law, we're both minors. It doesn't pay for them to pick up kids. I've learned to live one day at a time. There's Hertz, who's gone away and will stay away for months. My mother is off somewhere in London with a rabbi. Bella's been arrested. I have a couple of younger sisters who are with my mother. My stepfather wanted to take me along with them to London, but I'm too impatient to live in a rabbi's house. Naturally, he thought he'd get me married off to someone."

"How did he meet your mother?"

"Ah, that's a long story. He's some kind of distant relative. He wanted to marry my mother when she was still a girl. My mother's a beauty, much prettier than me. When we used to stroll in the streets, men would stop to stare—not on my account, but on hers. She's lived through a world of troubles and is still as lovely as a rose. Bella's pretty too, but she takes after my grandmother. And the really good-looking person in our family was my Waldbram grandfather. You never saw a handsomer man. Reb Mottele Lemberger, my stepfather, went to London some twenty years ago and married there, but he never forgot my mother. He's a pious man, but what is it they say in Russia? *Lyubov nye kartoshka* [Love has a way of growing]. When his wife died, he began at once to correspond with my mother. He's a rabbi in a synagogue. That's how it is in England. He has a good income. But he has a bunch of kids from his first wife. What would I do there? Sometimes I'm sorry I didn't cut myself loose from Poland. Here in Poland is where the first flames will burn. The revolution will come here too, but a little bit later."

"I wouldn't mind if it never came."

"So that's your view, is it? Well, you'll see. Skepticism is part and parcel of the capitalist ideology. Since life in any case makes no sense, what's the point of struggling against the bloodsuckers and the imperialists? The exploiters stand aloof, but try taking so much as a groschen from them and they'll fight like lions. England controls half the world, but it needs to add Palestine to the list. Having issued the Balfour Declaration, why don't they keep their promise? Why won't they let the people of the Bible return to their land? Ah, they can't fool me anymore. Sometimes I envy people like you."

"There's nothing enviable about me, Edusha."

"Don't sound so desperate. You'll become a rich colonist in Palestine or a famous writer. Everyone has problems when they're young which they forget when they're older. Never mind, socialism will create the new man—a man of conscience for whom a few groschen aren't his only goal. Till then, we have our troubles to endure, so to hell with it." Edusha winked at me.

Who knows, I wondered, maybe she wants to cheat on Lipmann? These people have no rules. I felt myself growing shy and scared by turns. It was one thing to kiss a girl like Sonya, but Edusha was an intelligent young woman, a high-school graduate. I had never made love to anyone like that.

I finished eating and thanked her as I got up to go to my room. Edusha give me a sidelong look. "I don't want to disturb you," I said.

"Wait a while, what's your hurry? You must have brought honeycake and brandy back with you from the wedding?"

"The men of the prayer quorum ate and drank it all up."

"How does a man feel who's stood under the wedding canopy? According to Jewish law, you're a married man."

"The whole thing was a farce."

"A farce like that can result in a bunch of kids. Before I met Lipmann, I was keeping company with a young man. We'd talked about getting married and were about to do it. He was a student at the university who came from a well-to-do family. A handsome young man with, as they say, all sorts of virtues. Then I ran into Hertz Lipmann and I knew at once that everything was over between me and Edek. No words were needed between Lipmann and me, we understood each other at once. I'm not even sure one can call that love. He's absolutely not my type. Besides, he's a dreadfully serious man who lives entirely for the revolution. Now he's gone to Russia, but if he had stayed here, sooner or later he'd have landed in jail. He has absolutely no sense of humor. For him everything is either black or white, and I'm completely the opposite. I can understand all points of view. I can even imagine how a Fascist feels. But some sort of intuition told me that Hertz would be my husband. When Edek telephoned me the next morning, he kept asking, 'What's wrong? What's going on?' To this day, I don't know what made him suspicious—evidently he could tell something from my voice. We met later that day and I told him, 'Edek, someone else has taken your place.' Edek's a tall man, a full head taller than I am. He stood there on the sidewalk and wept. I cried too. People stared as they went by, thinking we had just come from a funeral."

"What happened to him?"

"Three months later, he married a rich woman."

"Ah."

"Yes. That's the way life is."

"There is some sort of force that drives the world."

"There's no such force. Everything's nature. She has her laws and there's no escaping them. There was a feudal epoch, then it was the epoch of capitalism, and now it's time for Communism. It's as simple as that."

After a while I went back to my room and lay down, fully dressed, waiting. If the police came, I didn't want to have to dress in their presence.

Three things had reawakened in me the desire to live: the certificate that would take me to Palestine, finding a room in which to live, and the fictive marriage to Minna. But it was clear to me now that I had little reason for hope. Hope was the spur with which the world's will drove all men.

How many times before had I vowed to resign myself completely to fate? Now I felt guilty for having broken that vow and for feeling enticed by the crumbs fate had tossed me. "I'm a corpse. A living corpse," I told myself. "I'm still moving about here because I don't want to sadden my parents." I felt an inward trembling: If you don't want to sadden them, why don't you write a letter? I sat up and wanted to light the gaslight so I could search for pen and ink and conquer the passivity that had kept me paralyzed for weeks. But some sort of power would not let me get out of bed. An invisible power bound my hands and forced my head back on the pillow. Even to write a letter, one needs inspiration, and I felt hollow inside.

Finally, I got out of bed and fumbled about in the dark till I found a razor blade in my backpack. I put it under the inner sole of my shoe. I had no intention of languishing in jail, charged with being a Communist. If they arrested me, I would use the razor blade to cut my veins.

The telephone rang in the hallway. It was Sonya. She said, "You've already forgotten me, right?" And I replied, "No, Sonya dear, I've never stopped thinking of you."

4

SEVERAL days went by, but no police showed up to arrest me. Minna and I had finally applied for our exit papers. Each time I started a Hebrew lesson, we were interrupted. Meir Ahronson had ordered an old-fashioned traveling outfit for his daughter. Tailors came to take measurements and I watched Minna being fitted for a silk dress, a velvet dress, a white bridal dress. Minna and Zbigniew Shapira were planning a canopy wedding in Palestine as soon as she got her divorce from me.

While Minna was being measured for her clothes, I looked over her books and she allowed me to look through her album. I saw Zbigniew Shapira in all sorts of poses and moods—as a student, as an officer on horseback in the Polish Army, taking part in a hunt in Zakopane, where he won a prize. Zbigniew Shapira, not yet thirty, had talents without number. He spoke perfect Russian, Polish, German, French, and English. He was a skilled athlete and he had finished his engineering studies. He was a dancer, a piano player, and could mix in any society. Minna even bragged about the erotic conquests he had made before he met her. Not just rich young Jewish women, but also the daughters and wives of the Polish aristocracy.

Minna was behaving as if she was intoxicated. She repeated the Hebrew words I taught her, but promptly forgot them again. When she spoke of Zbigniew Shapira it was as if she was in the grip of a mania. I was now being paid not for teaching her Hebrew but for listening to her countless praises of him. "Have you ever seen a handsomer man? Is there so much as a single nerve in his body that isn't perfect? Don't his eyes express nobility, pride, intelligence?" Minna herself seemed to have lost her pride. She took Zbigniew's photograph out of my hands and kissed it. She confided intimate secrets to me.

I was witnessing a change—or perhaps the destruction—of a character. Yes, it was clear that Minna had given herself to him. What reason did she have to wait? She regarded his promise as holy. She had even been prepared to get pregnant, but he would not permit it. His enemies had made false accusations against him and wanted to drag him through the mire. Colleagues in whom he had boundless confidence had handed him papers which he had signed without reading them. A conspiracy had been started against him which, if it was ever exposed, would shake all Poland.

Minna had made a deposit on ship tickets, and I had received my interior passport. I had also paid money toward the purchase of my foreign passport. Barish Mendl, the fixer, performed wonders. He had connections everywhere, even in my father's town. The little fellow was not put off by anything. He could lift his telephone receiver and speak with a provincial governor, with high officials in regional commissariats, with the English consul. He spoke a Polish that consisted of truncated words. He had apparently never learned Polish grammar, with its declensions and conjugations, but he managed to make what he said sound important—as if it were beneath his dignity to speak the Gentile words clearly. There was no one whom he did not bribe. I heard him ask, "What sort of cognac does the nobleman like? What kind of stockings does his wife wear?" And he winked at me as he spoke.

Resigned though I was, I could not stop observing the people with whom I had to deal. Barish Mendl was short, and his wife was tall. He spoke quickly, but she drawled when she talked. The same scene was played out each time. His wife came in to tell him that the midday meal was ready, that the soup was getting cold. Barish Mendl would shake his head quickly to indicate No, as he blew cigarette smoke at her and shouted something into the telephone. His cigarettes lay in a pile on the table, but when he wanted a document, he would dig under them with a thumb and forefinger and retrieve exactly what he was looking for. Occasionally his daughter, a high-school student, would come in and ask him for money. She wore a black ribbed silk dress and black stockings. He would hand her a sheaf of uncounted bank notes, which she received without a word of thanks. Her dark eyes regarded her father and me with open contempt. I knew precisely what she was thinking: They're both a couple of kikes. The young woman suffered from the disease of the modern Jew, self-hatred. Even Minna, when she was praising Zbigniew Shapira, would say, "You know, he has nothing of the Jew about him."

It was not only the Gentiles who hated Jews; the new generation of Jews hated them as well. It was easy to see that Minna was embarrassed by her father. When he spoke to her, she listened with a half-guilty, half-pitying smile on her face. Though she understood Yiddish, she pretended not to understand it. Though she was planning to go to Palestine, she never lost an opportunity to announce that everyone took her for a Gentile. Edusha seemed to care about the Jewish masses—the shoemakers, the tailors, the hucksters—but she fled from Judaism, mincing no words about it. "What is Judaism? A relic of the Dark Ages. In a socialist society there will be neither Jews nor Gentiles. Instead, there will be a united humanity." She agreed with the Jewish Communists: "We don't need synagogues or studyhouses. We don't need Hebrew. All those religious stage props. The broom of the revolution will sweep away all that traditional garbage."

I met with Sonya again. Sonya's aged employers had gone away for a few days to a pension in Otvotsk. That evening, Sonya took me to a movie based on a Victor Hugo novel. I had heard about movie theaters over the years, but this was the first time I had ever been to one. Pictures danced before my eyes, and at first I could not make out what I was seeing. Some sort of hunchback who was as agile as a monkey was climbing about in the church towers. The figures on the screen seemed to be shaking with the ague and they moved their lips like mutes. The musicians played dazzling dance music—American jazz. Occasionally something went wrong with the projector and the screen was filled with sparks of light, like golden rain. I sat in the dim light, hushed and amazed at my own perplexity.

Later we went to Sonya's room in the house of her employers. We were careful to avoid the watchman as we slipped inside the gate. Everything was done secretly on my part. My coming to the house of strangers, eating their food, bathing in their tub, sleeping with Sonya in her landlord's bed and under his bed-clothes. Sonya even tried to get me to wear his pajamas. Sonya, for her part, decked herself out in her landlady's embroidered nightgown and made herself fragrant with her perfume and face powder. She also tried on her clothes—dresses of silk and velvet, fur jackets, scarves, muffs, old-fashioned hats trimmed with ostrich feathers from before the war.

We kissed, and every time the bell tower sounded, we listened attentively. Who could tell whether the old people might decide to come back sooner than they had planned. Sonya laughed but was afraid: she had turned on a night-light. Twice the telephone rang. The first time it was the old woman wanting to know if everything was all right; Sonya told her everything was in order. The second call was a young man from Sonya's town, a spats cutter. Sonya told me later that the fellow had wanted to marry her. She had walked out with him several times after the Sabbath afternoon meal, and apparently he could not forget her. He was going to see her tomorrow in the clothing shop.

Everything became fantasy—my marriage with Minna, my intimacy with Edusha, even my journey to Palestine. We were all playing roles in a comedy. I tried to prove to Sonya that withholding herself from me was hypocritical. But she said, "You're just an egotist, that's all."

Her employer was going to stay in Otvotsk over the Sabbath, so this time I did not sleep in my dark little room in Edusha's house. Instead, I stayed with Sonya. Nor did I telephone Edusha—the police might be tapping the line. I did phone Minna to tell her I wasn't feeling well. Since everything was temporary anyway, I might as well be temporarily free. In the morning Sonya went to her shop, but I lay in bed quite late. The telephone rang, but I didn't answer it. I ate the food Sonya had put out for me on the kitchen table. I brewed tea and drank it.

I found a blank postcard in a drawer and wrote to my parents. "Dear Parents: Don't worry. Everything's fine. I've been given a certificate to go to Israel. That's wonderful luck. I'll work there, and study too . . ." I promised them I would see them to say my goodbyes, that I would be a good Jew, and I swore eternal love.

I didn't know whether I was lying or telling the truth. I got dressed, then looked out the window into the courtyard. Snow had fallen and there were icicles dangling from the roofs. Here and there the frost had drawn trees and other patterns on the windowpanes. A Gentile woman with a sack over one shoulder was bending over a garbage can from which she pulled out a rag.

Once again I was struck dumb by the mystery of the world. What was it all about? What was happening here? Who spun the round world on its axis? Who moved the earth around the sun? Who sent the blood flowing through my veins, the thoughts coursing through my brain? I seemed to feel that there was a

God. He lurked near me, over me, in me. For the first time, I felt that He was strangely near. I could almost see His illimitable greatness, His eternal silence, His vast power over a cosmos for which He was responsible and from which He could not turn away for a second. He held the reins of the universe as if they were those of a restive horse that threatened to leap from its harness at any moment. Tears came to my eyes. "Dear God in heaven, forgive me."

He did not reply, but He heard me. As the books say, He had mastered His anger, but my recalcitrance was noted in His book of accounts, and punishment was sure to follow.

I prayed: "Father, reveal Thyself to me. Let me see Thee for an instant. My despair is driving me mad." He listened to that request also. Snow began to fall. God had more important things to do than to carry on a personal exchange with me, such as endowing each snowflake with its individual form. It seemed to me that I could hear God saying, "Wait, be patient. Each man has eternity before him."

5

AFTER Saturday, Sonya's employers returned to Warsaw and I went back to my dark little room. I was well fed and well rested, but my knees felt wobbly and from time to time what seemed to be sparks flashed before my eyes. I staggered when I walked, like someone risen from a sickbed, and I seemed to see everything as through a haze. I bumped into porters carrying baskets on their shoulders. I seemed to be invisible when, as I crossed the street, a droshky or an automobile just missed hitting me. In one of the bookcases at Sonya's, I had found a book entitled *Living Phantoms*, translated from the English. I devoured it all almost at one sitting, reading it until my eyes closed. When I woke, I resumed my reading. The book described powers which, even as a child, I had known to exist, but of which I had not dared to speak. Long before I was born, writers had investigated mysteries like fortune-telling, clairvoyance, premonitions, ghosts—dead mothers who warned their children of danger, dead fathers who revealed the location of lost wills, hidden money or documents. Even animals were known to have returned from the dead to say farewell to their beloved masters. Yes, there was such a thing as an astral body which could leave the physical body and drift through streets or towns and even cross oceans.

Reading this book intoxicated me. When Sonya spoke, I hardly heard what she said. My dreams turned edgy, filled with bizarre imagery, ambiguities, secret deeds. I woke with strange words and phrases in my head, but where they came from or what they meant I did not know. Even Sonya had a different aspect for me ever since I became fascinated by that book. Its presence among a pile of cookbooks and Paul de Kock's novels in the home of Sonya's old employers was incredible. But I understood why— it was the work of fate. If the pantheists were right and everything is God, then nothing in the universe is accidental. Millions of years ago it had been determined that I would read this thick book filled with the secrets of existence. Cause and purpose were one and the same. Every creature, whether a microbe or a seraph in the seventh heaven, had its mission. I rebelled against Spinoza's ideas. Why couldn't God have will, intent, feelings? What kept a God with unlimited attributes from creating souls, from rewarding and punishing? Why did God have to be a blind machine? There must be room within Him for Satan, ghosts, and demons.

I woke Sonya at night and we came together tumultuously, exchanging unrestrained caresses. We invented childish, funny new forms of tenderness.

Now she had gone back to work in her clothing store and I went back to my dark little room. On the way, I stopped at a courtyard where a blind man was singing a song about the *Titanic*, which had sunk some ten years before. Then I passed an open market. Was it possible that all those Jewish women had souls which had transmigrated and lived in previous epochs? Yes, that vendor of rotting tomatoes lived once as a man, a tyrant, or perhaps a pirate. And the punishment was to be reincarnated as a market woman in Warsaw. I, too, must have lived several lives through the ages and committed enormous sins.

I came to the gate of the house where I lived. I looked around to see whether there were any secret police about, but there was nobody lurking anywhere. I climbed the steps and knocked at the door. Edusha opened it. She was wearing a housecoat and slippers. She was amazed to see me.

"Where in the world have you been? I thought you'd gone to Palestine without saying goodbye."

"God forbid, since I owe you money."

"Where have you been? You probably went to live with your fictive wife."

"No, far from it."

"Well, come on in. Somebody named Dov Kalmenzohn phoned you. He wants you to call him."

"Oh . . ."

"Where've you been? I thought of you as a quiet type."

"What news of Bella?"

"Bella is still in jail. Damn the Fascist pigs! But there's some hope they'll let her out on bail."

I had been so engrossed reading *Living Phantoms* that I'd lost much of my shyness. When Edusha asked me where I'd been and what I'd been doing, I decided to tell her about Sonya.

She said, "It's a game for you, but women take that seriously. Not all of them, of course—there isn't a man that can pull the wool over my eyes. I know all their thieving tricks." We drank tea and talked. My absence of several days served to make us more intimate. After we had drunk our tea and were seated on the sofa and Edusha was scolding me for my careless ways, I put my arms around her. I expected her to be angry, but she merely regarded me with a mixture of curiosity and amusement. When I kissed her, she said, "Why did you do that? It won't work with me."

The telephone rang. It was Dov Kalmenzohn. "Where the hell have you been?" he wanted to know. "Go to the Ahronsons' at once. Then get in touch with me. There's something wrong there."

"What's happened?"

"Get a move on. I can't talk to you now."

When I walked up the stairs and rang Meir Ahronson's bell, I heard footsteps, but this time nobody opened the door. I waited awhile, then rang again. After I had rung several more times and knocked at the door, I heard hesitant footsteps. Meir Ahronson, wearing a bathrobe and a pair of run-down slippers, opened the door. His yellow pallor gave him a jaundiced look; his beard was unbrushed, his cap askew. He gazed at me with the uncomprehending look of a man who has just been awakened from sleep. He seemed not to recognize me. I said, "I'm Dovid Bendiger."

"Bendiger eh? Well, come on in. I'm in the midst of a disaster."

We went into the hallway, which now looked strangely barren. The huge Chinese rug was gone, exposing the worn brown and dusty parquet floor. Both the table that had been there and the chair in which I had sat on my first visit were gone. Meir Ahronson said, "You see what's happened. They've taken everything from me. I've been stripped clean. How is it written, *Arum yatsasi m'beten imi v'arum ashuv shama* [Naked came I from my mother's womb and naked will I go]."

"Who took it?"

"Our good Poles, the tax collectors. They came with two flatbed trucks and they emptied the apartment. All that's left are the beds. The monsters! You shouldn't visit Minna just now—she's ashamed to show her face. They demanded taxes for nonexistent income. I argued that there was no income; they argued that there was. You think they know what they're doing? They gave a couple of Gentile schoolboys the right to judge my business dealings. I say 'floor' and they answer 'ceiling.' They made me sign an official report that is as false as an idol. Today they listed my household articles; tomorrow there'll be a public auction. It's all a mockery. They just want to rid themselves of Jews, that's all!"

"I'm terribly sorry. I'll go now . . ."

"Wait a minute. I'll ask Minna if she'll see you. You'll excuse me. Now you and I are on the same level, poor folk together." Meir Ahronson went to Minna's room, knocked at her door, and went in. Another door opened and a pale Mrs. Ahronson, holding her lorgnette, peered out, then shut her door again. A moment later Meir Ahronson reappeared. "You can go in," he said.

He went into the room where I had seen Mrs. Ahronson. He groaned and muttered and shuffled as he walked. I knocked at Minna's door without getting any reply. I opened the door and saw a half-empty room. Everything had been removed from it —the rugs, pictures, furniture. There was a camp cot in the room. A scattered heap of books and manuscripts lay on the floor.

Minna was sitting on a kitchen chair near the window. She gave me an oblique look. There was a sort of exalted smile on her face, the look of someone who has lost all ambition, all shame. The word "Nirvana" came into my mind. She said, "Well, you can come closer."

I took a couple of steps nearer. Minna looked me up and down and said, "I've no idea where the Hebrew vocabulary book has disappeared to. They dragged it off somewhere. In any case, I can't study anymore."

"Well, you'll learn the language in Israel."

"Ha! What is it that the Bible says—'You've sown the wind and shall reap the whirlwind.' All of Judaism, here in Poland and everywhere else, is senseless. The Poles have a single goal: to drive out the Jews, and nothing more."

"A new chapter is being written in Palestine."

"Ha! I don't believe it. I don't believe in anything anymore. We're not a people. We're just a band of gypsies. Where did you disappear to so suddenly? Maybe you knew what was happening here."

"I was sick."

"You're a liar. I telephoned, and the young woman there—what's her name—told me that you hadn't slept in your room. What have you been doing with your nights?"

I said nothing.

"Never mind. You're a free man and can do whatever you want. There's just one thing—I want to leave here as soon as possible. It won't be long before both my parents die, and I don't want to be here when that happens. Someone will bury them. My father didn't even have the good sense to provide himself with a burial plot."

"Don't be so desperate, Minna. Things will turn out well, God willing."

"There is no God. What's holding up your immigration papers?"

"There's some kind of delay."

"I suspect your fixer is a crook. He keeps delaying matters so he can squeeze more money out of me. But he'll do better extorting money from the dead. There's nothing left for us to sell. It'll be a miracle if we have money enough to get to Constantsa."

"Would you like me to leave now?"

"Wait a minute. I can't offer you a place to sit. Pile some books up, won't you? They've even taken my portrait away, the idiots. What about you? I take it you don't have so much as a groschen."

"Please, Minna, don't worry about that."

"Kalmenzohn called, and I had to tell him the truth. It was predestined that I should endure this catastrophe before leaving Poland. I thought I would miss Poland, but now I detest it. I can hardly wait to escape. If the truth be told, I hate Palestine just as much."

"What do you like?"

"Zbigniew. He's the only one I love. All our misfortunes are my father's fault. As for my mother, the less said the better. What's wrong with you? You look as if you've been fasting."

"No. I eat."

"Where? We've sent Tekla away. There's no one left to brew tea. Well, since you want to go, you'd better go. But don't disappear again. Your certificate is now my only hope."

6

WHEN I went out into the hallway, there was Meir Ahronson. He walked to the door with me and looked as if he meant to confide some secret. "What did she tell you, eh?" he murmured.

"What was there to say? We're waiting for my papers."

"Maybe you could take her out somewhere. Why don't you go to a café someplace with her? For the time being, anyhow, she is still your wife, 'according to the laws of Israel.' "

"Oh, she wouldn't go anywhere with me."

"She sits there all day as if she's mourning the destruction of the Temple. Who cares if they took my window grates? They took them, very well, they took them. Who needs more than a piece of bread, a glass of water, and a place on which to lie? I've put an ad in the papers offering to rent rooms. We can rent three rooms. And when she goes, we can also rent her room. My wife and I can get along with just the kitchen and a bedroom. There's only one thing we want—Minna's happiness. What else have we got left? I've had my share of what the world calls good fortune—voyages, warm beds, first-class train travel, and all the rest of that nonsense. None of it is worth the powder to blow it up. Now it's time to experience poverty. Hee hee. In the present state of things, there isn't a Jew in Poland who won't lose his fortune. The Poles will take everything. That's what they want, all open and aboveboard."

I left the house and went to find Dov Kalmenzohn. I mounted the stairs and found things much as I had left them—the male and female Halutzim, the bundles, chests, rush mats, and ropes. People were speaking Yiddish, Hebrew, Polish. A young woman took a cigarette out of a man's mouth, took a deep drag on it, then put it back between his lips. His hair stood up, like wire. He took a long nail out of his pocket, placed it against one of the boards of a chest, and someone handed him a hammer. A young woman wearing glasses with thick lenses sat on a huge sack, reading a letter. Her slippers barely clung to her toes.

I asked one of the youths if he had seen Dov Kalmenzohn. "He's here, there, and everywhere," he said.

"He was here a minute ago," a woman with a Lithuanian accent said.

Just then Kalmenzohn, carrying a sheaf of documents, showed up. "I'm glad you're here," he said. "Come with me."

I followed him to a room in which bundles of magazines lay strewn on the floor. As before, he shoved a pile of papers off a chair, indicating that I should sit. "Perhaps you know what's happened to Meir Ahronson," he said. "It's not news. It's been a while since he went bankrupt. He never had any aptitude for business. After his brother died, everything turned topsy-turvy. What's your impression of Minna? A strange young woman."

"An only daughter."

"I knew her when she was at her most brilliant. I know Zbigniew Shapira as well."

"She talks about him as if he were God."

"A woman student committed suicide because of him a couple of months before he left Poland. She put the barrel of a pistol in her mouth and pulled the trigger. He's bad luck to anyone who has anything to do with him. He's an assimilationist through and through, and a crook to boot. I can't imagine what a person like that will do in Palestine. Minna tried to involve herself in

Jewish matters, but it didn't work. How are the Hebrew lessons going?"

"Not good."

"Her father is learned in the Torah, and his daughter might as well be a Gentile. What's the matter with you? You don't look well. You'll need strength in Palestine. Listen, we help our Halutzim earn money in all sorts of ways. What I mean is, people ask us to send them workers. The Halutzim won't turn down work of any kind. For one thing, they need the money; and then, it's good for them to get used to doing all sorts of things. If you want to earn some cash, we'll send you out. But you have to promise not to refuse the work, whatever it turns out to be. Agreed?"

"Agreed. Even if it means sweeping the street."

"Hm. Good. There's a young woman here who handles all that. Ask for Shoshana. The work won't make you rich, but every groschen counts."

I would never have believed that I could manage it. But I did. I opened the window, stepped out on the ledge, and began to wash windowpanes with a rag. The rooms inside the house had just been painted and there were paint spots on the windows which I scraped off with a knife. I looked four stories down and saw a narrow courtyard where the moist asphalt looked like water. My head was already beginning to ache, but I was determined not to give in to any weakness. What the Halutzim could do, I would learn to do.

I felt like vomiting. There was an evil-tasting fluid in my mouth, and my knees trembled. A voice—my mother's—warned me: "Get down." Young Binyomin, who had also come to wash windows, was smoking a cigarette at another window. He held on to the window frame with one hand while he scraped paint with the other. Occasionally he glanced humorously my way. He too came from a Hasidic family, but he had learned to be a carpenter so that he would be useful in the land of Israel. He had also been taught how to handle a rifle, so that he could serve as a guard. He had tried to convince me that all the misfortunes of the Jews resulted from the fact that they thought of weapons as "impure." There would be no pogroms if there was a rifle, a revolver, or even a sharp knife in every Jewish home. Binyomin had curly hair so black it looked almost blue. In his eyes, which were as dark as black cherries, there was always the hint of a smile. He was continually singing Yiddish, Hebrew, Polish, or Russian songs. He too was going to go through a fictive marriage with a young woman whom he called "my fixie." And he had left a girlfriend behind in his hometown.

I clung so hard to the window frame that my hand ached. I scraped paint with a knife and prayed, "Dear Father in heaven, I know that I don't deserve your pity, but please don't let me die this way." I vowed to give alms to the poor. After we finished cleaning the windows, we were paid and Binyomin took me to an eating house where they served cheap meals. He too was waiting for documents, but his situation was worse than mine. He had given up his Polish citizenship to avoid having to serve in the army. This youth from the provinces knew Warsaw better than I did. He had all sorts of connections and could get free tickets to the Yiddish theaters and free clothes from the Joint Distribution Committee. He said, "Listen, pal, a Halutz has to adapt, or else he's had it."

I understood that his adaptability was not a matter of policy but came from a sort of earthiness that some people are born with. He was full of stories about his town, his organization, his parents, his sisters and brothers, his girlfriend, Basha, who was also a Halutz. If Basha had had money to travel, he, Binyomin, would not have had to go to Palestine with a "fixie." But never mind, he would send for Basha. How could it be otherwise? They had sworn to love each other forever.

We hung out together all that day. In the evening, he took me to a place where there was a gathering of youths in shirts with unbuttoned collars. Short-haired women wore Stars of David around their neck and smoked cigarettes. A young fellow strummed on a mandolin and a woman sang a Hebrew song.

A pale-faced young man with a little blond beard made a speech: "How much longer will we ignorantly endure our exile? How much longer will we be uninvited guests at the tables of strangers? It's a fact," he said, "that after eight hundred years we are still second-class citizens in Poland. Most Jews in Poland can't even speak Polish properly. Is that normal? We must become a nation equal to other nations. We have a land, the land of Israel. We have a language, and the language is Hebrew." The speaker agreed with Max Nordau that a hundred thousand Jews must be sent to Palestine. He attacked Weizmann for being accommodating. He charged that England had turned the Balfour Declaration into a joke. He cited Jabotinski and pointed at a picture of Yosef Trumpeldor.

Later everyone sang "Hatikvah" and "There, in the Land." Though I agreed with everything that had been said, I still felt myself to be out of place. How can that be? I wondered. I have to belong somewhere. My hands hurt and my knees ached. Was I getting sick? Did I have a fever? I felt my forehead and it seemed to be warm.

Binyomin came by. "How do you like this crowd? A happy bunch. Come, I'll introduce you to my 'fixie.' " He took my arm and led me into another room where two young women were sitting on a bench. One was short, with a headful of curly hair, like a sheep. She had a book in her lap, *An Introduction to Biology*. Leaning against her was a taller woman whose face glowed. Her nose was short, her eyes were dark, and her hair had been cut *au garçon*. She had a cigarette between her lips and she was reading a Polish-Hebrew dictionary. There was a pencil stuck behind her ear.

Binyomin said, "Tsila, this is David Bendiger. We spent the day washing windows five floors above the ground. And this comrade's name is Yehudit," he said, indicating the shorter woman, the one studying biology. Evidently the taller one was the "fixie."

Tsila took the cigarette from her mouth and said, "You don't look like someone who could wash windows."

Binyomin smiled and a humorous look came into his black-cherry eyes. "Women have an instinct . . ."

Someone came up to him. "Comrade Binyomin, you're wanted on the telephone." He was gone for several minutes. When he came back, his eyes were more amused than ever. With a look of sly triumph, he said, "Well, pal, if you were planning to go home tonight, you have another think coming."

"What do you mean? What's happened?"

"Shoshana just telephoned. We're being sent out on another job."

"What kind of work?"

"Looking after a corpse!"

IV

THOUGH I knew my older brother Aharon's in-laws in Warsaw, I tried to avoid them. After I came back from the town where I had been a teacher, and spent the night sitting up in their home, I had had nothing further to do with them. It wasn't that I was angry with them. They simply had no place to put me. They were a family of five locked into a tiny space: mother, father, son, and two daughters living in one room with a kitchen and a sort of alcove. The daughters slept in one bed, the parents in another, the son on a cot. There was no room anywhere for a guest.

Another reason was that Aharon's in-laws were unhappy with him. He had taken their loveliest daughter, Ida, to Russia and nearly two years went by before they heard from her. Then they received a letter from my sister-in-law, telling them that she was in dire straits in Russia. My brother had become a writer, but he wasn't earning enough to support his family. Moreover, he was hanging out with writers and painters and rarely came home at night. Ida had had a baby boy, but Aharon had not even come home for his son's circumcision. Moreover, Ida hinted, my brother had a mistress.

My brother's father-in-law, Reb Laizer Tsinamon, never complained of Aharon to me. But his wife, Shayndele, had a good deal to say. She warned me not to follow in my brother's footsteps. "What's so clever about getting other people in trouble?" she said. "If you want to lead a dissolute life, don't get married."

I thought she was right, but there was no way she could

diminish my brother in my eyes. He had never wanted to be married. As far as I knew, he hadn't actually married Ida in Warsaw, and certainly he had not gone to a rabbi either in Kiev or in Moscow. I had last seen my older brother in 1917, when my mother, my younger brother, and I went to Byaledrevne, leaving Aharon and my father in Warsaw.

From the rare letters my parents received from Aharon, I gathered that he had lived through the pogroms in Russia, had endured marauding gangs, typhus, and hunger. He had written something for a newspaper in Kiev and worked on a magazine in Moscow. When he stopped being a Communist, he was persecuted by his fellow writers. Occasionally a greeting from him reached us. Sometimes I would see his name in a newspaper. Strangely enough, he had written a story for a Kharkov newspaper about the Kotsker rebbe.

I didn't own a picture of my brother, and couldn't rightly remember what he looked like, but he had become something of a legend to me. I dreamed about him at night. Dreamed that he talked with me about philosophy, taught me how to ride a bicycle, and rode downhill on a sled with me at an amazing speed. In my dreams, the sled had an unearthly quality and we slid into an abyss.

I had heard from his in-laws that my brother was trying to make his way back to Poland, but it was rare for the Soviets to let anyone out of the country.

I dreamed of my brother Aharon again that night. In the dream, he brought me a new bicycle and I wanted to try it out, but it was Yom Kippur evening. We were in a little town—not in Byaledrevne but in the town in Galicia where my father was now a rabbi. My brother insisted, "You can't ride on it now. Everyone's going to Kol Nidre."

How strange! On one side of the dream there was a little town. On the other there were automobiles, tramways, and shops as if it were Marszalkowsky Boulevard. I wanted to take my bicycle and escape with it to the other side of the dream. But the Austrian

Jews with their thirteen-edged fur hats and their mohair-lined fur coats warned me that if I profaned the sanctity of that day they would avenge themselves on my father. On the thresholds of houses, beggars sat holding bowls into which the members of the congregation dropped alms for the sick, for needy brides, and for the Burial Society.

Something woke me up. Striking a match, I looked at my watch—it was nearly nine o'clock. The telephone in the hallway rang again and I heard Edusha answering it. She opened the door to my room and said, "David, are you asleep? It's for you."

"Who is it?"

"It's your brother."

I could hardly believe my ears. I leaped out of bed and, in the dark, got into my trousers. By now Edusha and I were on familiar terms, but I was still too shy to let her see me undressed or barefooted. In the hallway my hand trembled as I picked up the receiver. My brother's voice said, "Little David, it's me, Aharon." For a while, we were both silent.

I held my breath; then I asked, "Where are you?"

"Here in Warsaw, in the home of Ida's parents."

"When did you get here?"

"A couple of days ago."

"How did you find out where I was?"

"From Susskind Eikhl."

"I was dreaming of you," I said. "Just a little while ago. I dreamed that you brought me a bicycle."

"Is that so? Susskind Eikhl tells me that you're entirely engrossed in Spinoza."

My brother spoke a Polish Yiddish, but now there was also a trace of a Russian accent in his speech. I felt a surge of delight mingled with a bit of fear. I was yearning to see my brother, but I was embarrassed by the complications in my life. He was nearly thirty, eleven or twelve years older than I. When I had seen him, I was still a boy just a little past my bar mitzvah. And still he called me little David.

There was no telephone in his in-laws' house and he had had to call from the home of a neighbor. We agreed that I would visit him at noon. There was brotherly warmth as well as a touch of adult irony in his voice.

I hung up the receiver, still unable to believe that what had happened was real. What shall I do now? I wondered.

I went back to my dark little room. I lighted the gas jet. Now I felt sorry to be going to Palestine. What was the point of leaving? For a long time I had been hoping my brother would come.

I went to the kitchen to wash and shave. Edusha was there, pouring water into the teapot. She said, "Congratulations on your good news."

"May good fortune come to you," I replied, according to the old formula.

"Invite him here. He has a pleasant voice," she said with a wink and a laugh.

I wanted to put my arms around her, but somehow the thought of my brother kept me from it. While he was not in Warsaw, I had felt myself to be an adult, self-reliant. His presence made me a boy once more. I had a strange feeling that he was watching me and laughing at me.

As if she read my hidden feelings, Edusha said, "Just because your brother's here, does that mean you can't kiss me?" I went up and kissed her, but differently from before, not like a man, but rather as if I were a child. Edusha caught that too.

"You kiss like a cheder boy."

Good Lord! Was there no way to conceal anything? Or was I one of those fools whose thoughts everyone could read? Was my skull transparent? But then, what was the meaning of my kisses, since she had a fiancé?

Edusha, singing a song about Charlie Chaplin, left the kitchen, looking back at me and sticking out her tongue. "This woman's a tease," I said to myself. "The devil's in her."

I started to shave. I mustn't miss a single hair of my beard or cut myself today. I wanted to look young when I met my brother, perhaps because I had accomplished nothing in the intervening years. I tried practicing Coué's system of autosuggestion and commanded myself to achieve a smooth shave. To help matters along, I used a new razor blade.

The teakettle came to a boil and I turned the gas off. When Edusha came back to the kitchen, she said, "Your brother arrives and you're on your way to Palestine. What's the sense in that?" We sat at the table and had breakfast together like an old married couple.

Edusha had found a job working in a furniture store, but she would not begin until Monday. She had received no letters at all from Hertz Lipmann. He had promised to write, but thus far there was only silence. Did that have anything to do with his Communist activities? Had something happened to him in Russia?

Though Edusha sang cabaret songs, she said that the revolution was more important than the trivialities of private life; but even as she spoke her eyes grew moist. Her mother and sisters were in London, Bella was in prison—in the women's section that was known as Serbia—and Edusha was all alone. She had behaved with me the same way Sonya had. I had intimate dealings with two women, yet had not tasted of the tree of knowledge, as they would say in Byaledrevne. Was this loose behavior typical of young women, or did it just happen to me? Maybe this was to be my lot forever.

I ate my roll and drank my coffee while all sorts of anxieties roiled in my brain. Perhaps I wasn't a real man? What if I was never able to write anything truly mature? Maybe it was already fated that I should fall from a window ledge. It had almost happened once before.

It struck me that while Edusha and I were talking and eating, there were hundreds of thousands of people who were waiting to die. Millions who were dangerously ill or breathing their last. I remembered how I had nearly died that night when Shoshana had sent us to the private clinic to guard a corpse. Binyomin had lifted the sheet covering the dead young woman, and I almost fainted when I saw a head of living black hair framing her white, unearthly mask. Her chapped lips maintained a shrieking silence. It made me shiver. I felt that the world was one great house of the dead.

I said goodbye to Edusha and left to find my brother. His in-laws lived on Panska Street, but I didn't take the streetcar. I walked in order to control my excitement. What was a brother, after all? Flesh and bones. My goal in life was to find the secret of creation, not to spend time with my family. When I looked into a store window I was frightened by my reflected face, pale as a corpse's.

I mounted the stairs and knocked at the door. My brother's younger sister-in-law, Lola, opened it. She was a tall woman with a large head, a hooked nose, and an excessively large bosom and hips. She was also bowlegged. In all her ugliness, I had discerned a certain beauty. She had retained a child's naïveté, while at the same time she had a glowing feminine aura. Her lips seemed to have been made for kissing. Lola had never got her high-school diploma; she dropped out in the eighth grade. She had been looking for a job for months now. When she saw me, her slightly protruding eyes lighted up.

Then I saw them all: my brother's wife, Ida; her father and mother; and their son. My brother looked almost the same, but his head was now bald and he was pale, as if from illness. His blue eyes looked keenly at me. We were both amazed at what the years had done to us. Now I saw wrinkles in his face that I had forgotten, and I saw how the features of my mother and her brother Gabriel were repeated in Aharon's face, with his high forehead, pointed chin, sharp nose, and hollow cheeks. Though I had forgotten them, the signs of his heritage showed.

"Well, you've grown up, that's right," my brother said. And I realized that I had almost forgotten the sound of his voice.

2

WE ate a home-cooked meal—noodle soup, meat boiled with carrots, apple compote, and tea. Spoons clinked against the crockery plates. My brother's child, whom he called Gershon and his mother called Grisha, slept in the alcove. With the exception of myself, they were bound together in an authentic family relationship. They were so full of things to say that I grew silent. My brother and his wife had lived through so much they hardly knew where to begin to tell their story. The mother-in-law, Shayndele, handed plates around and kept nodding her bewigged head, confirming the truth that women really come into their own when they become grandmothers. There were bags under her brown eyes, and her look was at once acerbic and clever. She knew everyone's faults. Her husband, Reb Laizer, had never learned how to make a living. In Warsaw he had been some sort of real-estate broker, but years had gone by without his having concluded any deals. He spent his time reading old newspapers or studying an almanac in which were listed all the fairs in Russia (pre-revolutionary Russia, that is). He visited the sick and accompanied the dead to their graves.

Reb Laizer Tsinamon—a good-looking man, tall, straight, with a brown beard and the imposing manner of a respected householder—was descended from a prosperous and scholarly family. As a boy, he had studied Torah with my grandfather. Shayndele, his wife, also came from a wealthy family and had been considered very beautiful in her youth. How these two had begotten a daughter as ugly as Lola was a mystery.

The older daughter, Khayele, was not ugly, but no match had yet been made for her, perhaps because she didn't have so much as a groschen for a dowry. She worked in a shop selling chocolates. Her brother, Max, the oldest of the children, worked as a printer for a Russian newspaper that still appeared in Warsaw. He had an awkward smile on his face and was quick to tell funny stories about the writers and printers on his newspaper.

I remembered Ida as thin, but she had put on weight in Russia even though food had been scarce. She told us it was because she had given birth to Gershon. She was a classic beauty with a Jewish woman's fluttering eyes. My brother was a head taller than she, and from the way she handed him his portion of meat, I could tell that she was in love with him and was happy to serve him. The looks of devotion she gave him were mingled with blame and seemed to promise forgiveness for all his sins, if only he would cease his foolish behavior.

Aharon turned to me and said, "I still don't know what you're doing in Warsaw."

"Well, I've got a certificate. I'm getting ready to go to Palestine."

"What will you do in Palestine? Eikhl says you're a writer."

"I'm trying."

"Who's the woman where you live? Eikhl told me some sort of story about her. Her sister was arrested?"

"It's her aunt."

"Her aunt? Be careful. What are you writing? Yiddish? Hebrew?"

"I've changed to Yiddish."

"Changed, eh? It appears we're all scribblers. I had hoped that you at least would grow up to be a practical man."

"The only other thing I could have been was a rabbi."

"We don't need that, either."

"What's happening in Russia?"

"Ah . . . they're cutting each other's throats . . . in the name of the revolution . . . in the name of the counter-revolution . . . in the name of the Czar . . . in the name of God. Now they're making speeches, dreadfully long speeches." He gave me a keen sidelong look in which I caught a glimpse of the lingering sorrow in my mother's eyes.

I said, "I read that you'd become a Communist."

"No."

When we had eaten, I went into the alcove to look at their baby. They had borrowed a crib from a neighbor and I studied him as he slept. I could see my family's look, as well as an adult seriousness in his tiny face. No doubt he was studying the Cabala in his dreams. I stood there for a long while, gazing at him. The others, too, came in to look. Then my brother said, "I've got to go to the Writers' Club to look for Susskind Eikhl. Do you want to come along?"

"Will they let me in?"

"You'll be with me."

I knew about the Writers' Club, but I'd never been there. Edusha had offered to take me, but I hadn't wanted to run into Susskind Eikhl. I was shy about meeting well-known writers— people whose names were printed black on white. One part of me was contemptuous of the scribblers continually rescuing the world with their paper prescriptions.

This time I went because my desire to spend another couple of hours with my brother overcame my shyness. Dressing to meet my brother and his family, I had put on a clean shirt and a necktie, a gift from Minna. Also, I knew I would never have a better opportunity than this to go to the Writers' Club. They might even give me a guest membership card, who could tell? I had heard that people who were not even writers went there to eat or to play chess. I had occasionally walked past the Writers' Club at night and looked up at its brightly lit windows. Discussions were going on there, arguments, people were enjoying themselves until late at night. The Writers' Club put on an annual masked ball, and there were banquets to honor writers from New York, Berlin, Paris, London, Buenos Aires. Actors and actresses were also frequently to be found there. I plucked up my courage.

My brother said, "Well, put on your coat." His mother-in-law, taking leave of me, said, "Don't be a stranger. Come see us again soon."

"Don't leave for Palestine without saying goodbye," said Khayele, Ida's sister. Lola, the youngest of the sisters, smiled. When I was studying at the rabbinical seminary, I had borrowed a copy of *Pan Tadeusz* from her. To thank her, I had kissed her as I was descending the stairs; that kiss was our secret.

It was some distance from Panska Street to the Writers' Club, but we went there on foot. My brother didn't have the money for streetcar fare and he walked quickly. He pointed out the changes that had taken place in Warsaw since he had left it. He knew every courtyard and every shop, and mentioned names I'd never heard of. He had spent the years of his young manhood in this city while I was still going to cheder. I had grown up, but he was still taller than I.

I remembered how he had taken me to cheder in the home of Moyshe Yitzhak at Number 5 Grzybowska. He was then sixteen years old; I was five. He had taken long strides and I had trotted after him with my tiny steps. Now as then, I was anxious about the people I would meet. I could read faces too well not to be anxious: mockery, misconception, contempt, greed. The women often laughed, but their laughter subsided when they were introduced to me, and they gave me maternal and sometimes pitying looks.

I said, "Don't tell anyone that I'm a writer."

"I'll be just as much of a stranger as you," he replied.

Little by little, he became more forthcoming. He said that within Russia much was being done for Yiddish—there were schools, publishing houses, libraries, newspapers, magazines, even higher institutions of learning. But one had to be a Communist to have access to any of it. And he, Aharon, had never been able to join. Maybe Marx and Lenin were right, but to become one of their disciples, to write pious Marxist articles, to make continual reference to the Marxist rabbinate, was not in his nature. He had not left one Hasidic court in order to join another. At least the Kotsker and the Gerer Hasidim believed in God. The Yiddish Communists had transformed atheism into a form of Hasidism—the same inward look, the same telling of

moral tales, the same repetition of Torah and the idolatry of their
rebbes. Each was idolized as a holy man: Lenin, Trotsky, Dzer-
zhinsky, Bukharin, Rykov, Kamenev. Each writer presided over
his own followers and had his own assistants. The Yiddishists,
it goes without saying, out-poped the Pope. They sang Communist songs of praise the whole day long and cursed the reactionaries with bloody curses. They kept boasting of what they
had done for the revolution. "What they write is no more than
barren word games," Aharon said. "Take that Susskind Eikhl,
whose scribblings are not to be understood; here in Poland, the
provincial youth think of him as a spiritual leader. The Poles are
certainly anti-Semites, but they're right when they say that Jews
spread Communism. In fact, Jews are always the first victims of
any revolution."

"What can the Jew do who has given up his belief in the
Shulhan Arukh?" I asked.

"History has its counsel," he said. "Come." We arrived at the
Writers' Club and climbed the muddied stairs. A little farther
up there was the Mizrachi office, which I used to visit when I
was studying in the rabbinical seminary. Later on, I got my letter
of recommendation from them to be a teacher. Ever since my
teaching career had collapsed, I avoided coming here. Now I saw
a "modern" rabbi on his way there: his beard was trimmed, and
he was wearing a fur coat, a hat, and galoshes over his shoes.
He carried a briefcase and was smoking a cigarette. Rabbis like
him had found a way to accommodate the secular world to Judaism. They did not want to wait until the Messiah came riding
on his donkey. They had dealings with the English and with the
League of Nations. They traveled to all sorts of Zionist confer-
ences. The rabbi looked at my brother and me. Each of us silently
negated the opinion we were forming of each other.

I thought we would have to ring the doorbell of the Writers'
Club, but my brother simply pushed the door open and we went
in. I paused on the threshold till my brother said, "Come on."
As I entered, I saw a great many faces and smelled restaurant

odors. The writers were having their lunch. There was the sound of clattering dishes, and waitresses were carrying trays. Beards wagged, and noodles dangled over them. Bald pates glowed; eyeglasses glistened. I had the feeling that I knew everyone. I remembered seeing their pictures in newspapers or in magazines. I recognized one musician who had long hair and the slanted eyes of a Tatar. He was struggling with the chicken on his plate.

My brother led me into a second, larger room, whose walls were hung with a brown linen of some kind. There were pictures hanging on the walls; the one above the piano was of Peretz. A gramophone was playing a popular song. A tiny man was dancing with a tall woman. Suddenly up popped Susskind Eikhl, who embraced my brother. Glancing at me, he said, "Well, here's the bashful but impertinent puppy."

3

MY brother was talking with Susskind Eikhl. I listened with one ear: they were maligning Russian writers who, despite all their Communist pieties, pulled every string they could to go abroad. A considerable number had managed to get to Paris, Warsaw, Berlin—and they were in no hurry to return. But Susskind Eikhl did want to return to the Soviet Union and let it be known that he had ties with important political figures. The talk veered to an anthology that Susskind Eikhl was planning to edit and an important literary conference in which my brother was to take part.

With the exception of myself, everyone in the room was a person of significance. Susskind Eikhl pointed them out to me: this one was a poet; that man was a journalist; the old fellow with the white mustache wrote Hebrew textbooks; the little fellow with the gold-rimmed glasses was a Hebrew poet. Susskind Eikhl said all this with ill-concealed irony. In his view everyone in the room except himself was a trivial fellow. He even accused my brother of distancing himself from the radical writers. "Even a blind man can see," he said, "that the reactionaries are in full retreat."

Susskind Eikhl then ordered tea and *kichel* for the three of us.

Good Lord, only yesterday the idea of being in the Writers' Club was unimaginable, and here I was drinking tea. Writers passing by looked my way; several of them stopped at our table and my brother introduced me. Each time it happened, Eikhl said of me, "He writes too," and winked.

I knew that I ought to have felt myself lucky. How long had I been wandering about Warsaw like a lost soul? Yet I sat there feeling helpless and knowing I was being laughed at. Aharon was hardly known here, and I was his brother.

On top of everything, I was afraid Edusha might come in at any moment. I knew that I would blush if she appeared. I was even afraid that someone would mention her name. I did all right as long as I was alone with a woman, but in a social situation all my cheder-boy shyness reappeared and I lost my tongue and stammered. I spoke foolishly, provoking laughter. Even now I felt myself blushing. I was warm, and my collar was moist. I had wanted to be here; it seemed to me I could spend hours watching the writers, but at the same time I felt fretful and wanted to leave. I had put on a fresh shirt, and yet my skin itched.

I wanted to participate in Aharon's conversation with Eikhl, but never had the chance to say a word. The two of them laughed and told jokes, and all I could do was sit and listen. I knew that Spinoza described my state as one involving affects. Yes, I was controlled entirely by feelings. Though I had carefully studied the fifth chapter of the *Ethics*, I still did not know how to control my emotions. Where was I to find ideas capable of driving away feelings? How could I free myself of pride, shame, depression?

No, Baruch Spinoza, yours are false remedies. The young man dancing the shimmy with the woman he had stolen away from the old writer she came with isn't using the advice you give in the *Ethics*. He feels secure because he's well dressed, speaks a fluent Polish, has a job on a newspaper and money in his pocket. I'm hot, but apparently he's cool. He dances slowly, deliberately. His shoes are shined, he's wearing bright spats, his trousers are pressed and have a razor-like crease. He has his arm around the woman's waist and is indifferent to looks from strangers. He's talking to her—undoubtedly trying to seduce her. She looks up and smiles at him with a sophisticated, coy, deceiving smile.

Will I ever be able to do what he is doing? Never. He's a worldly fellow and I'm a studyhouse bench presser. Though I've left the studyhouse, I haven't escaped it. Worldliness is not for me, but neither is the studyhouse. For that, I lack faith.

My brother sent inquiring looks my way and I sensed that I was embarrassing him. I was infecting him with my confusion. Susskind Eikhl also saw my condition, and a mocking look came into his eyes. Evidently he was considered a big cheese here, and was greeted by everyone. People came over to praise him and were given his amused thanks. They all tried to get into his good graces, even writers who wrote for the bourgeois papers, even the Hebraists. Here in the Writers' Club the revolution had triumphed.

Then the thing I had been dreading happened: Edusha came in and headed for our table. I was so horrified that I somehow forgot to blush. Susskind Eikhl rose and put out his hand. My brother also got up. I remained seated, petrified. Edusha had dolled herself up and wore a fur collar and carried a muff. Her hat made her look taller, older, even elegant. Her smile was coquettish, worldly, clever. She was wearing powder and lipstick. When Susskind Eikhl introduced her to my brother, he said, turning to me, "She is your landlady, after all."

"Ah, so that's who you are," Aharon said. "Earlier today we spoke to each other on the telephone."

"Of course."

"Well, you've certainly found yourself a pretty landlady," my brother joked.

This was not the Edusha whom I had kissed. She was now rather like the woman with whom the writer had danced the shimmy. She seemed to be well known in the Writers' Club. After she seated herself at our table, other writers came by and, pulling chairs over, sat down. Someone handed me a cigarette and I took it, though I did not smoke. I inhaled a mouthful of smoke and let it out slowly. Edusha said, "I didn't know you smoked," using the pronoun *du*.

"Ah," someone said, "the two of you say *du* to each other."

"They're lovers," Susskind Eikhl joked.

Edusha slapped his wrist. "What an idea! I have a fiancé." I knew that I ought to take part in this trivial conversation, ought to smile and toss in a clever word here and there, but my voice would not work and my face seemed to be paralyzed. I had but a single desire—to escape. At that instant the shirt on my back turned wet. I took a huge drag on my cigarette and realized that I had smoked almost the whole thing.

My brother said, "Uh-uh, he doesn't know how to smoke," and everyone burst into laughter. My brother went on: "When I left, he was a cheder boy, and now he writes articles about philosophy and Cabala."

"Really?"

One writer asked me what I was reading and whom I had studied, and I mentioned Spinoza, Descartes, Berkeley, David Hume, as well as the Ari and Moses Cordovero.

The writer said, "Maybe you have something we could print in our magazine."

"Yes, do print something of his," Susskind Eikhl called out. "Since he wants to be a writer, he might as well begin now."

"Bring it to me at the magazine," the writer suggested.

I saw him now for the first time. His hair was long, his face round. His spectacles had slid down to the tip of his nose. Instead of a necktie, he wore an artist's scarf.

Susskind Eikhl was called to the telephone. The round-faced writer continued to talk. "Usually we print literary essays. But Spinoza and Cabala—that's an interesting theme. What's your point of view? That Spinoza was a believer in the Cabala?"

"No. But he got his definition of God and the Creation from the Cabalists."

"Spinoza is usually considered to have been an atheist."

"Atheism is a sort of crippled mysticism," I said, without knowing whether I was expressing an original thought or had read this somewhere.

"What do you mean by that?"

"Blind nature has created all that we see, as well as all that we do not see—that's a mystical notion."

My brother said, "Davy, is this really you? Somehow I don't believe it. When you went away to Byaledrevne, you were still a little boy with red earlocks."

Edusha, who was watching me sympathetically, seemed surprised by what I was saying, but nodded agreement. She no longer looked like a sophisticated woman but, rather, like a schoolgirl from a Hasidic family.

The wet shirt on my back was drying out. I rubbed the stub of my cigarette against the ashtray; I no longer needed to smoke. My depression had lifted and my mood had changed to exaltation. Someone had offered to print one of my pieces.

The writer said, "Be here tomorrow at this time. We'll have lunch together."

"David, *mazel tov*," said Edusha. "Let this be an auspicious beginning."

Yes, fate was playing tricks on me. Like the damned in hell, I was being tossed from fire to ice. I drank the tea which I had allowed to get cold and took a bite out of the *kichel*.

Susskind Eikhl came back and I observed a change in his face. He looked serious, even worried. He stood for a while beside the table with a gloomy look. I could tell that he had just been told some bad news on the telephone. He took a cigarette out of a pack and lit it. "Edusha," he said, "I have to talk with you."

"With me? Certainly. Excuse me, please." She got up and went with him into the other room. The men at our table left shortly thereafter. The magazine editor offered me his moist, soft hand; then I was left alone at the table with my brother. He was silent for a bit; then he said, "Don't trust any of them."

4

I ASSUMED that Edusha and Susskind Eikhl would be back soon, but a good fifteen minutes went by and they still had not returned. What kinds of secrets do they share? I wondered. I wasn't in love with Edusha, but just the same I felt myself growing a bit jealous. Susskind Eikhl had taken her by the arm, and they had acted like a couple as they left the room.

I took the cigarette out of the ashtray, but I didn't have a match with which to light it. My brother also seemed to be waiting for Susskind Eikhl's return. He kept looking toward the door. To me he said, "If it isn't already too late, don't get involved with this crowd. They'll drive you crazy."

Susskind Eikhl soon returned, but Edusha was not with him. I guessed that he wanted to talk with my brother. I said, "I'll go now."

"Don't forget to be here tomorrow. It's just possible that he'll print your piece," Aharon said.

"I won't forget." Susskind Eikhl watched me but did not say anything. I gave him my hand. I went into the other room, where several writers were playing chess, and I watched them for a while. One of them said, "Ah, ah. Now where will you go? Your queen's *kaput*. You might as well say *Kaddish* for her."

"Don't anticipate," the other player said. "I'll move in a minute." And suddenly, in the melody of a Megillah reader, he sang a song of triumph.

I would have liked to watch them a bit longer, but a tall writer with a pipe in his mouth was giving me suspicious looks and I was afraid I would be told to go. As I started down the stairs, I was so exhilarated by the idea that I would be back tomorrow, and that someone might print one of my pieces, that I trembled, muttering, "Don't count on it. More than likely nothing will come of it."

God, the way things happen! I had a certificate, I was involved with women, my brother was here, they were talking of printing one of my things. It occurred to me that if I hadn't phoned Sonya that day and had taken the train to Byaledrevne, none of these things would have happened. I would be living now in some village, supporting myself by giving lessons.

Did this mean that everything was fated? Or was my being here simply a coincidence? What would have happened, for instance, if my mother had married the young man from Lublin who had been proposed to her instead of my father?

I started for home. Perhaps Edusha was already there. She had been a witness to my change of fortune. She had heard my invitation to submit something to a magazine. Whatever might have happened to Bella, Edusha would now treat me well.

I came to my gate and looked around to see if a policeman was anywhere about. I climbed the stairs and rang the bell, but nobody answered. Evidently Edusha was not yet home. I opened the door with the key she had given me. As I went in, I felt that I had become very mature.

Ever since Bella had been taken off to prison, I had lived as if the whole apartment was mine. I read Bella's and Edusha's books. I often lay down on the sofa where Edusha used to sleep. Practically everyone had stopped coming to the apartment, leaving me the only man in it. Sometimes it seemed to me as if Edusha and I had been cast ashore on some island.

The telephone rang and I ran to answer it, as Edusha had instructed me to do. She had put a notebook and a pencil beside the phone. It was Sonya on the line.

She said, "I hear that your brother's in town."

"Where'd you hear that?"

"Ida called me. Why didn't you let me know?"

Sonya was related to my brother's in-laws. Sonya and Ida had once been close friends. Everything was linked to everything else. I told Sonya that I had heard the news only that morning. That I had just now come from the Writers' Club. I bragged that there was someone who wanted to print one of my things. "Sonya dear," I said, "I'll be forever grateful to you."

"Yes, you'll be grateful to me, but you'll marry someone else. That's just my luck."

I made a date with Sonya for the next evening; then I lay down on the sofa and waited for Edusha to show up. My ears pricked up at every sound on the stairs. What's happened to her? I wondered. Was I in love with her? No, Edusha was not my type. She was too worldly, too left-wing, too modern for me. The only woman whom I could love and respect would have to be like my mother—a pious Jewish daughter. A young woman who could kiss one man today and someone else tomorrow could never have my respect. But what about me? Was my behavior any different?

I dozed off and dreamed. Then I heard the key turning in the outer door and woke up. The winter day had turned gray. The windowpanes showed blue, and when I looked out, it was snowing. Edusha came in, bringing with her a whiff of cold. She stood there in her coat and hat. I could hardly make out her face in the dim light. She said, "Why didn't you light the gas? Never mind, it's just as well. Has anyone telephoned for me?"

"No, Edusha. No one."

There was a muted quality in her usually lively voice. She took her coat off and laid it on the bed. She moved as softly as a shadow. I said, "Would you like to lie down on the sofa?"

"No. Stay where you are. Your brother looks just like you. Older, of course. And he's no milksop, the way you are."

"What makes you say that?"

"Ah, you pretended you didn't know me."

I wanted to say, "It's because I was shy." But what came out was "That's really insulting, Edusha."

"Well, never mind. I have more important things to worry about. David"—her tone suddenly changed—"everything's collapsing around me. Like a house of cards."

"What's happened?"

"I oughtn't to tell you. You'll just gloat. But I have to talk to someone."

"What happened?"

"Hertz has been arrested." Having said this much, Edusha burst into tears. She sobbed, and in the half-light I saw the anguish in her face..

I was silent for a while; then I said, "Where? On the Polish border?"

"In Russia."

I had an access of understanding. "The Bolsheviks arrested him."

"Yes. In Moscow." And she burst into tears again.

"How come? Why?"

"That's all I know. I don't know anything else."

She sat down on the bed, or rather, she flopped down on it. Edusha had said I would gloat over her news, but I felt no sense of triumph. Instead, I felt the sort of pain one feels whenever one becomes aware of an injustice.

Edusha was sobbing. She covered her face with both hands. I could see her shoulders trembling. I wanted to go to her, but I restrained myself. I said, "There must be some reason." And was instantly sorry for what I had said.

"What reason? He was loyal to the movement. He sacrificed his whole life to it. It must be that someone brought false charges against him. There are plenty of provocateurs." She wept even more intensely. I could feel my own tears welling up. For this young woman, one tragedy followed on the heels of another. The Poles had arrested her aunt; the Russians her fiancé. What a terrible blow Hertz Lipmann's arrest was for her.

I had heard of other such arrests. The newspapers printed stories about the whole population of peasant villages being deported to Siberia. Jewish merchants, rabbis, Hebrew teachers, and socialists had been shot. But I had not expected that they would imprison Hertz Lipmann. He out-Bolsheviked the Bolsheviks. Every word he ever spoke breathed animosity to the capitalist system. There was nothing he would not do for the revolution. What sort of people were these Reds? Beasts that devoured their own kind. I wanted to comfort Edusha, but I didn't know how and said the worst thing, "Edusha, let this be a lesson to you."

"What sort of lesson? There are provocateurs in every movement."

"It's the history of Robespierre and Marat all over again," I said.

"Please, I beg you, be still."

I went back to my dark little room. Edusha evidently sat in the dark, because if she had lighted the lamp in the living room a ray of light would have been visible in the hallway. She was silent—or she may have fallen asleep. I felt muted too. From my earliest childhood, I had heard people talk of the coming of better times, of the redemption of mankind. But no sooner had a man acquired a little power than the tyrant in him emerged. Into my mind came the image of Hertz Lipmann sitting in a Russian prison, rigid with fear, hungry, weary, suffering from lack of sleep, so overwhelmed by grief that there was no consoling him.

I fell asleep, and the next thing I knew, someone was waking me. I opened my eyes and for a moment was unable to remember where I was. I almost cried out, "Sonya," but then I saw Edusha standing near me.

"David, I'm scared." Her voice sounded ragged from much weeping. She shivered and her teeth chattered. I pulled her to me and she did not resist. I kissed her face, which was moist and feverish. She said, "What am I going to do now? Tell me, David. Is this the end for me?"

"How can you say that? God willing, you'll . . ."

"There is no God. There's nothing at all. Everything is barren and black. David, I'm choking to death."

"I told you that the Bolsheviks were killers."

"Who isn't? What is there left for me to believe? If something like this could happen to Hertz, then I want to die. When Bella hears the news in prison, it will kill her."

"Don't let her know."

"They hear about everything there. Since he's been arrested, the next thing we'll hear is that he was a provocateur. They'll say that there are other provocateurs ready to betray honest folk."

"You shouldn't be one of that crowd."

"To what crowd shall I belong? What is there left to hope for—the Balfour Declaration?"

"There's no need to hope for anything."

"Maybe you can live that way. I can't. If I have to give up hoping for justice in this world, I'll die. I've been thinking about it for hours. He sacrificed everything for an ideal, and now this disgrace. It's enough to break your heart. He'll die there before they can get to the truth of the matter."

"If he's destined to live, he'll live."

"I don't believe in all that twaddle about fate. Twenty million people died in the war. Twenty million! Why were they fated to die? Hundreds of thousands from both armies were sent to Verdun—sixty thousand of them died. A hundred and twenty thousand mothers and fathers got the dismal news that their sons were dead. And what of the wives? And what of those who died of typhus and cholera? And those who died of starvation? How can anyone not fight against a system that allows such dreadful things to happen?"

"The revolution killed three million."

"There was some point to their deaths. Oh, I'd do better to shut up. I'll leave if you want to go back to sleep."

"No, Edusha. Stay here."

She lay beside me, still wearing her dress and her shoes. I had no idea whether it was late in the evening or midnight. Edusha's breathing was labored, as if she had a fever. I had a hollow feeling in the pit of my stomach. Hunger pangs—I had not eaten supper. I felt like a hungry beast in its den, or like one of those primitives who lived in caves surrounded by wild animals, exposed to hunger and thirst and illness and the unreasoning hatred of their enemies.

I thought of my essay "Spinoza and the Cabala" and I burst out laughing. Spinoza who? What Cabala? *Homo sapiens* was just at the beginning of his evolution. The Ten Commandments were still only a distant ideal that might never be realized. My mother had wanted me to be a rabbi, a sage among the Jews, a people against whom a pogrom was directed every Monday and Thursday. Well, did being a writer among those same Jews make any more sense?

It struck me that it wouldn't be such a bad idea if I turned on the gas, making an end to us both. But I had parents, and Edusha had a mother. Besides, my brother had just arrived in Warsaw—some welcome I'd be giving him! The forces that govern the universe won't even let you die quietly, I thought. I asked Edusha what time it was, but she was asleep. She gave a snort, then a sigh.

I got out of bed quietly, careful not to wake her. A little bit of sleep was the nearest thing to consolation left for people like us. I went to the kitchen on tiptoe. Perhaps there was a bit of bread lying around somewhere. I felt about on the oilcloth that covered the kitchen table. Blindly, I opened a cupboard door, but all I found were tin plates. In another cupboard my fingers touched a bottle of something that smelled like vinegar, or vinegar concentrate. In the middle of the room, there on the table, lay half a roll.

I sat on the sofa in the dark and ate the roll, feeling bizarrely that I was a thief. I owed Edusha rent for my room and money for my meals. It was hard for me to believe that this same Edusha had, only this afternoon, arrived at the Writers' Club like a celebrity and writers had clustered around her.

I swallowed the last bite of the roll, but it merely whetted my appetite. My innards felt as empty as if I had been fasting for days. I went to the window and looked out on the blank wall. I studied the bricks for a while and wondered what thoughts a brick might think. If one took Spinoza literally—that God is expansiveness and thought—even material things must have their "idea," their spirit. The brick did not think brickish thoughts; its thoughts instead were the same as God's. The point was that a brick could not tell tales out of school.

I bent my head so I could see the bit of sky above the roofs. When I caught a glimpse of a star, I was as delighted as if I had been imprisoned for a long time, unable to see the heavens. Here over Edusha's roof there hovered a celestial body—not one of the planets, but a fixed pale green star that trembled and glittered.

My eyes made contact with a sun that had existed for hundreds or even thousands of years before its light had reached us, even though traveling at the rate of 300,000 kilometers per second. I stared at it and could not get enough of its light. Yes! What are you thinking, star? Surely you, too, have some sort of thought in your head, you who have greatness, distance, and perspective.

Why had they put Hertz Lipmann into the Lubyanka Prison? And why had those soldiers died at Verdun? What was the point of creating human beings if they were destined to end in blood and mud? Tell me, star—since I can see you, perhaps you can see me.

I watched until the star sank below the other side of the roof. The earth was doing what it always did, turning on its axis. No, I couldn't expect the star to carry on a conversation with someone like me. Stars need only to shine and be silent.

I turned back to the room, my neck aching from having bent my head. My hunger had somehow subsided. I heard footsteps and it was Edusha. "What are you doing?" she wanted to know. "Why are you wandering about?"

"Edusha, I ate what was left of your roll."

"You poor boy," she said. "I forgot to make you some supper. It's not your fault. I'll get something ready."

"No, Edusha, not for me."

"I'm hungry too. The stomach has its needs. Wait, I'll turn on the gas."

It was not so very late, just twelve-fifteen. The gas shed a harsh yellow light. Edusha brewed some tea and found half a loaf of bread, some butter and cheese. We sat at the table, chewing away like an old couple that had used up all their words long ago.

"What am I going to do now?" Edusha said. "There's no point in going to work in the furniture store. It makes no sense."

"They'll let Hertz go."

"No. Even if they do, they won't let him come back here. Or he may not want to come back himself. They suspected him of something over there. Maybe my stepfather will be willing to send for me from London. But what would I do there? He's already supporting my two younger sisters."

"Maybe you could go to Palestine."

"How? Your certificate is already assigned. Besides that, I haven't the slightest interest in going. Why Palestine? Because King David fought with the Phoenicians three thousand years ago? Palestine belongs to the Arabs, not to the Jews."

"Where should the Jews go?"

"They ought to stay where they are. If there ever is a just world, then there will be justice for all. And if we don't get justice, then Palestine won't help either."

That night we slept in Bella's bed. Our passions were charged with resignation. Edusha pressed herself closely against me. She was not asleep, but she was silent. We lay awake for hours, each immersed in his or her own thoughts. Then something occurred to me and suddenly I said, "Edusha, I can't say how I know this, but I'm sure that you and Stanislas Kalbe were lovers."

Edusha made no reply. She pulled away from me and moved

to the very edge of the bed. "You have no right to inquire into my past."

"No. But . . ."

"But what? I don't ask you what you do with Sonya or with that other woman—what's her name—your fictive wife."

"No, but what do you call love? You tell me that you're in love with Hertz Lipmann."

"Kalbe was before Hertz."

"Edek was before Hertz."

"I didn't love Edek, not the way I love Hertz. Why is it that men are permitted everything and women nothing? We're also flesh and blood. It's as simple as that."

"How can love exist in those circumstances? How can a man be sure that he's the father of his children?"

"He'll know. And if he doesn't, why that's just too bad. People like you have no business preaching morals."

"I'm not preaching, Edusha."

"Yes, you are. Here you are, sleeping with me, and you have contempt for me. Who created all these laws about love? People, not God. God wouldn't care if I had all the men in Warsaw— how can He, since He doesn't exist? Yes, I was involved with Stanislas Kalbe. If you don't like it, you can take the next train to your little town, where you can marry a rabbi's wife."

"Did Bella know about it?"

"Bella did the same thing." Edusha laughed.

"I'll go back to my room."

"Go ahead, little man."

I started toward my small dark room. I had become a man, but I was so nauseous I felt like vomiting. I was overwhelmed by grief and revulsion such as I had never known before. I understood for the first time the meaning of the word "defiled." I lay down on the iron cot and it seemed to me that I could hear my father's voice crying out: "Sinful Jew, may your name be cursed! See what happens when you turn from Jewish ways. You are worse than the Gentiles. I curse you! You are no longer my son and I'm no longer your father."

5

THE next day I was at the Writers' Club at the appointed time, but Getsl Slatkis, the editor of the magazine, was not there. The woman at the door would not let me in, and I was getting ready to leave, when Susskind Eikhl saw me. He told me my brother was coming to meet him, and asked me in.

People were eating lunch, and I saw the same faces and the same expressions I had seen the day before. The cross-eyed composer was once again gnawing on a chicken bone, with a noodle dangling from his black beard. We went into the next room, where Susskind Eikhl ordered lunch for me. One of the writers who had been hanging around Edusha came by and put out his hand.

I had forgotten my revulsion against Edusha, and having slept through the night, I awakened with a sense of conquest. I had actually had intimate relations with a woman. I said to myself, "Whatever may happen to Edusha, even if she lives to be a hundred, still she'll never forget there was once a David Bendiger." In some romantic way, I had the feeling I had made myself immortal. If my essay was also published, I knew I would count myself happy.

There was a link in my mind between being published and having had a woman. I could not remember where I had read—in Schopenhauer perhaps—that by means of sex one made contact with the *Ding an Sich*, the raw material of phenomena with the seed of truth that is concealed by the intellect's illusions.

On the way to the Writers' Club I had talked to myself as if I were quarreling with someone, even with my own father. I said, "I have not stood on Mt. Sinai, and neither have you. All your knowledge is drawn from an old book that someone wrote and edited. The Talmud itself acknowledges that the sages tried to suppress the Book of Kohelet. Even if one accepts that every word of the Torah is true, still there is nothing in it about the World to Come or of the raising of the dead. They added countless laws and made mountains out of molehills." My father replied, "Take one step away from those laws and you become a lecher, a libertine, an assassin. Who are the Jewish Communists who had the rabbis shot and the merchants, pious Jews? One day you'll learn the truth. I just hope it won't be too late."

I sat with Susskind Eikhl, who was saying, "Getsl Slatkis is a stinker. He tells a young man to meet him and then doesn't show up himself. A filthy fellow."

"What kind of magazine does he edit?"

"Twaddle. Bedbug journalism."

"I guess you know what's happened to Hertz Lipmann?" I blurted out, uncertain whether I ought to mention it.

Susskind Eikhl was instantly serious. "Yes, I've heard."

"What's your view of it?"

"It's hard to say. One never knows what's taking place there. But one thing is clear: if he hasn't done anything wrong, all will be well. In the Soviet Union they don't invent false charges against anyone."

"He seemed like an honorable fellow to me."

"Yes, but there are provocateurs. Here's your brother."

Aharon stood at the door. For the first time I saw how worn his coat was. He wore a soft cap of the sort one wears in summer. He looked thinner than he had yesterday, his face pale, his cheeks deeply sunken. His chin was sharply defined, like a boy's. For me Aharon had always been the grown-up brother. I was in awe of his height, his intelligence, his wide reading. While I was attending Chaim Yonatan's cheder at 22 Twarda Street, my brother was painting pictures, publishing a sketch in *The Jewish Word*, going to theaters, concerts. He was invited to the homes of people like Dinesohn, Levik Epshtayn, M. Y. Frayd. But here in the Writers' Club he was a stranger. Susskind Eikhl called to him, "Hey, Bendiger."

My brother spotted us—"Ah." When he removed his cap his bare skull reminded me of the young people who during wartime epidemics had been taken to disinfecting stations, where they had their heads shaved. There was a look of pride in his bright blue eyes, but I also detected a trace of anxiety. "Where's Getsl Slatkis?" he asked.

"Evidently the fool has changed his mind," Susskind Eikhl said.

"Well, it's no big loss. That magazine of his is shit."

At that moment Getsl Slatkis appeared in the doorway. He was wearing a loose coat that looked like a cape and a wide-brimmed felt hat, and he carried a walking stick with a silver knob. His artist's cravat hung a trifle askew. The long hair sticking out from under his hat, the briefcase he carried under his arm, his round face, his long sideburns, his wide-open eyes behind the lenses of his horn-rimmed glasses—all expressed an overwhelming desire for respectability that was mixed with childishness.

He made me think of a coddled only son who has been well groomed, dressed up, and then sent out to join the grownups. He was shaking his head and smiling apologetically. Mincing up to us, he said, "I'm truly sorry," in a high-pitched voice, and put a moist hand on my shoulder. I don't know why he made me think of a cat with a bellyful of mice. "Let me see your manuscript," he said.

I took the manuscript from my breast pocket and handed it to him. Getsl Slatkis wheezed a little as he smoothed out the pages, raised his eyebrows above the rims of his glasses, and smoked a cigarette. As he blew smoke rings, his eyes grew more thoughtful, worried, filmed over with sadness. For a moment I actually thought I saw tears of disappointment. At intervals his eyes would fix on a word, as if they were nailed to it.

Susskind Eikhl meanwhile winked several times, talked with my brother about a writer in Russia who played the role of a sort of literary Holy Jew. Then the talk shifted to the anthology that Eikhl was planning to issue in Warsaw and which would include Soviet writers. The Poles had put writers in jail for Communist activity, but Communism in literature was apparently considered kosher. In such matters different laws applied. In the left-wing magazines there were articles that said openly that the capitalist system was decadent, criminal, and a stinking ruin, and that one could only look to the East, to the Red Army, to the revolution, for hope. In those magazines Christianity, Judaism, Zionism, Hebraism, and all of Israel had been utterly exploded. They had even discovered the existence of a Jewish peasantry, though many Jews were merchants, brokers, intellectuals, and belonged to the very classes and conditions the revolution most wanted to exterminate.

My brother gave me a questioning look. We had escaped, he and I, from a world of religious lies, only to find ourselves in a web of secular lies.

Getsl Slatkis, after some hesitation, put the manuscript on the table. I had known from the first moment that he did not like my writing. He had been making the sort of wheezing sounds a grandfather clock makes before it is about to strike. "What shall I say, eh, eh, eh? A talented young man. Truly remarkable, but . . . but . . . the style. Not polished. Maybe if it were rewritten and . . . tidied up, so to say. Besides that—" and Getsl Slatkis broke off. He rubbed his thumb and forefinger together, waved his hand, and sat there. The weight of inexpressible or pointless words oppressed him.

I said, "It doesn't matter. Thanks for reading it. I know I've still got a lot to learn and . . ."

"I really would love to print a newcomer. We must have young writers. Literature needs them. But you see the times we live in. You're stuck somewhere . . . I don't quite know how to express it . . . somewhere in the past."

Susskind Eikhl snorted his one-nostril laugh. He lighted a cigarette quickly, readying himself to participate in a debate the minute he tasted the smoke, but just then he was called away to the telephone.

My brother lowered his head. "I haven't read the piece and I've no idea whether it's any good. But Spinoza was no Leninist, not even a Marxist. The Ari, too, never urged the masses to take to the streets."

"Ah, Comrade Bendiger, you'll pardon me . . . you've got it all wrong. One can write about the past, but from the point of view of a modern man. After all, something has happened in the three hundred years since Spinoza wrote. You know, Comrade Bendiger, that I have strong differences with the Communists, but still one can't deny that, eh, eh, the earth has moved. New forces have emerged—this last war and the awakening of social consciousness. The fact is that the eyes of the proletariat have been opened. How can one ignore all that? As regards the Cabala, one has to approach it from an appropriate perspective. No one any longer believes in God or in angels or in the Sephirot or any of that claptrap. Certainly not our readers. One has to understand the era in which the Cabala emerged, eh, eh, and the conditions that produced it."

"What conditions?" my brother asked. "The Cabala did not appear because Richard the Lion-Hearted wanted to capture Jerusalem."

"You'll never persuade anyone that the Cabala or any other religious movement appeared in a vacuum. One doesn't have to be a materialist historian to know that political and economic forces affect the ideologies of any era."

"Ah . . . those phrases numb my brain," my brother said. "I still can't see how Napoleon and the Kuznitser Preacher have anything to do with each other."

"You can't see because you don't want to see. I myself emphasize at every opportunity that the Communists exaggerate—even misperceive a variety of events in our lives; and I object especially to their negative approach to Jewish history and so on. You've just come back from the Soviet Union, so you know how they attack me there. They see me as practically a Fascist. In *The Kharkov Star* recently they called me an imperialist, and Mussolini's right hand . . . hee hee. And I'm in just as bad odor with the Zionists and the Jewish nationalists. No, Comrade Bendiger. One can't turn the hands of the clock back on two thousand years of history. Are you yourself a Zionist?"

"If I could bring myself to believe that Jews will be given a land of their own, then I'd be a passionate Zionist."

"No one will give it to them. Dreams of an addled brain, as they say in Poland, empty fantasies of a bourgeoisie that has completely lost touch with its base and builds castles in the air. The Jewish masses will stay in the lands where they find themselves and move with the mainstream of human progress, unless of course the Messiah should come. In that case, the Jews will all be carried off to the land of Israel on a cloud, ha ha!"

"Mr. Bendiger is wanted on the telephone."

My brother got up, but the woman sitting near the door laughed and winked. "Not you. The younger one . . ." I jumped up. I felt the blood rush to my face. There was only one person who knew where I was—Edusha. I nearly knocked the table over.

6

ON the telephone Edusha told me that Dov Kalmenzohn had phoned twice and that he wanted me to call him at once. Another woman, Minna Ahronson, had also called. "I guess she's your fictive wife, isn't she?" Edusha said, informing and questioning me at the same time. She laughed sarcastically, her manner at once intimate and sharp.

Getting a phone call at the Writers' Club had so confused me that I became half deaf. I had to ask Edusha to repeat every other word. I was certain that all the writers were listening to my conversation and were amused by it.

That morning at breakfast Edusha had quarreled with me, calling me a hypocrite, a provincial, and all sorts of other names. Sometimes she accused me; sometimes she apologized for herself.

She said she was not a loose woman but that she had blood in her veins, not sour milk. Why were men able to play around with any sort of drab? Why did no one point a finger at a man for yielding to his desires? It all came from the idea that a woman was no more than a useful object for a man. This was one more bit of debris from the capitalist system, from feudalism, from the Dark Ages. Edusha also admitted that she had never really loved Edek.

Why was she justifying herself so, I wondered. Why was it so important to her whether I thought well of her or not? Was it possible that we were at the start of a love affair?

Now, on the phone, her speech was a mixture of the prickly and the sincere. When would I get home? Should she make supper for me? Should she wait for me? Was my brother at the Writers' Club? "If he is, bring him along. No problem. I can get supper ready for both of you." I lied and told her my brother was not there. I would have been too embarrassed to say a word to her in his presence. I promised Edusha I would be home for supper. Her tone suddenly altered and she said, "Come as soon as you can."

As I started toward my brother, I felt my knees trembling. I had failed with Getsl Slatkis, but I had triumphed in my relations with a woman. Susskind Eikhl had said that he could get me a temporary membership card in the Writers' Club. After I had published a dozen pieces, I could apply for full membership. Who could say?—Susskind Eikhl might include my essay in the anthology he was planning.

I had the feeling my luck had changed for the better. From now on, only good things would happen. The only thing wrong was my shyness. I was still afraid of what would happen if Edusha showed up here. I was also afraid my brother would question me about our relationship.

Could anyone understand my perplexity? How would a writer describe these hidden anxieties? In the medical books I sometimes read, all personal complications were listed under the heading of nervousness or neuresthenia. They could be treated by means of hydropathy, rest in the country, or hypnosis. But the truth was that my mental processes were frightfully complicated, tenaciously mixed. I told myself that emotions contained within themselves more reality than the "adequate ideas" that Spinoza called mathematics and logic. The emotions are the essence of a human being, his soul. If all that was left after death were the adequate ideas, it would mean there was no trace of the soul's immortality.

My brother was alone at his table. His eyes bored through me. I had the feeling he knew my most secret thoughts, all my weaknesses and confusions. Though he was older than I, still we were like those identical twins who, though two bodies, yet have a single psyche.

While I was at the phone, someone had turned on a Victrola. The journalist with the bright spats and the sharp crease in his trousers was dancing once more with the woman with birdlike eyes and a beaked nose. The music coming from the record was an impudent squeaking song whose foreign words I did not understand, but it seemed to be saying, "We have contempt for everyone. We spit on God and on humanity. We have lost all shame. We have returned to the nakedness of the time before the Fall."

My brother asked, "Who phoned you here at the Writers' Club?"

I blushed. "It's something to do with my certificate," I lied.

"Sit down. That Getsl Slatkis is a scribbler who has climbed onto the revolutionary bandwagon. You can't know what's been happening in Russia. What I didn't know is that it's the same way here. I'm in a bad spot." Suddenly his tone changed. "I had counted on finding some work here. I can't stay at the Tsinamons' any longer. They haven't room enough for themselves. I have to find an apartment somewhere. If I don't . . ."

He stopped short. It was the first time that Aharon had ever confided in me and it made me uncomfortable. "Susskind Eikhl talked about a benefit evening for you," I said.

"What's the good of a benefit evening? I have a family of three now. I don't know, maybe I ought to let our parents know. Mother is likely to show up here, and where would I put her? Why don't you tell me how things are with them? How come Father ended up in Galicia?"

"He came to Byaledrevne in 1918. Grandpa was dead by then. Uncle Gabriel was made rabbi, so there was no place for Father. He found an opening for a rabbi in some little town, practically a village."

"You've been there?"

"Only for a day. They wade about in mud up to their knees. All of them are followers of the Hasidic Rebbe of Belz."

"Ah. Nothing's changed here, but there, there's another sort of fanaticism. Maybe you've heard about what happened in the Ukraine?"

"Yes, the Petlyura pogroms."

"I lived through it all. The gangs, the harassment. Everyone beat up the Jews. Anyone who had a hand or a foot used it as a weapon. The wonder is that the Jews survived. We paid the highest price for the revolution. Later on, Jewish commissars shot Jews at every hand. Street urchins were given unlimited power and used it to vent their rage on the Jews."

"Yes, I know."

"You don't know. There's no way you could know. A Jewish Chekist is as evil as any Ukrainian hooligan. Jews were dragged before a firing squad for having put on phylacteries or for selling thread. What were the Jews supposed to do? Work in factories in their declining years? Work on the Sabbath? I tried to say something, but it was as much as my life was worth. I can hardly believe that I got out of there alive."

As painful as his words were, they made me feel a childish pride that my brother was talking to me as if we were peers. I said, "Maybe you could go to Palestine."

"Come on. What would I do there? There's no way that I could become a field worker at the age of thirty. Besides, nobody has given me a certificate. I have a wife and an infant child. In

Russia, Ida worked in a hospital, but it's hard to find a job here. I have no passport and no other documents. I can't even enlist."

"I know a fixer who can get you whatever you need."

"I don't have the money to pay him. What's happening with your certificate? Do you really mean to become a Halutz? And how did you get one?"

I gave my brother all the details, and as he listened he shook his head. He began playing with a spoon, which he balanced on the edge of an ashtray. "She might become your wife in fact," he said.

"How? She's madly in love with her fiancé, Zbigniew Shapira."

"What will you do there?"

"I don't know."

"You don't look too well. Are you anemic, or what?"

"No. It's just my natural color."

"Do you ever see a doctor?"

"No."

"I guess Father's turning gray?"

"When I saw him last he had only a few gray hairs in his beard."

"How old are they now? In Russia, they took Jews of Father's age and shot them. Or put them in jail with murderers and hooligans—all in the name of Karl Marx and Lenin. I couldn't believe that Jews would be so bloodthirsty."

"That kind, anyway."

"What's the point of being a writer? Write for whom? Every time I pick up my pen I put it down again. And here the young folk sit, comparing each other's talents. All of them are red-hot left-wingers. Take this Getsl Slatkis. I hear that he owns houses in Warsaw, he's a rich man. Susskind Eikhl's a good enough fellow. He wants to help me out, but he's one of them as well."

"He's idolized in the provinces."

"What can you expect from those young people in the small towns. The Poles will have nothing to do with them. Nobody wants them. You can't live among nations forever as a minority.

After two thousand years, the problem is more acute now than it was in the time of Rome. Well, let's go. Ida's father has made supper for me."

We left the Writers' Club and walked silently through the streets. They were filled with beggars, cripples, round-shouldered Jews in torn coats. They seemed not so much to walk as to shuffle along on their patched boots. The look in their eyes seemed to be saying, "Whither goes the Jew?"

We passed Aharon Sardiger's synagogue. We heard a suppressed murmuring and smelled rotting rags and old urine as we passed the gate. A bell sounded in the church at Gushibov, either calling Gentiles to Mass or because they were carrying out a corpse. A hushed dismay hovered over the town. The snow had melted and was transformed to mud. A horse pulling a wagonload of barrels fell. Women wearing head shawls called, "Hot beans!" "Potato puddings!" "Peppered peas!"

My brother asked, "How much longer can this last? Well, take care of yourself." He put out his hand.

I had accompanied him as far as Panska Street. Evening had fallen. In the windows of the decrepit houses, gas lamps were beginning to be lighted. In dark little shops, potatoes, onions, and butter were being weighed on scales. I felt a pang of hunger and the mood of evening. I looked about for a drugstore or a sausage shop where I might find a phone and call Dov Kalmenzohn, but by the time I found one, the people at the Halutz house told me he had gone home. When I called the Ahronsons' the phone rang several minutes without being answered. I was about to hang up when I heard Meir Ahronson's voice—strangely soft and tender. "Hello. Who is it, eh?"

7

"MR. Ahronson, this is Dovid. Dovid Bendiger," I said, raising my voice the way one does when speaking to the deaf.

"Who? Who is it?" Meir Ahronson asked again. It was clear that I had woken him.

"Excuse me," I said, "I didn't think you'd be asleep so early in the evening. This is Dovid Bendiger, your daughter's Hebrew teacher." What I nearly said was, "Your daughter's fictive husband."

Meir Ahronson was thoughtful for a while; then, "Well, what is it?"

"I've been told that your daughter's looking for me. May I speak with her?"

"Looking for you? Why is she looking for you? It's Tisha Bov [a day of mourning] here in my house."

The old fellow's lost his mind, I thought. What I said was, "If she's at home, will you be good enough to call her."

"I don't know. I'll see. It's all over. What's your name?"

"Bendiger."

"Of course. Well, I'll look."

I held the phone and I waited a long time. It seemed to me that I could hear the slapping sound of Meir Ahronson's worn old slippers. Then there was a dead silence. He's turned senile, I thought. I was about to hang up when I heard a snorting and banging, then a noise as if someone had moved a chair, after which I heard Minna's voice. I could hardly recognize it. It was as low and feeble as her father's.

She said, "*Tak* [yes]," with that mixture of fatigue and distress one hears from someone who has just been roused out of sleep.

I began at once to apologize. "Minna, they tell me you've been looking for me. I hope I haven't disturbed you."

There was a long pause; then Minna said softly, in a voice without energy, "Where are you? I want to see you, but not here at home. Maybe I can come to your place."

"To my place? I live in a dark room. Besides . . ."

"Well then, come here. My mother isn't well. Maybe we can go somewhere together."

"Good. I'll come right away."

I left the tavern where I had gone to make the telephone call and went to the end of Leszno Street and then to Iron Street. A damp wind was blowing, cold and biting. I put my collar up and my hands into my pockets. It must be that Minna's mother was dying. The thought came into my head: The last time I saw her, Mrs. Ahronson had looked at me through her lorgnette, her face quite yellow. My brother's despairing words, the cold, the gloomy lamps from which streaks of mist trailed, the leaden and inert sky—all this affected me deeply. The wind struck my face, got into my sleeves, under my collar, up the legs of my trousers.

Am I getting sick? I wondered. I started to run, and I realized that my shoes, on which Rafel the shoemaker had put half soles and heels not two months ago, were once again worn down. There's no point to life and no reason to cling to it, I thought.

I climbed the badly lighted stairs and knocked at the door, but no one replied. Perhaps Mrs. Ahronson had died. A thought struck me, bringing fear with it. Ever since that night when Binyomin and I had guarded the young woman's corpse at the clinic, my schoolboy fear of the dead had returned. I rang the bell again, heard steps, and then the door was opened—by Mrs. Ahronson! Her face was yellow, and she gave me a look of mute accusation. I said, "Your daughter asked me to come up."

"Well." Mrs. Ahronson pointed to another door which I had not noticed. Minna had been given another room. A solitary lamp was burning in the huge and empty hall, perhaps as a light for renters coming to look at the rooms.

When I knocked at the new door and got no response, I opened it and saw Minna sitting on the sofa. She was surrounded by strewn bedclothes, there was a kitchen table in the room, and heaps of books were piled on the floor. The window was covered with a green shade, and the room was filled with shadows. I greeted Minna, but she made no reply. I said, "Minna, if I'm disturbing you, I can come back tomorrow morning."

"You're not disturbing anyone. After all, I asked you to come. Here's a chair, sit down." It was a wicker chair, the kind people use in summer country houses. I sat down. Minna gave me an oblique look, the look of someone about to sneeze or to tell a joke. She said, "You ought never to have had anything to do with me. I'm nothing but bad luck."

"What's the matter?"

"Zbigniew Shapira has married someone else."

I was speechless. I stared at Minna and saw that her pallor was that of a sick person. But her eyes were smiling and there was a wry twist to her lips. I tried to swallow the lump that rose in my throat.

"Are you telling the truth?"

"Yes, the truth."

"Ah . . ."

We sat in silence for a while. Minna's eyes had turned darkly earnest, her upper lip quivered, and she said, "I'm sorry to have dragged you into this mire. But it doesn't essentially change our situation in any way. I still want to go to Palestine, and you may be sure that the moment we get there I'll give you your freedom. All the same, it seemed to me that you had to be told the truth. My father's prattling reveals everything anyway. He and my mother are against my going, naturally. But I'm of age, and there's no way they can force me to stay."

I looked down, embarrassed by the shamefulness of her situation and astonished by the surprises that fate kept setting before me. Only a few days ago, Minna had been saying that Zbigniew Shapira was her chief consolation, the only light shining in her darkness. Meir Ahronson's words came to mind: "It's Tisha Bov here in my house."

I knew that I ought not to say the words I was about to say, but my malice would not let me restrain them. "What will you do in Palestine now?" I knew that my question was tactless, almost gross.

Minna raised an eyebrow. "Get a pistol and shoot him."

"No, Minna. You're a respectable Jewish woman."

"Ha! How am I Jewish? In no way. But that won't affect you. No one will blame you for my sins."

"If you really mean what you say, I can't possibly take you with me," I said, surprised at my own words.

"There speaks the Jew. Don't be afraid. I won't shoot him. He won't be there anyway, since he married a rich English tourist. My father's a dreadful man, but he predicted disaster for me. I can just imagine what you think of me, after all our talks."

"Minna, you're one of the finest women I ever met." It was as if someone else was speaking through me. "It's said that those whom God loves, He punishes, and that may be . . ." I stopped.

Minna smiled and said, "Then God must love me a lot."

"Yes."

"It's all nonsense, nonsense. I haven't sent for you so you could give me compliments, though I thank you. Ah, he's slain me utterly, and I can't even hate him. It's all tied in with my fate. Think of it this way: Two people are wrecked on an island and one of them is fated to be murdered. Even if the other one isn't naturally a murderer, he will kill his fellow—since he knows it is fated. It would make no difference to you in any case whether I was married or not," Minna said in an altered tone. "Just as long as I continue to pay your expenses, our situation remains the same. I want to hear you say so directly. So that there won't be any misunderstanding later."

"Certainly. You're the person I know, not Zbigniew Shapira."

"You make the name Zbigniew sound funny. As you say it, it sounds Yiddish. Yes, of course, what difference does it make to you what I do when we get there? In any case, I can't stay in Warsaw, that much is certain. When did you last talk with the fixer?"

"I have to phone him tomorrow. The passport is waiting for me at the government office."

"Ah. There's nothing more I can do right now. But we can leave as soon as you get the passport and the visa. I won't pack a thing, absolutely nothing. Maybe you know someone who'd like to buy my bridal outfit? I begged my foolish parents not to spend money on fancy things. It's as if I had a presage that the whole thing was a joke. It seems to me that I mentioned this to you once, or am I just imagining things?"

"Yes, Minna. You did mention it."

"There may be a prophet hidden inside each of us, but we tend to be deaf to such warnings. As I was being fitted for my wedding dress, something in me kept asking, 'Why, Minna? Why? You'll never marry him.' Isn't that strange? How could I have known it? If my parents had put money aside with which to pay taxes, the government wouldn't have taken our furniture away. The only things they didn't take are these rags. I still think Zbigniew Shapira is an interesting man—but he's too much of an egoist and a charlatan. I regret nothing, nothing at all. I wouldn't even mind if he had left me pregnant. If only I were! Well then, so that's how we'll leave it. We'll travel to Palestine. Back to Grandfather Abraham's land. Is it true that your brother's come back from Russia?"

"Yes."

"Why didn't you tell me? The woman where you live—I'm sure she's your lover—told me. Why have you kept it a secret? What harm can your brother's being here do me?"

I did not know what to say. "You're a little bit like Zbigniew Shapira—in your own way," Minna said. "Yes, it occurred to me just this minute." She laughed, and her eyes glowed with the pleasure of her discovery.

My inner dybbuk, or whatever irrational force dwelt within me, made me say, "Yes, but it's me you stood with under the bridal canopy."

Minna's features froze. "Don't be a fool."

V

MY passport was waiting for me at the government office, but there was a delay. I needed a release from the tax office showing that I owed no back taxes. The English consul also required that I produce a certificate of good moral character. I suspected Barish Mendl of creating the delay so he could extract more money from us; he spoke unclearly, through his nose, and his manner was sly and deceitful. But it may be that I imagined this. Minna had paid him in advance, which no doubt had been a mistake. I knew he was involved in some sort of speculation: I had heard him apologizing over the telephone and promising to cover a bad debt. Barish Mendl spoke a mixture of Yiddish and Polish as he drew deep drags from the cigarette he left perched on the edge of an ashtray. He snarled at his wife, and when his daughter came in to ask for money he said, "I don't run a counterfeit factory!" She had given him a spiteful look as she left, taking little catlike steps.

My brother was now traveling to several towns in Galicia, where he gave talks and readings from his work. Susskind Eikhl had also passed on to my brother the jobs he was unable to do. The fact that Aharon had just returned from the Soviet Union gave him a certain cachet among the leftists. My sister-in-law, Ida, had found a job in a clinic. Edusha, now working in the furniture store, was away from home all day.

I telephoned Sonya and she told me that the spats maker from her hometown, with whom she had walked out on Sabbath afternoons, had proposed to her. He had just bought a sewing machine in Warsaw and he intended to open his own shop in their small town. Sonya went into a long monologue: "What's the point of staying with my employers, letting my pigtails grow gray? I'm not getting any younger. I'm earning my own living, but I don't even have my own room. My bosses still treat me like a servant. I've been in Warsaw nine years and what have I got to show for it? Warsaw men expect huge dowries, and the truth is, I haven't saved any money. Mendl will give me a home, he wants children, he wants to lead a normal life. But . . . I'm not in love with him. He's a nice enough fellow, but he's soft. And a constant complainer. He talks like a book and hums like a bee. And second, I've gotten used to the big city. When I think of that empty marketplace, and those unpaved streets, my heart sinks. Immediately after Purim, the place turns into a mire and one slogs about until Shevuoth. At night you light your kerosene lamps. After they're married, the girls turn into sickly women who say mean things about each other. Well, what's left?"

"What will you do, Sonya?"

"I don't know, David. Mendl wants a clear answer, but I keep putting him off. I can't just bury myself there. If one has to suffer, better to do it in a Jewish land and for an ideal."

"Do you really want to go to Palestine?"

"Maybe you can get me a certificate. A village would be better than a small town."

"Sonya, you know I haven't got any pull."

"I can do everything—milk a cow or work for the Halutzim. David, I want to ask you something, but you have to promise me you won't say no. I want you to meet Mendl and tell me what you think of him. There are times when I think he's quite personable, and then all at once he seems dreadfully provincial and a fool. He reads Yiddish literature and repeats what he's read. Foreign words. He starts a conversation and ends up heaven knows where. It's all deplorable. He wants to be thought enlightened and hasn't courage enough to wear a modern hat. He goes about with a little Jewish hat stuck on the top of his head.

When he's about to sit, he takes out his handkerchief and dusts the chair. He's acquired three gold teeth, and when he opens his mouth, they dazzle my eyes. He talks about his father, a sick man, night and day. How much can a man say about his father? His father has to like me. If he doesn't, that's the end of the match."

"No, Sonya. It's not a match for you."

"What is there for me? Only women come to the store where I work. If I stay any longer, all I'll get is older and grayer."

I promised Sonya that I'd meet with her and her spats maker. After I hung up the phone, I started pacing from the bed in which Edusha now slept, and in which Bella had slept before her, to the window that looked out on the solid wall. I'd become a complete householder and made myself tea on the gas ring when I wanted it. If I got hungry, I opened the kitchen cupboard and found some bread or butter or a lump of sugar—whatever else might be there. I had stopped recording the number of meals I had eaten and how much rent I owed Edusha and Bella.

I went into my dark little room and turned on the gas jet. The books that Stanislas Kalbe had left behind were still on the shelves above my bed—textbooks on integral and differential calculus, analytical geometry, trigonometry, physics. He had graduated from Warsaw's Polytechnic. He had slept with Edusha and with Bella, and then had accepted a job in Danzig. Evidently he had married a rich young woman there. I resented him because I was behaving just like him.

His name sounded brutal to me—Kalbe. And why should a Jew be named Stanislas? I hated his books, which I could not understand, and on whose title pages his name had been stamped. To spite me, Edusha talked of him continually. Stanislas took her to the opera, where they sat in the loge; to the Café Zemianski, to the Café Europejski. He had even taken her to the races once. Though Edusha loved to talk about rescuing the proletariat, she behaved like a bourgeoise, and it evidently pleased her that Stanislas Kalbe had a rich father. "Even if I were in love with her, I wouldn't marry her," I said to myself. "Let her get herself another Hertz Lipmann."

I looked through Edusha's bureau drawers and found an album with a picture of Stanislas Kalbe standing between Edusha and Bella, his arms on their shoulders. He had curly hair and a square face. There was an ordinariness to his features; it showed in his impudent smile, his broad nose and thick lips, his cleft chin. A feeling of revulsion for Edusha rose in me. I vowed not to make love to her again. With the help of God, I would pay off my debt to her—with interest.

I started to plan a novel. There was no money to be made writing essays on Spinoza, but a successful novel could make one rich. It didn't have to be long—a hundred to a hundred and fifty pages would be enough—but it must be made so exciting that the reader couldn't put it down. There would have to be love in it, but not necessarily the love of one man for one woman. Where was it written that a man could love one woman only? Why not write a novel in which a man was in love with two women, or even three—that would be something new in literature. Or maybe I could have one of the women in love with several men. Neither Sonya, nor Edusha, nor even Minna would make an appropriate heroine for such a novel, and they'd be sure to recognize themselves. I could not be the hero. It would have to be a mature man, a practiced Don Juan like Zbigniew Shapira. Yes, that was the right idea.

I had a notebook lying on the dresser. I took Edusha's pen and ink and started to write. When I finished a full page, I was not pleased with what I had done. What, after all, did I know about Zbigniew Shapira? What did I know about universities or the army? How could I create the hero of such a novel, a synagogue scholar who hadn't so much as a crust of bread to his name? When I reread what I had written, I tore the page to bits and flushed them down the toilet.

I lay down on the sofa and yawned. It was cold in the house and I felt a chill run down my spine. How could you write if your hands were freezing? I was hungry too. Instead of concentrating my thoughts on my work, I fantasized a dish of groats and beans with mushrooms into which potatoes had been sliced. It seemed to me that I could smell the odor of meatballs and fresh bread coming from neighboring apartments.

I closed my eyes and lay there in a darkness of my own. Why not die and put an end to all the torment? I invoked Nirvana, or Death, or *Bitul Eyvrim*—the cessation of the members, as the Hasidim call it. I wanted to enter a sphere where there was no anguish, no yesterday, no tomorrow. I wanted to retreat into a part of the elements of which I was constituted. As I dozed off, I dreamed about things for which there are no words or concepts. I became a creature who stretched like rubber; I was partly an elastic spring, partly a lung, partly fear, partly language. I turned into this unknown thing—an embryo, perhaps, in the process of growing.

A sound woke me.

Edusha had opened the outer door with her key. She came in, saying, "So you're sleeping away your days."

"How was it at work?"

"Ah, work. Couples come in, buying beds and mattresses, thinking things will be the way they used to be. What about you? When do you leave for Palestine?"

"I still don't know. I have the passport."

"And what about your lady? What's the point of her going?"

"Edusha, I don't understand anything anymore."

"You'd be better off doing something. A writer should write, not lie around dozing in the middle of the day. What book is that? Oh, *Analytical Geometry*. Do you understand that stuff?"

I made no reply. I couldn't remember bringing the book with me into the living room. Lately, I had been doing things automatically. Edusha paced back and forth. "Did the postman bring any mail?" she asked.

"Nothing."

"What are they doing to Hertz over there? He's no provocateur.

Why would he do such a thing? Provocateurs don't spend months in Polish prisons. If Hertz is a provocateur, then there's nobody you can believe. I've written a letter to the Russian consul, but they don't reply. Come, help me make a snack."

I went into the kitchen with Edusha. She put rice on to cook. She had bought some ground meat and asked me to cut up onions. "Guess who I ran into on the streetcar today?"

"I can't guess."

"Edek. He's put on weight. How did he manage to get fattened up so quickly? Strange. We used to be quite close, but he was like a stranger. How can someone turn so cold?"

"Evidently it's possible."

"No. I never loved him. It's your fault too."

"How is it my fault?"

"There's nothing to be done. One gets used to it. If you hadn't come that afternoon and rented the room, I wouldn't have known that you existed. Now that your brother is in Warsaw, you will sooner or later end up in the Writers' Club. I talked to Susskind Eikhl on the phone today, and he sent you his regards. He's decided you and I are engaged. It's too funny for words."

"What does he say about Hertz?"

"Ah, he keeps silent, like the rest of the dogs. They've already forgotten him, his good comrades. As if he had never existed. It's as if he's been liquidated!"

2

SHOSHANA got Binyomin and me a job as packers at a notions store that had closed when its owner died. We piled the bundles onto a handcart, which we took to the apartment of the owner's widow. It was hard work. In addition, we angered the professional porters, who attacked us, saying we were taking away their livelihood. A porter threw one of our bundles into the gutter. Binyomin had to call the police. Some women bystanders sided with us and shouted abuse at the porters and told them that we were Halutzim and were working to help a widow.

Because we had to work so fast, I soon became tired. Despite the cold, I broke out in a sweat. Binyomin laughed at me, and young women called out, "Better go back to your synagogue." I hadn't realized I was so weak. My heart beat wildly; my hands seemed paralyzed. When I walked, I wobbled. Binyomin said, "What will you do in the Land? Stand swaying before the Western Wall?"

We worked the whole long day. When it was time for us to be paid, the widow said that she didn't have any money. She had had to pay a promissory note that her husband, may he rest in peace, had signed without her knowledge. She had had to pay out all her available cash, and told us to come back after the Sabbath. Binyomin asked me to go with him to the soup kitchen, but I begged off even though I was hungry. My fatigue was so great that my eyes kept closing. I had to lie down. It was all I could do to get back to Edusha's house on Leszno Street.

On the way back, I felt a pressure in one of my shoes. My left heel was being rubbed by a piece of leather. I stuffed paper inside the shoe, but this only made it worse. I stopped beside a gate and examined my shoe but found nothing wrong with it. The same shoe that for these long months had left me in peace had now acquired a murderous power. The skin under my sock was rubbed raw. Each step I took was painful for me.

I opened the door into the dark hallway and felt a current of cold air that smelled of gas, mold, and dirty laundry. Edusha had not yet returned from work. I searched for matches with which to turn on the gas, but they had disappeared somewhere. I did not take my coat off. Instead, I took my shoe off and lay down on the sofa. I was so weary my eyes closed at once, but I kept being awakened by the cold. There was a breeze blowing through the living room, as if someone had left a window open or a windowpane had been broken. I rested for a full hour, but my knees still ached. My feebleness astonished me.

Am I really so sickly? I wondered. If that's true, I'm going to spoil the certificate which would gain entry to Israel for someone who would be useful to the Land. Besides, if I go myself, I'm likely to die there of hunger.

Evidently I had caught cold. First I had chills, then fever. My nose was so stuffed that I could hardly breathe. My handkerchief was moist and dirty. I wanted to take my sock off, but it was stuck to my foot. Several days had gone by and I had not moved my bowels. My belly was hard and swollen. Was such constipation possible? It struck me that ever since I had moved in, I had avoided using the toilet because I was still embarrassed in Edusha's presence.

I felt a pain in my side. I wanted to go to the toilet, to make an effort to move my bowels, but I was afraid of the dark. The face of the young dead woman beside whose body Binyomin and I had watched appeared before me in the dark. "Oh God, this is the end," I cried aloud.

I heard the scraping of a key in the keyhole. I knew very well that it was Edusha, but what if it was the dead woman who had come to warn me? I sat up and listened attentively. I called, "Is that you, Edusha?"

"Why haven't you turned on the gas?" she called from the hallway.

"I couldn't find any matches."

"They're in the kitchen."

Yes, it was Edusha, though her voice had altered. I didn't get up from the sofa until after she had lighted the gas jet in the kitchen. Now she came in and turned on the living-room light.

She stood there in her worn coat (she always saved her good one for holiday occasions), and was wearing a hat that looked like an overturned pot. Her face looked cold, wet, a trifle smeared. "David," she said, "I've lost everything today."

"What have you lost?"

"My belief in mankind."

I wanted to ask, "What happened?" but I hesitated.

Edusha took off her coat and hat. She smoothed out her disheveled hair and glanced at her face in the mirror. After a bit, she knelt down, opened the door of the heater, and lighted a fire. I brought in some coal from the bin in the hallway. We worked silently together, like husband and wife. Edusha had lighted some kindling, but it had not taken, so the coals did not burn. An acrid smoke filled the room. Evidently the vent was stopped up. Neighbors had complained that months went by and one never saw a chimney sweep. Edusha scratched more matches and lighted some newspaper. She rearranged the kindling, put her hand out for a piece of the coal I had broken up with the dull side of a meat cleaver, and said—as much to the heater as to me—"It was Hertz who betrayed Bella."

"What! I don't believe it."

"It's true. He is a provocateur. He was working for the Defense Ministry."

I had sat down to help Edusha with the heater and now I got up. The fire had died again. The print on the burning newspaper pages glowed for a moment before turning to ash. Edusha too got up. There was a crooked smear on her face that extended from her forehead halfway down her nose. "Edusha, it can't be true."

"That's what you say. All of my innards are churned up," Edusha said, pointing to her belly.

"A provocateur doesn't go to Russia."

"He went there as a spy. But we have our counterspies. They found his name on a list of Defense Ministry agents. The very thought that such a man once touched me will drive me mad."

"That's what revolution is like."

"You mean the counter-revolution."

"It's all the same."

"At least you're openly against it. An informer's an ugly creature. I hope he gets what's coming to him over there—and a bit more."

"I can't believe any of it."

"I don't feel well." Edusha ran out into the hallway. I heard her throwing up in the toilet. The telephone rang and I hesitated, wondering whether I should answer it. By the time I lifted the receiver, there was no one on the line. In the kitchen I filled a glass and gave it to Edusha. She swallowed once and made a grimace. "How can one live in a world like this?"

Edusha gave up trying to light the heater. We sat in our coats and ate a dry meal, bread and cheese. Frost-etchings grew on the windowpanes. The gas flame snored. I told Edusha that her face was smeared, and she wiped it with her sleeve, but that only made the smear wider. She broke off a bit of bread and sprinkled it with salt. She lifted her head, then bowed it again, avoiding my eyes. She seemed to me to have grown older and smaller, with the look of a middle-aged woman who has let herself go. Her head trembled. She had about her a sadness that was as ancient as the Jews. Or perhaps it was a female sadness. After supper, Edusha asked, "Do you want me to make up another bed for you?"

"Why a separate bed?"

"Oh, I have the feeling that I'm unclean."

In bed we put our arms around each other and lay there quietly. Our feet were cold. Edusha put both our coats over the bedspread, but we couldn't get warm. Outdoors, it was perceptibly colder. The window frames rattled in the wind. We heard the bells of a fire engine and an ambulance's siren. Someone's place was burning and firemen had to leave their beds and go out into the bitter cold.

I was practically certain that Hertz Lipmann was not a provocateur. The Party must have concocted the story of his guilt when he was arrested in Moscow, but there was no way I could prove this to Edusha. I knew Hertz Lipmann would have willingly made a false accusation against anyone, if the Party required it of him. Edusha pressed herself closer against me, partly to warm herself and partly to find protection against the world's wickedness. She sobbed in her sleep for a while; then she said, "When

Bella hears about it, that'll be the end of her. Tell me, David, what am I to do now? I won't be able to believe anyone anymore. Who knows, maybe you're a spy too."

"Yes, Edusha. I'm an agent of the Defense Ministry."

"What can you tell them—that I hate injustice?"

"The secrets of the Kremlin."

"In the Kremlin they're trying to create a world without exploiters, without informers, without spies, without slavery. Is that wrong?"

Edusha turned her face to the wall. I was facing the room. The moon must have paused in the bit of sky visible between the blind wall and the window, because a greenish-silver light shone through the frost on the windowpanes. I could see everything in the room—the heater, the table, the chairs—even the picture of Rabbi Akiba Eiger that had been hanging on the wall when Edusha's father was alive. I dozed off, started awake, and then I slept again, only to wake once more. It occurred to me that Hertz Lipmann was probably dead. He had no further use for a better society, for a revolution, for Leninism. I wondered what his thoughts had been when his former comrades set him up against the wall. And if there was such a thing as the release of the soul, what was his soul doing now? Was it possible that his spirit was hovering here and heard what Edusha had said about him? A wild thought occurred to me: It was too cold here even for a ghost.

In the morning, quite early, someone knocked at the door. Edusha put on a coat and went to open it. I heard her murmuring for a long time to someone in the hallway. The room was as dark now as if it were evening. After a while Edusha returned, pale with the cold. She said, "I have a visitor."

"What kind of visitor?"

"Hertz's sister. I've put her in the kitchen. What am I to do with her? There's no end to my troubles."

3

B ARISH Mendl, the fixer, phoned after Edusha had left for work and informed me that all the necessary documents were ready. Minna and I could leave the country whenever we wanted. But there were some new expenses—a deposit that amounted to more than sixty American dollars. He said that he couldn't release the documents until that debt was paid. As far as I knew, Minna had covered all his expenses in advance. As always, he muttered incomplete words, unfinished sentences. Words fell from his mouth like peas. I wanted to say, "Swindler, why are you harassing a couple of unfortunate people?" What I said was, "I'll call Miss Minna."

"Ah, do it quickly, or all my work will have been wasted."

I phoned Minna several times, but nobody answered. What's happened, I wondered, have they all died?

The water pipes in the kitchen were frozen. I could neither wash nor shave, nor was there anything in the house to eat. As I put on my clothes, I knew they could not keep me warm enough against the freezing weather outdoors. I could no longer stay in this cold, gloomy apartment, but at the same time I had nowhere else to go. Slowly I descended the stairs and went out into the courtyard. Icicles hung from the eaves. Overnight all the windowpanes had been frosted over. My nose turned numb in less than a second. It felt as if it were made of wood. I started off to Minna's house. The street was all but deserted. The rare passersby hurried, emitting puffs of vapor from their nostrils. Sleighbells jingled. The sun, as if it were made of tin, gleamed above the rooftops. "Siberia," I said as I walked. By the time I reached Minna's gate, I felt that I could take only a few steps more.

My legs were numb as I started up the stairs. "What'll I do if she's not home?" I asked myself. And anyhow, how could she help me? I could live only for the moment. As always, I would have to find someplace to get warm and a bit of food to eat. I rang the doorbell, but I heard no footsteps. I waited awhile, then I rang again. I felt myself growing stubborn. I was sure there was someone in the apartment. I would not leave this door until someone came to open it. After considerable ringing and banging, I heard steps, and the door was opened on the chain. A single darting yellow eye looked out from under a disheveled eyebrow. It was Meir Ahronson, Minna's father.

I said, "Excuse me, but I have to talk with Miss Minna."

"Oh, it's you."

Slowly, clumsily, he undid the chain. Even so, he only half opened the door. He said, "What do you want with Minna? Everything's finished."

"I have the documents," I said. "Everything's ready."

"Ready, eh? She has no one to go to. Well, come in. We keep the door locked because we get unwelcome guests. They think there's something left to take."

He was wearing a torn and spotted cotton bathrobe and a pair of run-down slippers. He looked eighty years old, pale and shrunken. His speech had altered as if he had lost his teeth. And indeed his mouth was empty; evidently he had removed his false teeth. When I went in, the door of the room that had formerly been Minna's opened and the man who had rented the room came out. He was wearing a wine-colored bathrobe, had curly blond hair, and did not seem to be a Jew. He returned to his room almost at once and shut the door. Meir Ahronson had never seemed as small as he now appeared to be. I towered above him like a giant. He gave me a partly mocking, partly pleading look. "What do you think you'll do in Israel, become a Partition Jew? And pray for us at the Western Wall?"

"There are enough Partition Jews without me."

"Then what will you do? Plow the earth with your nose?"

"I hope I'll find something to do."

"What, for instance? Minna isn't well. She's still in bed. The truth is, she has no reason to get up. Come into my room for a while. I have something I want to say."

Meir Ahronson led me into his bedroom, sat down on the edge of the bed, and indicated a kitchen chair. He spoke with the hesitation of one who is unsure how to begin a conversation, though certain he will get to say what is on his mind and that his listener will hear him out.

"Now, what is it . . . oh yes. Palestine. I never heard the word in my day. Why 'Palestine'? Palestine derives from the Philistines. And what about the Philistines. As far as the Gentiles are concerned, the Philistines are the rightful owners of the land of Israel. I'm only saying this because, now that Zbigniew has pulled off that stunt of his and has gone off God knows where, what's my little Minna going to do there? She speaks Polish, not Hebrew. She's no laborer, either. I had two grown daughters, and when I lost the first one, this one became the apple of my eye. I could have arranged a good marriage for her. I set aside a good dowry and other things for her. But *Yoshev ba'shomayim yitsakhek* [He sits in heaven and laughs].

"But then came the war, and after that the Polish government. The Russian ruble became worthless. Even now I have thousands of formerly valid bank notes. I have no idea why I still keep them. The Russia of old will never return. I had money in the German state bank too. They've taken a nation and turned it into rubbish. Well, that's how it is. My daughter insists on going, but where's the sense in it? Since the only reason the two of you got together was to deceive the English, she'll be left over there without a country, without a home, and without an income. What's the point of putting a healthy body into a sickbed? Do you understand me?"

"Yes, I understand."

"Here in Warsaw, despite everything, she has a place to stay and she could be a teacher. She says she doesn't like teaching children, but what does she like? When you can't climb over, you must crawl under. I'll tell you the whole truth. My wife and

I have nothing more to lose. If I'm fated to spend my last years in an old folks' home, then so be it. I was rich long enough. It's time to get a taste of poverty, hee hee. My wife, poor thing, isn't well. I hope she can carry on for a while longer. She gets weaker day by day. Well, I can't look after the whole world, but I hate to see my Minna going astray. What about you, is it true that you want to be a writer?"

"If it depends only on my will, then yes."

"You have to use your will. You also have to have . . . what is the word? . . . talent. One person writes well and it has a flavor, while the other can't make his words stick together. Do you think you can make a living one day by writing?"

"Not immediately."

"But what will you eat in the meantime? The belly won't wait. It makes its own demands."

"Yes, I know."

"Is it true that your father is a rabbi?"

"Yes."

"Where?"

I named the little town.

"When you don't sleep at night, you think all kinds of thoughts. Since the two of you have been married according to the laws of Israel, and since you come from a pious family, why shouldn't you be married in fact? Don't think that I've said a word about this to Minna. She's still too upset by what that Zbigniew, that sinful Jew, that scoundrel, has done to her. I knew from the beginning that there would be no bread baked from that dough. That fellow is a swindler and an adventurer; he'll have ten more wives and will rot in jail. I no longer have a dowry for my daughter. She's a poor young woman, but she's a good child, educated, intelligent. A bit too intelligent. If I were your age, I'd marry a girl like her and look for some way to earn a living. She'd be a help to you. I sent her to the university and she's well-read, knows French, plays the piano. What'll she do in Palestine all by herself? I want to derive some pleasure from her life before I die."

I had lowered my head. At that moment I would have given anything for a roll and a cup of coffee. Meir Ahronson's heartfelt words had moved me strangely. I could hardly restrain my tears. I was hungry, shabby, without a profession, and an honorable Jew, a former rich man, offered me his daughter, a university graduate. I said, "She won't have me."

"How do you know that? If she pleases you, talk directly and clearly to her. She has her wedding outfit and all that. My wife is dying of grief. She might recover if she knew that Minna was not going to be left alone. You would be saving a soul."

"Well, I'll talk to Minna."

"Don't let her know that we spoke. She's dreadfully proud. Since you're a writer, you ought to know how to talk to a worldly modern young woman. Who knows, the whole thing may be heaven-sent."

"I'll speak to her."

"Yes, do talk to her. And if it's fated, it will happen. If something comes of it, I'd like you to stand under the wedding canopy once again. It's permissible, it's not considered a sin—I know of a case where it was done. For years now, my wife has had only a single wish: to live to see her Minna under the wedding canopy. God willing, it won't be too late. She's been bedridden now these many days. Doesn't leave her room. Hardly eats a thing. Well, what's the point? My wife has beautiful jewelry. We hid it from the villains. And she'll give it all to Minna. What does an old woman need jewelry for? We've rented a room to a boarder, but he'll move out if we ask him to. He's a count, an impoverished count. They've also been ruined—the nobility. He has a job somewhere as an inspector or something."

"Dov Kalmenzohn says that you're a scholar?"

"I've studied. Do you realize that fellow Zbigniew was a peasant when it came to Jewish matters? In my view, a young man who can understand a page of Gemara is better than one who can shine on the dance floor. In the face of everything, let's remain Jews."

"Yes, I understand."

"Go on. Talk with her. But she must never know that I suggested it. God forbid, in her grief she might harm herself or become my worst enemy. Well, good luck."

I went out of his room. I felt dizzy. I was afraid I might faint. The floor was bobbing up and down as on a ship. The walls whirled like a merry-go-round. I seemed to see a blazing flower before me, but I managed to make it to the door of Minna's room, and I knocked.

4

NOT hearing a reply, I knocked again. When I knocked the third time, the door opened of its own accord. Minna was asleep in her bed. I stood there for a while staring at her. Asleep, she looked younger than usual and strangely peaceful. The winter sun shone on her brown hair and there was the trace of a smile on her lips. She was apparently dreaming a happy dream. The bedsheet reached only to her hips. I could see the embroidery on her nightdress where it covered the lower part of her breasts. I felt that Minna had become once again what she had always been—rich, untroubled, a cherished young Jewish woman whose every caprice must be indulged. For all I knew, she was dreaming that she was reunited with Zbigniew Shapira. Ought I to go away, or ought I to wake her? It was late in the morning, nearly noon.

Then Minna opened her eyes. Seeing me, she smiled. Apparently she did not recognize me. I said, "Excuse me, Minna, I thought that . . ."

"I stay awake at night and doze by day. Do you have some news?"

"The documents are all ready."

"Good."

"Barish Mendl wants more money."

"Ah. I don't have any more. Come closer. Sit down here, on

the chair. I lie here thinking, and then all at once my eyes close. How is it outside, cold?"

"Bitterly cold."

"We have central heating. The landlord can't keep any single tenant from getting heat. If he could, he would certainly shut ours off. What time is it?"

"It's almost twelve."

"That late. Ah, I'm sleeping my days away. I was dreaming that I was riding a horse. I used to ride with Zbigniew. Who let you in, Papa?"

"Yes."

"Have you had breakfast?"

"Yes. No."

"You look frozen. How much does he want?"

"Sixty American dollars."

"Barish Mendl is a thief. But why should he be honest? I'll call and tell him I'll turn him over to the police. I have a friend who is a lawyer. Actually a friend of Zbigniew's, a former captain in the Legion. If he speaks to Barish, he'll ease up on us. He's not going to relish telling a courtroom about his dealings. When will you be ready to go?"

"Tomorrow, if you like."

"Wait. Everything has to be done just so. My parents are giving me trouble. They don't want me to go, but I'm determined to leave. Even if I have to die, I'd rather die abroad than here. Do you have things to pack?"

"Almost nothing."

"It's better that way. I won't take much besides some dresses and linen. My mother wants to give me her jewels, but I won't take them. I'll simply be a servant or whatever else they want me to be over there. What about your girlfriend? Is she still in jail?"

"It's her aunt who's in jail, not she."

"Oh, her aunt. Will you send for her after you get to Palestine?"

"Minna, she and I are not intimate. I live in her house and

she treats me well. She's a fanatic Communist and wouldn't dream of going to Palestine. She wants to achieve the revolution here, in Poland."

"They have too much energy. That's what makes them so wild. If they were as weary as we are, they'd simply want to rest."

"How will you rest in Palestine if, on the very day you get there, you have to go looking for work?"

"You're right. But in the meantime we'll be traveling by boat, and one can always jump off a boat."

For a moment there was amusement in her eyes. They became grave once more and she said, "Go out into the hallway and I'll get dressed. We'll take care of everything today and get it all done."

I had been unable to propose to Minna. I wasn't even sure that I wanted her. In the popular novels I had read, the romantic hero always got down on one knee, kissed the hem of his lady love's garment, and made a feverish speech. But those novelists ignored the kind of hero who was hungry, weary, had no place to sleep, and had no idea with whom he was in love. The truth is, I more or less wanted every one of the women I had met, but I felt no compulsion to act. I waited, ready to accept whatever fate sent me. I knew that no matter what I said to Minna, it would be true only while I was speaking. How had literature overlooked situations and characters like these? What was the point of a Romeo who had not yet chosen his Juliet and might never choose her? Because of the fiery loves those novelists portrayed, young women like Edusha ended up sleeping with men who chanced to come by looking for a room. And how strong was Minna's love for Zbigniew? How long would their relationship have lasted if another and greater "right young man" were to show up? The writers, like the politicians, were liars and made generalizations that did not correspond to the facts.

I stood in the hallway, fearful that Meir Ahronson would ask me for an account of how I had fared. No, I had been unable to ask Minna to live with me. I wasn't even sure how much longer I would live. I owned nothing but a batch of manuscripts of whose weaknesses I was well aware. I began to pace back and forth, silently, so that Meir Ahronson would not hear. There was something else—the soles of my shoes were worn out. As I paced, I imagined that I was in a prison and the hallway was the room in which I had been condemned to live for twenty years. Well, what if—as a result of a capricious set of circumstances—the world was destroyed and all that was left was this apartment? With whom would Minna choose to live? With me or with the impoverished count who had stuck his head out of his door? Perhaps with us both. And how much food was there left in the apartment, and how long would it last? And how likely was it that, in such circumstances, people would turn to cannibalism?

Even as I was musing on these matters, I was astonished at the things a mind can think. A new literature must arise, a literature without prescribed laws or rules of initiation. And with an end to the distinction between literature and philosophy. It would present people with all their deeds, thoughts, caprices, and insanities. Though literature has always studied character, it has almost always ignored modern man's characterlessness. Suddenly I had an impulse to write. It seemed to me that if I had a table, paper, pen and ink I could write a masterpiece on the spot.

The telephone rang and Minna, in bathrobe and slippers, came out. She seemed at first not to know who it was on the telephone, but after a while it appeared from her words that a doctor was on the line and that someone was sick and helpless. Then I heard her say, "I'm terribly sorry, but we no longer have a relationship." To whom could her words refer? She spoke more quietly now, almost in a murmur, and her tone grew more friendly. She ended by promising something, and hung up the phone. Then she announced—to me and everyone else—"Zbigniew's mother died in her sleep today."

"Oh."

"I'll have to go over and see what I can do. She was entirely alone."

"In that case, I'll go away."

"Wait, why don't you come with me? Someone has to arrange for the funeral. They have almost no relatives. I really don't know what to do. He's killed her—that's the pure truth."

Minna went through a door that led to the bathroom. Once again, I took to pacing back and forth. Well, this old woman's needs had been met. She was no longer cold or hungry, and did not have to worry about rent money. One way or another she'd be buried, and worms and microbes will do what they do. In the real world nature has an answer for every question. Through wars, epidemics, sieges, and revolutions, it is able to get rid of myriad beasts and people without number. And now nature's broom had swept away Zbigniew Shapira's mother. The name of the broom was death—which answers all questions, solves all problems, straightens whatever is crooked. I now remembered that I had put a razor blade under the insole of my shoe, and I removed it. If it slit one of my arteries, that would be the end of all my problems.

Nearly half an hour went by before Minna came out. She was fully dressed, wearing a hat and coat. On the stairs I had a frivolous impulse. Acting with the courage that stems from frivolity, I said, "Minna, since you no longer have Zbigniew Shapira and I too have no one, why don't the two of us really get married?"

Minna stopped. "Are you serious?"

"We're both desperate. What can we lose?"

"It's true, we have nothing to lose. But I'm five years older than you are, and more than that, we're not a good match. Did the idea just come to you here, on the stairs?"

"I saw you lying in bed and I . . ."

"You really do have something of Zbigniew in you. By your own account you saw me lying in bed and . . . Well, let's go. You're right about one thing. I'm truly desperate."

She put out her gloved hand and took my arm. I trembled and was seized by a sudden fear. I also had an access of adventuresome self-confidence, and it struck me that this was the same feeling a murderer might have after having successfully committed a murder. Slowly, and with measured steps, we went down two flights of stairs silently, immersed in our own thoughts. On the second floor, I stopped and let go of Minna's hand. Taking her by the shoulders, I said, "Let's do foolish things together."

She looked at me, stunned. With a sad smile, she said, "Yes, my whole life has been a chain of foolish acts."

5

ONCE we were outside, the wind and the cold seized me again, but it was not as bad as it had been earlier. Minna took my arm and insisted we take a streetcar. The mother's apartment was at 131 Marszalkowsky Boulevard. In the streetcar Minna said, "Poor fellow. You don't have the right clothes for winter. That's not a winter coat you're wearing."

"It doesn't matter."

"How can you go about wearing so little? Some want so much for themselves, then there are others who don't have a thing. Zbigniew had three fur coats, not just one. Ah, I have to laugh." And indeed Minna laughed, putting her fur-covered purse to her mouth. I thought, watching her, that she looked very Gentile. Pale skin, a short nose, green eyes. Her laughter revealed a naïveté, almost a childlike quality, of which I had not previously been aware.

Twenty-three or twenty-four. That's not so very old, I thought. True, she and Zbigniew Shapira had been lovers, and she was madly in love with him. She's not like Edusha, who slept with Stanislas Kalbe simply because he rented a room in her house. And Minna isn't looking after the proletarians of the world.

We got off the streetcar and started up the steps of Mrs. Shapira's building. The night I spent sitting beside the corpse in the clinic had reawakened all my childhood fears. At the same time, I had become almost immune. "It's the middle of the day," I said to myself, "I'm not alone. Besides, Mrs. Shapira was an old woman." Somewhere I had got the idea that the aged dead were less to be feared than those who died young.

Minna rang the bell and a small thin woman with blond hair opened the door. She had large earrings in her pierced ears. She seemed girlish, but her face was very wrinkled. Minna said, "I'm Minna Ahronson. Dr. Barabander phoned me."

"Yes, I know. Auntie spoke of you on the day before she passed away. She said she wanted to do something for you to make up for the injustice you've suffered. Please come in."

"This young man will be going to Palestine, and he's taking me with him on his certificate. His name is David Bendiger."

"Please come in. Mrs. Shapira was actually my great-aunt. I was able to be with her for these last few days, but I have a job and have to get back to work. I'm afraid of losing my job." Her features darkened, and a tear appeared in her left eye. We went into a living room in which there was old furniture, a worn rug, and a frayed velvet sofa. It had the dusty smell of an apartment whose windows were rarely opened. And yet the sun shone through those windows. Each bit of furniture seemed to breathe usefulness and comfort, as if the pleasure the old woman had taken in it had survived her death.

Then I noticed a parrot. He was perched on top of a huge cage, looking at the visitors. His feathers were a mixture of faded yellow, faded green, and other pale colors. His beak appeared to have been broken and then healed over. I approached him, but he did not take fright. He merely waved one of his wings. The woman said, "He's a complete orphan now." She burst into tears and felt about for a handkerchief.

Minna said, "May I look at her?"

"Of course."

She took Minna's arm, and both women went into the bedroom where the corpse lay.

I sat down on the sofa. All at once the parrot, in what sounded very like a man's voice, said, "Parrot monkey." For some reason this moved me. Good Lord, I had no idea I had so much affection for birds.

Quietly I paced the apartment. And yet I felt uplifted, proud. I can't go on living alone, I thought. I'll drop with exhaustion. Very well then, let me marry. She comes from a good family. Her father is a scholar. My parents would be pleased. In fact, it would be a better match than the one Aharon made.

I had forgotten that I was hungry. I spoke to the parrot, who bent his head and turned it to one side as he listened to me. "You've no idea how lucky you are," I told him. "You have a place to live. You have food and water. You're warm. You have no need of a certificate. You're not required to become a Jewish writer. There is only one thing you lack—a lady parrot." It occurred to me to wonder whether I could take him with me to Palestine: raising an orphan is considered a good deed among Jews.

I assumed that Minna would return soon, but more than a quarter of an hour passed, then a half hour. The two women came out of the bedroom and paused in the hall, where they were whispering. From the few words that reached me I gathered that Mrs. Shapira's grand-niece wanted to send word to Zbigniew Shapira of his mother's death, but she did not know his address. A while later both of the women came into the living room. The grand-niece said, "You'll forgive me for not introducing myself. My name is Mrs. Rena Kulass."

"Pleased to meet you. I'm David Bendiger."

"What will you have to drink, Mr. Bendiger? Tea, coffee, or cocoa?"

I had trouble finding my tongue. "Whatever you give me will be fine, thank you."

"I've made coffee. You'll have some too," the woman said, turning to Minna; then she left the room.

Minna said, "The old woman talked before she died and said she loved me like a daughter. How dreadful everything is! Someone has to arrange a funeral and there's no money for it. She had a little money somewhere, but it's so well hidden nobody can find it. She may have to be given a pauper's burial."

"Why is that so bad?"

"Ah, if she had known that was to be her end, she would have died three times over. What's wrong with you, you didn't shave today?"

"The water pipes were frozen where I live."

"All I hear lately is poverty, dirt, misfortune. There was a time when I heard about good things only. I have the feeling that all the malevolent forces in the world have turned on me. When I looked at the dead woman, instead of feeling sorry for her, I envied her. She looks so gentle, so much at peace. We shared a destiny. We loved a person who did not deserve our love. But she's resting at last. What you spoke about earlier—it's utterly absurd," Minna said in a changed tone.

"I understand."

"What is it you understand? You're too young, still almost a boy. The fact that you're poor doesn't trouble me at all. Now I'm also poor. And in fact, Zbigniew owned nothing but debts and hopeless, fantastic plans. But I felt protected with him. With you, I would feel like a mother. You don't look as if you could or would want to do physical labor. You have no trade or profession. Together we would make the most forlorn couple imaginable."

"You're right, it's true, but . . ."

"But what? If only you were five or, say . . . eight years older. Zbigniew is thirty-one years old. He's crazy, but he's a man. Besides, you write in Yiddish, a language no one except a few primitives can understand. It's not a language at all. Only a dialect, a mishmash. Even if you had the greatest of talents, no one would ever hear of you. Why don't you learn to write in Polish?"

"I can write in Hebrew."

"You told me yourself that there were more writers than readers in Palestine."

"Yes, it's true. But . . ."

"I don't know if I'll stay there. I'm going to leave Warsaw— that much is clear. Later we'll go over to the fixer. I'll shake him up a bit, as I told you. I don't plan to pack more than a single suitcase. Lately I've become a true fatalist. It's clear to me that the world is ruled by powers stronger than we are, and the best we can do is to yield to them. The situation I'm in now is so strange. If anyone had predicted it, I'd have thought he was making a foolish joke. But here I am. Officially, I'm your wife, and you no doubt suppose you have certain rights over me."

"No rights, God forbid."

"What can you possibly like in me? I'm in a tangle of depressions."

"That alone . . ."

"Ah, you're not in much better shape than I am. My mother has a little Yiddish phrase: 'Two corpses go dancing.' "

The door opened and Mrs. Kulass came in carrying a tray on which were coffee and cake and a little pitcher of cream. She put it down carefully on a table near the sofa and said, "My aunt was hospitality itself. The moment anyone came in, she was there with goodies. If her spirit is still around, I'm sure it wants her guests treated her way."

The three of us sat down to drink our coffee. I had a desire to down the cake all at one swallow, but I remembered that in a home like this, one had to be mannerly. I drank quietly, took small bites, and paused occasionally, the way the others did, with the result that my hunger increased. I felt my stomach stir and I was afraid it would rumble. I was reminded of the mourners' feast that Jews gave in ancient times and which now the Gentiles had taken over.

How unforeseen everything was—how strange the situations in which I found myself! How could one anticipate what was to come—not merely what the future might hold, but what might happen within the next hour or two.

We sat in silence for a while. Then Rena Kulass said, "I have to be gone for several hours. It's truly a matter of life and death. Could you possibly sit here until four o'clock?"

"But we were going to go to the fixer," Minna said, speaking partly to herself and partly to me.

"We can send Mendl a telegram," I replied.

"Well, if it's a matter of life and death," Minna said, "but you have to be back at four."

"Certainly, I'm not going to run off and leave you here with a corpse. Everything in life is hard. Even arranging for a grave," said Mrs. Kulass. "Why is everything human so complicated? Animals live and die so simply."

"An animal doesn't mind being buried in a pauper's grave," I said, startled by my own words.

Both of the women laughed. The parrot flapped its wings. Rena Kulass nearly spilled her coffee. Her eyes took on a youthful look and I could see that she must once have been beautiful. She did not look old; rather, she had become wrinkled before her time. After a bit, Mrs. Kulass said, "She would not mind either, but burying her in such a grave would trouble me. As for Zbigniew, he's gone and he couldn't care less. One way or another Zbigniew manages to avoid all responsibility."

6

BEFORE Mrs. Kulass left, she showed us where there was food in the pantry—bread, eggs, butter, cheese, cake. Sick as Mrs. Shapira had been, she had maintained a proper household.

Mrs. Kulass said that her aunt had died at the right time.

"Had she lived a few months longer, she would have had to be sent to an old people's home—or she might even have been driven into the street. Despite all the community agencies, there is no place to put a forsaken old woman. Hospitals keep the sick waiting to be admitted until it is too late. The agencies do what they can, but nothing is ever done right. When it comes to a crisis, nobody knows where to turn."

Mrs. Kulass put on a ratty fur coat, a shabby felt hat, and put her hands inside an old muff. Earlier she had powdered her face so that it now looked smooth. It was apparent that the chance to leave the house for a few hours had raised her spirits. Evidently she had noticed that I was hungry, because she urged me several times to eat.

As soon as she was gone, I went into the kitchen and grabbed some bread. A while later, Minna came in and said, "Would you like me to cook you something—an omelette, perhaps? After all, in some sense I am your wife."

I told her that I was satisfied with bread and cheese, but Minna put on one of Mrs. Shapira's aprons and busied herself at the stove. She fried a couple of eggs, then turned on the heat. The living room had been warmed by the sun, but the kitchen was cold. Evidently Minna was also hungry, because she prepared food for herself as well.

We sat at the kitchen table eating bread, cheese, fried eggs and drank coffee. I had eaten four or five slices of bread without satisfying my hunger, so I reached for still another slice. Minna, rummaging about in the pantry, found some apples and dates, which I ate. They served to swell my stomach. As a result, where I had been hungry before, I was now exhausted.

We went back into the living room and I lay down on the sofa. Minna found a shawl somewhere.

I had been living for the last few months in rooms that were either completely dark or where perpetual twilight reigned. It was only now, in this room illuminated by the winter sun, that I realized how much the constant darkness had contributed to my depression. It was not for nothing that the mystics identified the good with light. I closed my eyes and dozed off, thinking, How good it is to be well fed, to rest, and to be with someone. I also wondered how it was that I could feel so good in an apartment in which there lay a corpse.

After I slipped into a dream, I opened my eyes again. I thought I had dozed off only a moment, but the clock showed that I had managed to lose half an hour. Minna sat, her legs crossed, deeply engrossed in reading a book. I could not tell whether she was smiling because the book amused her or because it was so badly written.

Watching Minna, I realized that I really did not know her. Her features were continually changing. It was impossible to tell whether her hair was chestnut-colored or perhaps blond. Were her eyes gray, blue, green, or perhaps brown? There were times when she looked like a woman of thirty, and other times she resembled a high-school girl. I also had the impression that she was content with her own society. People like her, it seemed to me, could not possibly be unhappy.

I got up, and eager to look out, I went to the window. I studied the courtyard walls, the rooftops, the windows. What force keeps all the bricks in place and has kept them there for so many years? I wondered. What keeps all those millions upon millions of molecules from flying off into space? It's not gravity or magnetism. There is matter continually at work which takes no account of what it is doing. That smoke rising from the chimney, for example, has never heard of time, space, qualities, or quantities. It doesn't even know about existence. But for the moment, it's here. Soon it will disperse without knowing it has done so, because it is a gas. One wisp of smoke will not yearn for another. Mrs. Shapira, being dead, is like that smoke. The tragedy of the dead is that they don't know how lucky they are. If one of the dead could know how immeasurably fortunate this was, he or she might want to die a second time from sheer delight.

I turned away and went to Minna. "What are you reading?" I asked.

"Oh, one of the old woman's favorite novels. Every second line has been underlined."

"May I look?"

"Yes. I've had enough."

I leafed through the book for a while. There was a dried flower which the old woman had pressed between the pages. I put the book down, bent over Minna, and, taking her by the shoulders, pulled her up out of her chair. She looked inquiringly at me, but she made no resistance. I kissed her forehead and her cheeks, her hair and her throat. She said, "What are you doing, foolish boy?"

"Ah, I love you."

"You're a liar. You don't even know how to kiss."

I kissed her on the mouth and she kissed me back. We kissed for a long time. It was as if we were testing which of us could hold his or her breath the longest. I was overwhelmed with desire. Minna struggled with me, pushing me away. I half led, half pushed her toward the sofa. She cried out, alarmed, "The door isn't shut." I wasn't sure whether she meant the outside door or the door to the living room. For a moment, I had an impulse to put the chain on the outer door, but I was afraid to go through the dark hallway. I was a step away from triumph and did not want to lose it.

At that moment the outer doorbell rang, and it was clear that I had missed my opportunity. The forces that controlled the universe had, as they so often did, prepared a surprise for me. Minna pulled away and gave me a look that was part triumph and part astonishment. She started toward the door, but cast a backward glance as she went. One of her stockings had slipped down and she stopped to fix it in the doorway. I looked after her, feeling like someone who has just sustained a terrible injury from which he will never recover.

I listened attentively. Had Rena Kulass come back so soon, or was it someone from the Burial Society?

Then, strangely, the living room grew dark. Evidently the sun had been obscured by a cloud. I experienced a surge of fear. Maybe the dead woman had brought on the darkness in retaliation for my lack of respect. There was an interval in which I heard no sound. Minna had disappeared in the dark hallway where the rugs were piled on top of each other. Then I realized that, waking or sleeping, the thing I most feared had happened—I was alone with a corpse. More than that, I had the impression I had lived through this scene in one of my nightmares. I wanted to call out to Minna, but restrained myself—the sound of my own voice would have frightened me. I waited and heard the beating of my heart.

Finally Minna returned. She carried a letter in a bluish envelope. Her face was pale and she looked both sad and amazed. She said, "David, God exists." This was the first time she had ever called me by my first name.

"What's happened?"

"The postman's brought an express letter from Zbigniew. He's in Berlin."

"In that case, send him a telegram at once."

"Shall I open the letter. It's for his mother, naturally."

"His mother will never read it."

"No."

She started to tear open the envelope. Her hands trembled, and it was some while before she got the folded letter out of the envelope. As she read, her eyebrows arched. There was anger in her face at the same time as she smiled. Once in a while, she seemed to sneer and made a grimace of revulsion. When she had finished reading all four sides of the letter, she turned back to the first page and studied it again as if she were looking for more text in the margins. She looked at me and said, "I'm not a pious woman, but this letter makes me want to thank God."

"What's in it?"

"I'm healed, completely healed. He's the worst human being I ever met. My poor parents are right; much righter than they can imagine. I'm a fool, an absolute idiot."

"What has he written?"

"He writes his mother he never knew joy until he met this . . . person of his. Nearly word for word it's the very same thing he said to me. A charlatan, a filthy liar and a charlatan."

"That should be good news for you."

"It's not good. From now on, I'll never believe anyone. What am I to do now? I'll be embarrassed before Mrs. Kulass because I opened the letter. One thing is clear, we must send him a telegram. Let the scoundrel know that he has murdered his mother. And make him pay for the funeral. The gigolo has married a rich woman whose husband abandoned her. Wait, I'll write out the telegram. We mustn't waste a minute. Maybe you'd go to the post office to send the telegram."

"You'll stay here by yourself?"

"I'm not scared. She never harmed anyone when she was alive. Now that she's dead, she's even less likely to do so. But let's wait until Mrs. Kulass comes back. He's not likely to leave Berlin until tomorrow, and it may even be that he won't come at all. He risks being arrested here because he's a swindler, a crook. Well, I'm cured. As far as I'm concerned, Zbigniew Shapira is a corpse among the dead."

Minna put the letter down and shuddered. She gave me a strained, angry, sneering look as she said, "Now you can kiss me."

VI

HERTZ Lipmann's sister had received news of her brother. It was not in Moscow that he had been arrested but in Nyesvizh, as he crossed the Russian frontier. He had evidently made a mistake in giving the password—either that or the Soviet border guards misunderstood him. After many complications, he was at last released from prison and his sister Irike received a letter from him from Moscow.

I got this news from Edusha. Hertz Lipmann had sent her a telegram. The story that Hertz Lipmann was a provocateur and that his name had been found on the rolls of the Defense Ministry's agents was, it turned out, invented by a fellow named Adam Kronenberg who was soon going to be tried by a Party court.

Edusha wept as she told me the story. "You can be driven mad by all this stuff." If she—Edusha—had not gone off the deep end, it was proof that she was stronger than iron. She said we must both forget what had passed between us. We could still be friends, and that would have to be enough. Since Hertz Lipmann had turned out to be an honorable man, everything was changed back to the way it had been. It seemed to me that there was something false in all this, but Edusha's tears were real.

After she stopped crying, she broke into sobs again. She apologized continually: "I was left an orphan; the war turned everything topsy-turvy. I was misled by my aunt's example. I've never met the man who would really suit me. Edek was nothing more than a Warsaw fop. As for Stanislas Kalbe, well, yes, he once lived here."

Edusha let me know that she would prefer to marry me rather than Hertz Lipmann. Then she kissed me to show me that we had to part. From now on we would have to behave properly.

My brother Aharon gave me some money with which to pay Edusha a part of what I owed her. I suspected Susskind Eikhl had had a hand in that transaction. He put all sorts of opportunities to earn money in my brother's way. Though he was a leftist, still he had connections with rich people in Warsaw, salon Communists who financed left-wing publications. Susskind Eikhl knew that Edusha couldn't let me stay in the dark little room, and give me my meals, without charging me.

The truth is that my situation had improved somewhat. Every few days I got sent on jobs by Shoshana, Dov Kalmenzohn's secretary. Binyomin liked to work alongside me, perhaps because I listened to his stories and because I told him things about myself. In fact, the two of us had lived through similar tragicomedies. We had both had love involvements with our fictive wives. Binyomin had left a young woman named Basha behind in his hometown and had married a fictive wife, a Halutz named Tsila, who would be paying his expenses. I had met her on that night when Binyomin and I went to sit with the corpse. Tsila had graduated from high school and had studied at the university. She spoke Hebrew and smoked cigarettes. Binyomin and Tsila had not only kissed but were on the verge of becoming man and wife in earnest.

Good things happened to me. A young man who edited a review called *Tsvit* [*Blossom*] had taken my essay on "Spinoza and the Cabala." The magazine did not pay; in fact, the author had to pay something. I knew that in the history of literature a great many writers had begun their careers by publishing in such little magazines. For example, Romain Rolland's famous novel, *Jean Christophe*, had begun publication in such a magazine. I had rewritten my essay and my brother had edited it. It had already been set in type and I was reading proofs.

When I considered the matter, I knew very well that the desire to see one's name in black and white, in print, was a sterile lust, a form of affectation. But oh how eagerly I reached at night for a match when I woke, as I often did, to light a candle so that I might read my printed name, David Bendiger, once again. I had entered the family of literature. If I could publish nine more essays, I would become a member of the Writers' Club.

I began to fantasize about what else I would write—several novels, many short stories, even a play that would be called *The Certificate*. The characters would include myself, Edusha, Bella, Minna, her parents, Binyomin Hesheles, Tsila, Basha, Sonya, Hertz Lipmann, my brother Aharon, Zbigniew Shapira, Barish Mendl, and the spats maker who wanted to marry Sonya. Perhaps Dov Kalmenzohn could be included as well. But how was Act One to open?

This much was certain: the third act would have to take place in Palestine. I bought myself a notebook in which to write down ideas, themes. I also wrote out a program of things to do—when to get up, when to write, when to read.

But how could I keep to a program when I didn't have a proper place to live and no income and no clothes?

It was strange that I had received a notice to present myself before a military committee though I was still two years or so short of twenty-one. I was sure this was because Barish Mendl had given the draft board my name; he was angry at Minna's refusal to give him the additional money. My passport was delayed at the government office. Minna had already put a deposit down on the tickets. Everything involved money.

Zbigniew Shapira did not come to his mother's funeral, but I knew that Minna had gone to meet him in the free city of Danzig. Her father, Meir Ahronson, told me about it himself. He said, "What's the point of it, eh?"

Though I myself led a licentious life, the licentiousness of the women nevertheless shocked me. How could Minna go off to meet Zbigniew, after having had a relationship with me, and when he was married to someone else? Somewhere in the world there had to be people who would take love seriously. If women behaved like men, then we would have another generation like the one that was destroyed by the Flood. Or, to put it another way, would men be able to indulge themselves if every woman was really faithful?

Minna had gone away quietly all by herself, probably to meet Zbigniew Shapira at a Danzig hotel. As for Edusha, she was going to be reunited with Hertz Lipmann.

Sonya invited me to have lunch with her and Mendl. Her aged employers had gone away on a trip, and Sonya was playing hostess. Mendl was a short, stocky fellow with a look of kindliness in his dark eyes. Sonya had apparently terrified him with how important I was. He stammered when he spoke to me and did what he could to use foreign words and phrases. He kept saying, "That which," "Above all," and "Generally speaking." He removed his small hat from his pomaded head and put it back on again. He scratched his neck under his stiff collar, smoked cigarettes, and sucked mints to make his breath smell good.

Mendl brought news from his hometown. Little was being done there for culture. The fanatic Hasidim had broken into the library and torn up literary books. A Zionist delegate from Zamosc had been invited to speak, but the Communists disrupted the meeting; every time he started to say something, they hooted and whistled. A rich American Jew came to town who wanted to donate money for a course on "The Development of Civilization," but the rabbi sent for him and, together with the rest of the town's fanatics, persuaded the American not to donate money to "freethinkers."

To put an end to such exalted talk, I asked Mendl to tell me about spats-making machinery. He promptly described the machine he used and how one passed the leather through it; how the leather must be cut to the shoe, how one had to be careful not to cut off a finger.

When Sonya brought in the food, I noticed she had put on a new dress. The conversation naturally turned to the Jewish situation. Mendl had served in the Polish Army and fought against the Bolsheviks. He had been wounded, yet the Polish soldiers continued to call him "Bolshevik," "Trotsky," and warned him that the time would come when they would massacre all the Jews. Even when the Polish soldiers treated him well, Mendl was uncomfortable with them. He couldn't tolerate their language, their lascivious speech, their stories which continually turned on the spilling of blood. Even officers used the language of the gutter. They drank brandy out of water glasses, made jokes about death, illness, and the sufferings of animals and humans. And in peacetime were things any better? Jews were hated and oppressed in all sorts of ways. On the train Mendl had taken to Warsaw, a Jew had been beaten; the Gentiles had tried to throw him off the train. Mendl said, "It'll never be any good here."

"In that case, why don't you go to Palestine?" Sonya asked.

"They won't give me a certificate. The spats maker's trade doesn't exist there."

"Then who makes spats there?" she said.

Mendl did not reply. He began to pick his teeth with a toothpick. A bit later he said, "The Jews don't all have to go to Palestine."

Sonya took me aside and whispered, "Well, what do you think?"

"He's a decent fellow."

"I'll have to sleep with him, you won't."

Mendl and I said goodbye to Sonya and went off together. Mendl was to spend the night at an inn on Franchishkaner Street. He told me he had paid for a private room, but that on the very first night two other beds had been made ready in his room for other guests. He said, "Words have no meaning in this country."

As we parted, I shook his hand. He pressed my hand twice. "Say a good word to Sonya about me," he said. "Sonya thinks the world of your opinion."

I waited for a night streetcar, and though I stayed half an

hour, it did not come. Sonya had asked me to come back to spend the night with her. I had no desire to return, and moreover, the watchman would not let me in anyway.

What's the point of marrying if women behave like this? I wondered. How can a modern man know if his children are his? Some years ago, I had read Strindberg's *The Father*. At that time I had not fully understood the problem and had merely appreciated the beauty of his style, the authenticity of his dialogue, and the mystery that lay behind the words. Now suddenly I understood the tragedy of modern man. He had undermined his own foundations and had turned the mother of his children into a whore.

Whenever a young man got to know me, the first thing he talked to me about was his dealings with girls and women, how every man was deceived. The women demanded money for clothes, shoes, jewelry, summer houses, and then gave themselves to the nearest passing stranger.

My father used to speak of intellectuals as playboys and used to curse the Yiddish writers as poisoners of youth. Now I understood his point of view. But how could one maintain the purity of the family without believing that the Torah was given to the Jews on Mt. Sinai?

I unlocked the door of the apartment and found that Edusha was still awake. She told me Dov Kalmenzohn had telephoned to say that unless we left within a week, he would give my certificate to someone else. Edusha said, "What's the biddy waiting for—Count Potocki to fall in love with her?"

Edusha had had a letter from Hertz Lipmann. He had told her that he could stay in the Soviet Union if she would join him. He had written, "You know that I'm not sentimental, but I've literally kissed the soil of our socialist nation."

2

I TELEPHONED Minna several times that day, but was told she was not at home. I called Dov Kalmenzohn and he agreed to hold my certificate for another few days. I had to explain the whole situation with Minna. Kalmenzohn replied, "If she's still having anything to do with such a phony, she's not what we want in Palestine."

Somehow the winter had gone by without my being aware of it, and spring was here. Oh God! If I'd survived this winter, I must be stronger than steel.

Edusha had lost her job in the furniture store. Aunt Bella had been released on bail from prison. She and a whole group of Communists whom the prosecutor had lumped together were to be tried later. They could only be tried together, since the prosecutor claimed they were all members of a single conspiracy.

Bella came out of prison as haughty as when she went in. She had received packages in jail from Edusha and from the Party. She was evidently a functionary of some sort, because she was not required to do any work. As soon as she got home, the telephone began ringing continually. Susskind Eikhl resumed his visits and even brought my brother.

One evening I heard my brother's voice in the living room. When I went in, everyone laughed. My brother went with me to look at my "salon," as he called my dark little room. He took a book down from a shelf and said, "Who is this Stanislas Kalbe?"

"A former tenant."

"Another do-gooder!"

"No, just a rich young man."

"What's happening with your certificate?"

As my brother asked that question, the telephone rang and some instinct told me the call was for me. I ran out into the hallway, picked up the receiver, and it was Minna. It seemed to me that her voice had altered. There was amusement in her voice as she said, "Are you still there?"

"Where else would I be?"

"On the moon . . . or on Mars."

She said that she had to speak with me. She wanted me to come to her house at once. I was eager to go because I felt uncomfortable in the presence of my brother and Edusha. Susskind Eikhl watched me with an amused look in his eyes. Bella had asked me whether I had behaved properly. They all knew I had spent weeks alone with Edusha in the apartment, which led to all sorts of quips. I tried to practice self-hypnosis to keep from blushing and made use of Emile Coué's formula. In the library I had found a translation of a book on self-hypnosis by Charles Badouin, I had read Pallot's *The Development of the Will*, but in my brother's presence I lost my courage. I blushed and turned pale. I had trouble talking, and when I did say something, the words came out clumsy and foolish. I had turned into a schoolboy once again and I was playing the role of a naïf.

I snatched up my coat and started to make my farewells. Bella said, "Why are you running off? Your brother's here. He came especially to see you."

"It's an urgent matter."

"It has to do with your certificate?"

"It's been withdrawn, the certificate," Edusha interposed. "His fictive wife went off to Danzig to see her former lover."

I threw Edusha an angry look. She had no right to chatter about the secrets I had confided, but she wanted to impress my brother. She flirted with Susskind Eikhl and slapped him teasingly on the wrist. It was clear to me that she was making herself ridiculous, but perhaps she was being attacked by the same emotions that were troubling me.

My brother asked, "Where are you going?"

"He's had a phone call from a young woman," Edusha said.

"You've got two beautiful women here at home."

"Nobody values what they have at home," Bella said.

"Make a man of him," my brother said. "I sometimes think he's still a schoolboy. It wasn't so long ago that I led him off to school. It seems like only yesterday."

"I'm beginning to understand why a thousand years is as one day to God," Bella said.

"If you're up in Seventh Heaven sleeping, even a million years doesn't amount to much," Susskind Eikhl said. "I gather that, according to Einstein, even time is an illusion."

"I think you mean Kant," I said. "For Einstein, time is relative, but it has nothing to do with illusion."

"Look at him. Talks just like a grownup," my brother said, amazed. "Then you understand Einstein's theory?"

"I've read a book about it. I myself believe that time is neither relative nor an illusion. Neither time nor space exists."

"Just the same, a woman carries a child to term in nine months, not in ten."

"It isn't time itself that matures the infant but a variety of processes. It isn't time that ripens an apple but the sun. A person doesn't age because of time but because there are changes taking place in his heart and his veins. Time is no more than a designation, the way this house is designated as being on Leszno Street."

"My brother's really perking up," said Aharon.

"One can change the name of the street, or even the name of the town, but nine months remain nine months."

"Only if you compare a woman's belly to the trajectory of the moon around the earth. The comparison doesn't hold water."

Bella gave me an angry look. "Try sitting in jail for a while, young fellow, and you'll see that time does have significance. Each day seems as long as a year and the winter nights drag on like an exile. Try working fourteen hours a day, the way they used to work in the factories, and you'll know that time is not merely a designation."

"It was the work that tired them, not time."

"Foolishness and quibbling," my brother said. "Really, David, you ought to be ashamed to repeat such blather. Immanuel Kant sat in Königsberg and never budged. And even though he did not believe in time, his watch was as punctual as everyone else's. He was never so much as a second late to his classes at the university. Well then. And what is space?"

"Emptiness. Nothing."

"But there is more nothing between Warsaw and Moscow than there is between Warsaw and Radzymin. How can there be more of nothing?"

"He's an utter child," said Bella. "He crams himself with all that book stuff and thinks he's eating holy noodles. Time is nothing. Space is nothing. Next you'll say that money's nothing."

"Money is something."

"Well, thank God. But where is it to be found? And be good enough to straighten your necktie."

"You call that a necktie? It's a string, not a necktie," Susskind Eikhl said, and snorted through one nostril.

Everyone laughed. I noticed that Edusha did not quite participate in the laughter. She sent me questioning looks, evidently annoyed that I let myself be teased.

I wanted to justify myself. I wanted to compare time and space to the number zero, which acquired value only when it was set beside other numbers. But I was aware that Minna was waiting for me. Besides, they wouldn't understand me. Having spent my nights digging at these ideas, I had come to the conclusion that the categories of reason were no more than symbols and that they could be represented by other symbols or names. Humankind needed to orient itself continually by signs, or by an address. Time and space were no more than the memory's indicators. All of human existence was no more than a huge address book.

I left the house and went to Minna's. After what had happened between us, I had begun to love her. But her journey to Danzig to see Zbigniew Shapira had spoiled things. She had betrayed both him and me, and made a mockery of her feelings; of the entire tragedy itself.

I climbed the steps to the Ahronsons' apartment and rang the bell. Meir Ahronson, who opened the door, was wearing the same shabby bathrobe, the same worn slippers, the same flattened cap as the last time. His wrinkled face had a yellowish cast. It seemed to me that even his beard had shrunk. His right eye was shut, as if it were blind. His left eye under its shaggy eyebrow regarded me with keen amusement. He said, "Well, now what? You're still here? I thought that by now you were at the Cave of the Fathers."

"You know that I can't travel to Palestine without your daughter."

"I'm damned if I know what my daughter wants. What made her run off to Danzig in the midst of everything? Your entire generation has lost its head."

"Evidently she's still in love with Zbigniew Shapira."

"Ha! That's not love, it's madness. She's shamed us all. Well, if you live long enough, you live to be shamed and scorned. But I pity my poor wife."

"God will help you."

"Where? Not in this world."

I knocked on Minna's door and found her sitting on the paint-flecked wicker chair. She looked thinner and younger, and in some way foreign. She was wearing a dress I'd never seen before and her hair had been either combed or cut differently. She had a cigarette between her lips. Her legs were crossed so that her knees were exposed. She emanated worldliness and the self-confidence of one who is indifferent to everything but her own needs and caprices. The look she gave me had in it the same sense of amusement that I saw in her father's. "Well, and how is the Don Juan of Byaledrevne?"

"How is Zbigniew Shapira?" I replied.

"Mad, as always. Sit down, here on the bed." I sat down on the edge of Minna's bed. She looked me over, hesitantly. "I'm sorry to have to tell you this, but I've had to cancel my plan to go to Palestine. In my present situation I have to ask you for a divorce," she said, attenuating her words. "I'm sorry, truly sorry, I've dragged you into a mire."

"What's happened?"

Minna knitted her eyebrows. "Oh, it's a long story. I don't know quite how to begin. But what difference does it make to you? My life is such that it's beyond clarifying. If you divorce me, you can travel with someone else. Maybe with the young woman from your hometown, the one you really love. You told me about her—what's her name?"

"Lena."

"Yes, Lena."

3

MINNA talked as she smoked. Sometimes she grimaced, sometimes she smiled. She said, "It's not in my nature to tell intimate things about myself to anyone. If anyone had told me that I would reveal myself this way to you, I would have thought him absurd. But after what has passed between us, we can hardly regard ourselves as complete strangers. And then, in some sense, you are my husband.

"I had to talk with him. I had to see him," she said in an altered tone. "Much of my agony came from my inability to understand his motives. That is . . . I both did and did not understand them. It was only in Danzig that it became clear to me that Zbigniew had hypnotized me. That I had all the symptoms of one who is hypnotized. That happens when, though your mind is entirely clear, you are nevertheless compelled to obey someone else's dictates. I thought that, if we were to meet again, he would remove the spell that he had cast over me. What is a spell, after all, but a form of hypnosis? And that's why I went to him. When I got there, he was waiting for me at the train station. He looked handsomer than ever. His new wife—she has a strange name, Eulalie—was not with him. She's a daughter of a rich family in Germany, but she lives both in Lausanne and in Paris. Her parents are now in America. They conduct important business matters all over the world. Her first husband was a French Army officer; she's had a second husband too. Zbigniew is her third. That's what she says. For all I know, he is her fifth or her tenth. She's mad about him and squanders money left and right."

Without knowing why, I asked, "Is she . . ."

"Is she Jewish?" Minna completed my question. "Yes, she is. Or anyhow, her father is. But her other two husbands were Christians. But what does religion mean to people like that? She could become a Muhammadan tomorrow. When I met her, it seemed to me that she and Zbigniew were wonderfully suited to each other. How could it be otherwise? Each of them is ready to stride across dead bodies for the sake of their own pleasure. Besides, she's rich, so she can afford her cynicism. I've never met a woman as cynical as she.

"Where was I? Yes, he was alone when we met. The first thing I did was to tell him I was married. He turned very pale, and that gave me a moment of satisfaction. He asked, 'And where's the lucky fellow?' I said, 'He's a yeshiva student from a small town who wants to be a Yiddish writer, and he's five years younger than I am.'

"He stared at me, then asked, 'Why did you do it? Why did you do it?' I had to laugh. We went into a café and sat there until closing time. Later he telephoned his wife and she joined us.

"Now don't be embarrassed by what I'm about to tell you. When she came in, she flung her arms about me and kissed me as if we were sisters. Is she beautiful? It's hard to say. She has a sort of degenerate beauty. She suggested neither more nor less than that I come to their hotel. She was very straightforward about it: 'We have a wide bed. It'll accommodate the three of us comfortably.' I gazed at her, and it struck me that he had hypnotized her as well. Though she was herself thoroughly perverse, he was the source of it all. Or it may be the other way around, and she had seduced him.

"All my life, I've tried to train myself not to be surprised by anything. But the surprises come anyway. You meet someone who looks different, is different, thinks differently—as if he or she came from another planet. Only a week before I thought that if I were to meet this woman, I'd choke her to death or plunge a knife into her breast. And yet here we were, sitting together, and she was calling me by my first name. I had no idea that a woman like this could exist. I had never encountered such a woman in Polish literature, not even in French literature. Evidently Zbigniew had praised me to the skies, because the next thing she did was to suggest, quite openly, that we all go on a round-the-world journey together."

"Are you going to do it?"

"I don't know. All I know is that I can't break up with him. That's the terrible truth. Logic has nothing to do with it. We were together in Danzig, and later in Zapat. And guess whom we talked about? A good deal of our talk was about you. That was strange enough. As I said, I told him all about us, and he was fascinated. He turned immediately into a Jewish nationalist, a Zionist. He wanted me to telephone you at once and ask you to come to Danzig. He offered to find a translator for your essay, or to send you to Berlin to further your studies. She got excited too. They imagined that you had the black hair and the burning dark eyes of a typical Jew. When I told them that you were fair-complected and had blue eyes, their enthusiasm cooled a bit. But then their excitement returned. Naturally, everything with them has to do with moods. They are nationalists one minute and cosmopolitans—or whatever else pops into their minds—a moment later. There's something wild and infantile about her, and he too turns foolish in her presence. They sleep by day and are awake at night. They drink champagne for breakfast. My guess is that she takes drugs. One thing is clear: I have no reason now to go to Palestine, it would be utterly senseless."

"Dov Kalmensohn sent me a telegram. He said that if we don't leave for Palestine at once, he'll give my certificate to someone else."

"I'm sorry about that. Oh yes, we can leave the country and

go to Berlin, where we can get a divorce. I know very well what you're thinking about me, but you haven't yet learned just how demonic the power of love can be. I was dead the whole while Zbigniew was gone. Or, to put it another way, I was a corpse in motion, animated by some force like galvanism or some similar power. But the moment I saw him again, I came alive—literally. I suffered. No one who has not had my experience can know just how deep my anguish was. But it was the anguish of one who was alive. Not the petrified dullness of death. The truth is, I have no need to justify myself to you. Nor will I justify myself to my parents. How can I possibly make excuses when I know that they are a thousand percent right."

"What do you mean to do?"

"We've made an agreement—the strangest agreement ever made between a man and a woman. I told him, 'I'm in your hands. Do with me what you will.' I said it in front of her, and both of them swore that they would not abandon me so long as they lived. Crazy, isn't it? But life is filled with madness. They want me to go with them on their trip around the world. They want to spend long periods of time in China, Japan, India. She has a daughter by her first husband who's staying with her grand-parents in Lyon. But the grandmother isn't well and can't look after the child any longer. The French I studied in school will prove useful now. Yes, if you want to call things by their right name, I'll be her daughter's governess. I don't believe that even in Dante's *Inferno* anyone has ever imagined a punishment quite so ingenious as this one. But I've accepted it because it allows me to be near him."

Minna's eyes shone. She had the look of someone who has come to terms with disaster. She smiled.

I said, "Why would his wife agree to such a thing?"

"I don't know, and it may be that I'll never know. And perhaps she doesn't know why either. Millionaires—those who have tasted all of life's pleasures—suffer from boredom. Who knows? She divorced two husbands, and when I asked her why she had done it, she replied, 'I don't know. It got tedious. I've forgotten why.' I know I ought not to be the one who says it, but she's quite a sympathetic person. She's taken my man, but I can't dislike her. And that, in and of itself, is a dreadful surprise to me. As far as my parents are concerned, I've all but cut myself off from them. I've turned myself over to the Devil utterly."

"I think we have to go to Dov Kalmenzohn so we can explain matters to him."

"Yes, of course. We can go at once. Oh yes, there's something important which I forgot to tell you. Something that will utterly blacken my name in your eyes. I took money from my parents to pay for my trip. There was a time when I thought of my father as a rich man, but compared with what I've seen over there, we were poor even in the best of times. Zbigniew's wife squanders money, and so does he. He never thought it was sinful to take money from other people, no matter who, no matter when. I tell you this simply to reassure you that you won't have to suffer financially from my decision. I'll cover all your expenses."

"No expenses. If I get the certificate, someone else will pay them."

"Yes, of course. But one can't always be sure. What will you do if you don't get the certificate? My impression is that Kalmenzohn was acting on my behalf."

"Yes, that's true."

"Come, let's go outside. I feel uncomfortable in my own room. My parents treat me as if I were an enemy."

We went down in the elevator. I realized that Minna was wearing an elegant new yellowish fur coat. She looked rich. When we were outside, she said, "My dear friend, I won't go with you to the Halutzim unless you'll have something to eat with me. You look very pale and, if you'll excuse my candor, downright famished. Are you fasting?"

"No, but . . ."

"Come, we'll have something to eat. And a cup of coffee. Though it's still cold, it's spring. I don't know whether men feel this way, but when spring breezes begin to blow, bringing with them scents from God alone knows where, I get all wound up. The feeling is properly called 'spring fever.' I sense that good luck is nearby, but where? Come, we'll go into Number 38. We ate there once."

"Thank you."

"What will you do if you don't get the certificate?"

"I don't know. I may have to go back to my town in the provinces."

"If you have an emigration passport, we can get you a visa to Germany, or at least a transit visa. Once you're there, you can always get an extension on your time. Or even get a residence permit."

"What would I do in Germany?"

"I don't know. But anything's better than to settle down in some small town. One can't depend on them . . . but I've already told you. They've both expressed a desire to help you. I mean Zbigniew and his wife."

"But I would never go to them."

"Ah, why not? I'm the one who's made a shameful choice, not you. You haven't done a thing to be ashamed of."

We went into the café, and Minna ordered rolls, cheese, an omelette, and coffee for me. She ordered cocoa for herself. The sun was shining, and I observed that there were already some flies in the café, humming around the chandelier. Mixed with the smells of coffee, herring, and milk were other odors, of earth, forest, and river.

Minna was silent for a long while. Occasionally she glanced at me as I sat there eating. Then she said, "I could have loved you, if only you were ten years older, but you're still a boy, a downright boy. But I'm not sorry for what we did."

"You shouldn't have told Zbigniew Shapira about us."

"You don't like that. But you don't know the sort of person he is. People like him have severed all connection with the old rules. What was beautiful they regard as ugly, and the other way around. I think the idea's expressed in *Macbeth* somewhere. It seems to me that all mankind is moving in that direction. Take today's music and dance—even the hats the women wear. In Germany, there's a popular play called *Pleyte*. I think it's a Yiddish word. What does it mean?"

"It's used to mean 'bankrupt.' "

"Yes, the person in the play has gone bankrupt, and he acknowledges it himself. I'm an example of the same thing. I'm bankrupt in every sense of the word—completely, absolutely."

4

IT seemed to me that my life was without coherence, or like a tangled novel that had stretches of bleakness and tension, a book too painful to read, too fascinating to put down.

Bella told me directly and clearly that I had to vacate the dark little room. She intended to put her own bed into it. I went to see Dov Kalmenzohn, who told me that my certificate had been withdrawn. He was irritable when he spoke of Minna, but he let me know that I deserved a considerable share of the blame. The British consul had already informed the Polish commissariat that he had withdrawn my visa. The government office had consequently delayed issuing an emigration passport. Minna thought it was Barish Mendl who had betrayed us, but finally, what difference did it make?

Minna wanted me to divorce her because she neither could nor would travel on papers that indicated that she and I were married. Everything had to be done quickly, because Zbigniew Shapira and his wife were waiting impatiently in Berlin. Before leaving Warsaw, Minna wanted to place a tombstone over Mrs. Shapira's grave and to sell the furniture and other objects that were left in the apartment. The old woman had a safety-deposit box in a bank somewhere, but Zbigniew did not know where. In addition, a quarrel had broken out between Minna and Rena Kulass. Zbigniew telephoned from Berlin daily. He had hired a lawyer in Warsaw, actually the same former captain of legionnaires with whom Minna had threatened Barish Mendl.

The events that followed proceeded at a feverish, hallucinatory pace that no one seemed able to control. Minna and I went to a rabbi on Kupyetska Street and he gave us a divorce. We sat on a bench, and the scribe wrote with a goose-quill pen. Our witnesses were two Jews who were learning how to seal marriage contracts with the appropriate script. The rabbi sat turning the pages of a book and sighing. We nearly did not get the divorce, because Minna could not be sure whether her Jewish name was Miriam or Mindl or both names together. The marriage contract was in Barish Mendl's office, and he swore that he couldn't find it. Minna telephoned her father, but Meir Ahronson appeared suddenly to have become deaf. Minna, speaking to me in Polish, said that she had always hated Judaism, and if they intended to make trouble for her now, she would convert to Christianity. Meir Ahronson was suddenly able to hear what was wanted of him and said that Minna's name was Minna Mindl, and that she had been named after a grandmother. I could hear him scolding Minna on the telephone, shouting, "You're not my daughter anymore, and I'm no longer your father."

We sat on the bench and Minna spoke to me in Polish. "What is it these Jews want? Why do they trouble the world? What makes them so sure that they know what God wants? And why, if they are so pious, are there speculators who buy up whole blocks of houses with inflated currency? It's true that most Jews are poor, but it's that small number of rich adventurers who create anti-Semitism."

As for herself—Minna said she had no real relationship with them. If the truth be told, she had no relationship with the human species itself. She had but a single wish—to forget. To stupefy herself with an opiate or some other narcotic so that she would no longer remember anything. "In fact," she said, "you don't really need a divorce, because I'm dead." She took my hand and then released it. The rabbi's wife opened the kitchen door and sent baleful glances at us, because people who were getting divorced were not expected to sit together or whisper to each other. The rabbi tugged at his beard and said, "It's not too late. You can still be reconciled."

Everything was done according to religious law. Minna put her hands out and I handed her the divorce. The rabbi told Minna that she would have to wait ninety days before she could be married again.

Once outside, we took a droshky to the lawyer's house. Oh, spring was truly here. The swans in the Krasinski Garden were out on the lake and children were throwing bread crumbs to them. The trees were in blossom. Birds were chirping. Sunlight glowed in the gutters. Was it possible that Purim had come and gone and I had not known it? Yes. I had completely lost a Purim. I might as well have been a convert, a Gentile.

Something within me murmured, "*Vayhi ba'yemei Akhashverush* [Now it came to pass in the days of Ahasuerus]." And suddenly I saw my father, my mother, and the short thick candles we lighted on the evening of the Purim feast. The loaf was partially sliced at one end; the table was laden with Purim baked goods that would be distributed to relatives and friends. I experienced a nearly physical pain. Was I so far gone that in Warsaw, the most Jewish city in the world, I had overlooked a religious holiday? Yes, I had abandoned God and He had abandoned me.

Minna took my arm. "What is it, young fellow?"

"Oh, nothing, nothing."

"Who knows? Maybe we're making a mistake. We might have been happy together."

The lawyer we went to made us wait in his hallway for three-quarters of an hour. Then he called Minna into his office while I waited in the hallway for another half hour. Then he called me in and gave me papers to sign. I signed them unread.

His windows looked out on a garden. The parquet floor shone.

Each sheet of paper on his mahogany desk had been smoothed out. Portraits looked down at us from the walls. In the corners of the room there were vases filled with flowers. This was no chancellery, it was merely a parlor. The lawyer was a tall, portly man with a snub nose, a square chin, and a short neck. The blond hair on his head stood up like a brush. He gave off a sense of ease and strength such as I had never known or imagined. Like me, he had lived through the war. He had even been wounded at the front. But he was in his own home, in his own country. He was dictating something to a secretary. He spoke on the telephone, clearly, easily, with a firm voice, with the calm of someone free of pressures and entanglements.

"Yes . . . fictive . . . certificate . . . to bring more Jews into Palestine . . . I understand."

He said goodbye to Minna and kissed her hand. Then he gave me a huge warm paw.

Outside, evening had fallen. It was cool, but it was a coolness stirred by warm breezes. Water flowed through the gutters. I smelled leaves and flowers. Minna took my arm and we strolled for a while, with no goal at all. I had no idea what street we were on. Through the curtains on the windows one could see the glow of chandeliers. Somewhere a piano was being played. Behind those balconies, behind those curtains, deeply rooted families survived, and neither wars nor occupations could budge them. Below, the wet asphalt street glistened like a river in which the passing cars and droshkies were reflected.

I felt terribly tired and at the same time had the sense that time had never begun and space had never ended. Life had always pulsated; death forever lay in wait.

We came to a café and Minna said, "Let's go in. We'll have something to eat."

The restaurant looked too elegant for the way I was dressed. I adjusted my tie and buttoned up the coat which, a little while later, I would be unbuttoning. The well-dressed patrons raised quizzical eyebrows and exchanged glances on seeing us come in. My shabby jacket was an ill match for Minna's fur.

We took a corner table and sat down. There was a mirror opposite in which, all the while I was there, I could see my image—my collar frayed at the edges, my loose necktie, the dangling wisps of what was left of my red hair, the pallor of my face, my sunken cheeks, my thin neck, my keen blue eyes, the curl of my lips. I'd been married and, as luck would have it, divorced as well. I had had a certificate and it had been taken away. I was having a snack with my divorced wife, who never stopped talking about Zbigniew Shapira. She said, "He deserved it, deserved it utterly. It made me happy to tell him that I'd been with someone else. He turned as pale as this tablecloth."

"Miss Minna, the tablecloth isn't pale." Minna glanced at the tablecloth.

"Why do you call me Miss Minna? I'm no longer a miss. We'll have to invent a new word for someone like me. The lover of someone who has married someone else so that she can go to her lover who has married someone else. Then she gets a divorce so that she can become a governess to her lover's stepdaughter. Isn't that funny? Try putting that on the stage! Tell me, just what are you going to do after I've left the country?"

"I've already told you that I have nothing specific in mind."

"Just the same, you'll have to go somewhere and do something."

"Go back to Byaledrevne. Teach Hebrew . . ."

"If you want to leave the country, you don't need an emigrant's passport. Come to Danzig with me. From there, it's easy to smuggle yourself into Germany."

"No, Miss Minna, I'm not going to drag along after them."

"Everyone drags along after someone. They lie down in a doorway crying, 'Let me in or I'll die.' My poor mother clings to my addled father, I cling to Zbigniew, Zbigniew has latched on to his millionaire . . . and so on. The truth is, we ought not to have divorced each other. You could have come with me as my husband. Zbigniew would not have objected to that at all. On the contrary . . ."

"Too late, Miss Minna."

"Why? We could remarry." The waiter brought cheesecake and coffee. Minna said, "Where will you go from here? To your dark little room?"

"It's not mine any longer. I have to vacate it in a day or two."

"Where will you go? Move in with my parents. They have another room to rent. And when I'm gone, they'll rent out my room as well."

"You know that I have no money."

"I'll pay for the first three months. I'll give you the money and you can give it to them. They won't take anything from me. My father calls me a street whore, and maybe he's right. But it's not easy to find a tenant. They're afraid of all sorts of complications. That count who moved in left after a week. He had a wife with whom he had quarreled, and then they made up. All these troubles will kill my poor mother. Move in with them; my father loves you, he can talk Talmud with you, or Yiddish. As far as he's concerned, you're his son-in-law. He's not likely to have another son-in-law ever. Move in. It'll be good for all three of you."

"That would be a funny situation."

"Everything I do is funny. Come, let's go home. I have money and you can give them a deposit. Maybe you can find something to do in Warsaw. I feel guilty where you're concerned. You've lost your certificate because of me. Oh God! I hurt everyone—my parents, and you, and myself as well. What I'm about to do will put a stain on my character forever. I feel—literally—as if fate were driving me to destruction. And I have the bizarre feeling that Zbigniew may have regretted the whole adventure. I'll arrive only to find that they've gone away somewhere. I'm caught in a spiderweb. Finish your cheesecake and let's go. I can't sit still any longer. It's as if there were a motor whirring inside me. I've never experienced anything like it."

VII

THE telephone rang early in the morning and Bella came to tell me that it was my brother Aharon. I got into my pants and went into the hallway to the telephone. Aharon's voice trembled as he said, "Father has come to Warsaw."

"*Father?* Where is he?"

"He's here, but we have no place to put him. I heard a knock at the door, and there he was."

"When was that?"

"Last night. I could hardly recognize him. He's gotten smaller—or maybe I'm imagining it. With these pious Jews, nothing has changed in hundreds of years. I opened the door and there he was, holding his prayer-shawl sack and carrying the same little valise he used when he went to Radzymin. He's got hemorrhoids and has to have surgery. He hasn't got any money at all. We had no place to put him, and at the same time he refused to eat anything here. I telephoned you, but you weren't at home. I can't tell you what it's been like. My father-in-law offered him his own bed, but Father couldn't possibly sleep in the same room with a woman. He wouldn't even drink a glass of tea here, though the Tsinamons keep kosher. I haven't slept a wink all night. I wanted to take him to a hotel, but he wouldn't have it. I haven't any money anyway. What's to be done? I'm absolutely desperate. Maybe you could take him somewhere."

"Where?"

"Have you any money?"

"Not a penny."

"What a mess! Come right away. He keeps talking about you. If you haven't shaved, then don't. He's given me a long lecture about my beard. I had to put my hat on and recite the evening service with him. Ida put a kerchief over her hair. The whole house is topsy-turvy."

"Where did he sleep?"

"We gave him our alcove. Ida and I slept on the living-room floor. The noise woke the baby and we couldn't get him back to sleep. Then Father insisted on our hand washing and all the rest of it. The truth is, I've nearly forgotten all those injunctions. He was about to go to sleep when he asked whether the mattress contained any forbidden linen-and-wool mixture. How would I know? It's enough to drive you mad. I finally persuaded him to eat a bit of dry bread. He brought no clothes with him but a shirt and his four-cornered undergarment. Not even a bathrobe. Jews like him have learned absolutely nothing. I've just taken him to a synagogue; he was determined to be with a prayer quorum. And I'll have to fetch him when he's done. He seems to have forgotten what Warsaw is like. He evidently never knew any other part of the city except our street. If he stays here, it'll literally be the end of us."

"I'll come at once."

"I've got to go make corrections for the printer, so I won't be here. They're holding the proofs for me."

"I'll get there as soon as I can."

Soon after I hung up the receiver, the phone rang and Edusha answered. She said it was for me, and when I asked who it was she said, "An old man."

Could it be my father? Could he have got my phone number? Was he calling me from somewhere near the synagogue? No, that was impossible. I picked up the receiver and asked, "Who is it?" There was no reply and I said, "This is David, David Bendiger." It suddenly occurred to me that it was Meir Ahronson. There was a rattling mixture of sighs and stammers. I heard him ask, "Is it you, Dovid?"

"Yes, Mr. Ahronson. It's me."

He was silent for a while; then he spoke clearly: "Dovid, could you come at once? Something's happened here."

"What is it?"

"I can't tell you on the telephone. Please come at once."

"Mr. Ahronson, my father's just come to town and I have to go see him. He's waiting for me. What's happened?"

"I can't tell you on the phone. When can you get here?"

"Maybe by noon."

"It has to do with Minna. She's done . . . something. Well . . . come when you can. Excuse me." With that, Meir Ahronson hung up. Edusha, standing in the living-room doorway, asked, "Was that your fictive father-in-law?"

"Yes, Meir Ahronson."

"What's happening? Your fictive divorcee's having a baby?"

"Edusha, it's not funny."

"Why not? They're all off their rockers. They can't live alone and won't let anyone else live in peace. What's happened, eh? Anyhow, I'd like to meet your father. Some of the times when you went off to see your fictive wife, your brother told interesting stories about him—a naïve man, but an honorable one."

"You know that my father won't look at a woman?"

"You do enough looking for the two of you. Well, that won't do the revolution any harm." Edusha hesitantly closed the door.

I thought, Well, she's back on intimate terms with the revolution. I didn't know what to do. Should I go to my father, or should I run over to the Ahronsons' to find out what Minna had done? Maybe she had killed herself, or tried to. I remembered her saying, "One can always jump off a ship."

"I'm ready for all sorts of trouble," I said to myself. It seemed to me that in the midst of all the turbulence what I felt was indifference, a sense of fatalism, a certain stillness. If only I had a clean shirt to wear! I was embarrassed to visit my brother's in-laws wearing a wrinkled shirt. The hooks on my shoes were twisted and the soles were worn again. Everything was all contrary—my father's reproofs, the in-laws' comments, the ironic looks I got from Lola. No, I had not shaved, but my father would consider me shaven just the same.

I dressed slowly. I would be leaving Edusha's tomorrow or the day after tomorrow. I'd already stopped taking my meals here. Yes, but if Minna was dead, I could hardly move in with her parents. My mother used to say that nowadays people were cruel. Now I saw how right she was—even about me. I was not concerned about anyone. I could do whatever I wanted—leave it all behind, run off where I liked. I realized that if I had money for a train ticket, I'd go to the station and leave them all behind, even my father.

I put my coat on and went out. I wasn't hungry, and yet saliva filled my mouth. I went into a grocery store and bought a roll, eating it as I walked. I had gone some little distance along Iron Street when I was overwhelmed by curiosity to know what had happened to Minna. There was not much I could do to help my father, I thought, justifying myself. I turned back hurriedly— nearly running. I ran up the three flights of stairs and rang Meir Ahronson's doorbell. Mrs. Ahronson opened the door to the length of the chain. Her face looked yellow and blotched here and there with green. The whites of her eyes, too, had a yellow cast to them. "What do you want?" she asked.

"Mr. Ahronson phoned me. He asked me to come."

"What for, eh? Wait a minute."

Mrs. Ahronson shut the door and angrily pulled the latch to. I studied the door which, until that moment, I had never really examined—a broad door decorated with carved molding, with a mailbox and a brass plate on which the name M. AHRONSON was incised. The wood was painted a mixture of brown and red. "And yet whoever made the door must have intended to give someone pleasure," said the chatterbox within me, the compulsive thinker. "The Marxists hold that behind every *exchange* value lies a *use* value. If no use is made of all these carvings and decorations, the work has been a waste."

I heard footsteps, and when the door opened there stood a woman in her late twenties or early thirties, a slender woman with a long nose and hollow cheeks. She wore a dress with a high collar. It failed to hide a deep scar under her chin—the sort of healing scar one sees after an operation. She wasn't dressed like a nurse, but something about her—an air of authority—reminded me of a hospital supervisor. She wore low-heeled shoes and a fashionable dress whose sleeves reached her wrists. Her light brown hair was worn in a bun, and her gray eyes took my measure with insolent familiarity. She said, "Miss Minna is ill. Seriously ill."

"What happened?"

"Are you David Bendiger?"

"Yes."

"Come in."

When she opened the door, she made a movement with her arms as if to keep me from going farther. Casting a backward glance, she said, "Mr. Bendiger, Miss Minna has had an accident. A dreadful accident. She's in bed now, and the doctor says she must have rest, complete rest. She has been talking about you, and she sent for you, but I'm afraid your visit will only disturb her. I'm related to Minna. I'm Miss Sabina Ahronson. My father and Minna's father were brothers. Until recently, I've been working as a supervisor in the Jewish Hospital in Tshiste."

"What happened to Minna?"

"Ah. She came home yesterday. Suddenly she had a nervous breakdown. She began screaming and tearing at her clothes, at her wedding outfit. She did something to her throat as well but, thank God, it's not serious. They called the emergency service, and they treated and bandaged her."

"Is she asleep?"

"No, she's awake. Indeed, she's quite normal now. But one can never tell. She keeps asking for you. The doctor says she'll be all right, but you have to avoid anything that will make her angry. In these cases one can't be sure how a patient will respond.

There is always the danger that . . . My uncle thinks it would help if the two of you could talk things out. I'm aware of the whole situation; it's unbelievable."

Miss Sabina spoke softly, sadly. When she had need of Polish words, she gave them an unusually distinct pronunciation, like a teacher of diction. Somehow it had never occurred to me that Minna had relatives in Warsaw, since she had never mentioned any.

I said, "You must do what you think is best."

"Go in to her. But if, God forbid, she becomes hysterical, please leave the room at once. My impression is that she's calmed down completely. I've had years of experience with psychotherapy and I've seen all sorts of cases. I think she'll be fine."

"Thanks so much."

"Wait, I'll tell her you're here."

2

MINNA, her throat bandaged, lay in bed. She was propped up on cushions. It seemed to me that the room had been cleaned up and some furniture had been added. Books were no longer lying about. There was even a rug on the parquet floor. Minna had never looked so fresh and young as she did this morning. On a chair beside her bed there was a velvet-bound book with gilded pages—Novalis's *Hymns to the Night*—and half a glass of tea with a slice of lemon. Miss Sabina showed me to a chair and said, "I'll be out in the hall. If you need me, call."

"I'll be completely calm," said Minna to her relative in a voice that sounded strangely clear and normal, coming from someone who had just had a nervous breakdown. "You can go to sleep."

"Well, we'll see. Actually I'm not sleepy. In my profession, one learns that sleep isn't nearly as important as people think."

"What can be better than sleep?" Minna asked.

"Many things. Well, I'll be going. If you'll take some advice, Minna, don't get too involved in particularities—and all the rest . . .".

"Don't worry, everything will be all right."

"Call me if you need me." With that the door squeaked shut behind Miss Sabina.

"She's a typical old maid," Minna said. "She's my cousin, but years have gone by without our seeing each other. Suddenly she shows up and behaves like a sister. I asked my father to call you. He said your father was in Warsaw. He's come, no doubt, to see your brother."

"My father's not well. He needs an operation."

"Everyone has his troubles. I'll never understand what happened to me yesterday, nor do I want to understand it. It wasn't me but literally someone else."

"Ah!"

"Sit down. Have you had something to eat?"

"Yes. I've eaten."

"The doctor gave me a sleeping pill. But I woke early this morning and I've been thinking things through. The real fault lies, as always, with my mother. Though she's in perilous health herself, her single worry is that I'm not going to make use of my wedding outfit. She nagged at me so long that something in me burst. It was only later that I realized what I had done. I'm embarrassed because I couldn't even die successfully."

"There's no reason for you to die."

"Best not to talk about that. But since I can't die, I'll just have to live. David, Zbigniew mustn't know what happened here—at least not yet. I was going to call him today at his Berlin hotel, but I can't speak to him from here. For the time being I've got my cousin nursing me around the clock. I've sent for you to ask you to do two things. First, I want you to send Zbigniew a telegram. I wrote it out this morning with a pencil. I hope you'll be able to read my handwriting. The second thing is, if you lose the room you're in, you can move in here. The count has vacated his room. He removed his things in the middle of the month. His wife came and helped him to pack. It's all very funny. I'll give you money so you can make a deposit. My father was very pleased and excited when he heard that you might move in. My mother doesn't like you very much, but then she's suspicious of everyone. She has paranoid fantasies. She'll have to be sent to a hospital soon in any case. She has jaundice, and who knows what else."

"I don't want to move in if she's against it."

"She's no more against you than she is against everyone else. She's frightened of strangers. That's her peculiarity. At least she won't worry that you'll rob her. My money's there, in the lowest of the albums. There on the shelf. Will you hand it to me, please?"

I gave her the album. When she opened it, I saw a bundle of bank notes, including American dollars. Minna raised herself up and reached under her pillow, from where she took a piece of paper and a pencil. She counted out money, then counted the words she had written, after which she corrected the text of the telegram once more. She kept glancing at the door, prepared to hide what she was doing in case her cousin came in. It struck me that I had never seen Minna so calm, serious, and practical as this morning. She handed me two bundles of bank notes and said, "Put these in different places. This money will cover the cost of the telegram; the rest is enough for a single month's rent. Ask my parents how much they want for the room. We've already talked about it; they won't overcharge you."

"Really, Miss Minna, if you can worry about me at a time like this, you've got to be the noblest woman I've ever met."

"Please don't praise me. If you'd been here yesterday, you'd have seen what I'm capable of. My first impulse was to attack my poor mother, but the Good Lord kept me from such an ugly end. If I'd harmed her, I couldn't have lived for another day. My father would have died too. So you see, there is God's mercy even in such cases."

"I didn't know you were religious."

"I didn't either. It seems to me that the last time we spoke I talked like an atheist. Well then, now you see another contradiction. If someone can leap completely out of his skin, then let's have no further talk about consistency. If only I had ended it all. All that really happened was that I destroyed some clothes which had cost my parents a fortune. I also did a certain amount of harm to myself. If my neck is scarred, I won't be able to go to Zbigniew. He's a dreadful aesthete, an absolute perfectionist. When we walked in the streets and a cripple passed us, he shut his eyes. That's what he's like."

"When do you want me to pay the rent—now?"

"No, a little later. Maybe tomorrow. I don't want them to suspect anything. Don't go yet. There's something else I want to say. What's going to happen to you after I've gone? You have to eat too. And your suit looks worn out. Especially your trousers—do you sleep in them?"

"No, but they don't get pressed."

"You can't neglect yourself that way. If you want to be a writer, you've got to be properly dressed. Can't your brother help you?"

"He's broke too. And he has a wife and child."

"Why did he come here if he can't find any work to do? Evidently yours is a family of bohemians. Mine, too, is baked of the same dough. My father gave a factory away for nothing. As long as I've known him, he's been a consistent loser. He squandered not only his inheritance but my mother's dowry as well. Thank God, he doesn't have anything left that he can risk.

"I want to tell you something else. My younger sister did not die a natural death. She committed suicide. When she had an appendicitis attack, instead of going to a doctor, she went dancing. I'll end the same way, but I'll have to wait until they"— Minna pointed to the door—"are gone. One more funeral, one more week of mourning, that would be too much for them. If you move in, you'll be here a great deal. I'm talking to you as if you were family—I don't quite know why. I lay here all morning thinking only about you. Besides my family and Zbigniew, you are the only one I feel close to. I used to have girl friends, but it's been years since I've been close to anyone.

"Strange as it may seem to you, I spent more time with Zbigniew's wife than with him. There are some things one can't talk about with someone of the opposite sex. Men have no patience with the things women talk about. And they don't understand either. Yes, I'm dreadfully lonely and that's why I do irrational things. You won't believe me, but I worry about you as if I were your mother or an older sister. I ought to have married you for real. For one thing, you're dreadfully young. And then I think that you're not really capable of loving anyone. Or, to put it better, of *committing* yourself to anyone. That's what tells me you're really a writer."

"I'm committed to you."

"No, you'll forget me as soon as I'm out of sight. And it's better that way. There is one thing that seems strange: I'm not a homely woman . . . or at least I wasn't homely when I was young. Besides, I'm no fool, and I've had an education. And yet with all that, no one has ever loved me. Zbigniew's behavior had nothing to do with love, though now he swears by all that's holy that he'll love me till the day he dies. Well, you can go now. Be here tomorrow to pay the month's rent. And bring your things, if you have any."

"I don't have anything."

"That'll make it easier for you to move."

Impulsively I said, "Miss Minna, may I ask you something?"

"What do you want to know?"

"You don't have to reply, and don't be angry at me for asking. No matter what you say, my good opinion of you won't change."

"What do you want to know?"

"In Danzig, Miss Minna, in Danzig did you and Zbigniew . . . You know what I mean."

"Yes, I know what you mean. But why do you want to know?"

"Because I'm a writer."

"You're a strange young fellow. Yes, I did. And his wife knew about it. But I wouldn't let her involve me in the perversions she wanted—in orgies, as a matter of fact. I'm not quite that decadent—or perhaps I didn't have the courage to be. But I lived in their hotel, only a few doors down from their room. He is the only man for me. What I did with you was nothing more than an act of desperation—sort of a moral suicide. I thought I had been healed of my love for him and that what I did would help me end my dependence on him. But it didn't work. He called and I ran to him like a dog whose master beats it. It still responds to his whistle and runs to him, eager to lick his boots."

"Then you'll still be his mistress."

"I'll do whatever he wants."

"May God help you!"

"How can God help someone like me? Well, now you know everything. Don't forget to send the telegram. Come here, kiss me. In case we don't see each other again, try to think well of me."

"Why won't we see each other again? You're not that sick."

"You're right. If the doctor would let me, I could get up. But I feel that in some way I've come to the very last margin of my existence. They say that life is hope, and I've lost all hope. Yet I've retained desire, which seems inexplicable. In a situation like mine, one can die in spite of good health. I have the feeling that that's what happened with my dead sister. She loved someone who cast her off and she arranged to die. Now that I speak of it, it strikes me that her lover was a sort of Zbigniew, of a slightly lower class. Be here tomorrow morning. Come here and kiss me," she said again.

I bent over Minna and kissed her on the forehead, then her hair, her eyes. She kissed me back, murmuring, "A boy. Truly a boy . . ."

3

AFTER I sent the telegram off to Zbigniew Shapira, I went to meet my father. The door of the in-laws' apartment was opened by Lola, who looked amused on seeing me. I went into the alcove and there was my father. He was a short, stocky man with red sidecurls and a red beard, in which there were signs of gray. His shabby hat had a spotted hatband. Through his open coat, his broad ritual undergarment showed. There was an open book on a small table as well as a scarf that my father was using as an *eruv*. When he saw me, a look of childlike delight came into his blue eyes. He made a movement, as if he meant to get up and embrace me, but he stayed seated, regarding me with a mixture of embarrassment and wonder. He was ashamed of the way I was dressed and of the situation in which we found ourselves. I wanted to kiss him, but he put his hand out by way of greeting. "It's you," he said, "it's you."

"Father!"

"The Lord be praised, we meet again. When Joseph's brothers met him in Egypt, they did not recognize him because he had acquired a beard. But you . . . you're easy to recognize."

"I don't shave . . . I use a scissors," I said, quickly inventing a lie.

"Why should a Jew be ashamed of his beard? Man is made in the image of God. Well, sit down, sit down. I've been here since yesterday. I've kept asking about you, but evidently you live far away. I've completely forgotten what Warsaw is like. I went to a synagogue to say my prayers, and a young man brought me back here."

"Father, I hear you're not well."

"Ah well. That's why I've come, I have to see a doctor. Your brother had to leave. You should have come sooner, but I guess you were delayed."

"I had to send a telegram."

"Oh? Where?"

"To Berlin."

"A business matter, eh?"

"Not exactly."

"Ah well, may God speed the matter. One thing, though—never forget that you're a Jew."

"How can I forget it?"

"Aharon tells me that you've gotten some sort of permit to go to the land of Israel. You wrote to us about it. Are you really going?"

"No, nothing has come of it."

"The land of Israel is no small matter. It's been said that anyone who doesn't live in the Land has (God forbid) lived the life of an idolater. But under what circumstances can that be said? Only in the case of an individual who goes there to commit sins, to display his unbelief."

"But I'm not going."

My brother's father-in-law, Reb Laizer Tsinamon, came in and greeted me coldly, nodding his head at me and at my father. Then he mentioned a doctor who was a hemorrhoid specialist, but one had to pay him in advance. He told us how he too had had hemorrhoids on which Dr. Soloveitchik had performed an operation. Salves and other such remedies were only temporary expedients. "A boil has to be cut," he said with finality. Having made his pronouncement, he turned and left the room. Then his wife, Shayndele, came in. She stood in the doorway regarding us with a look that was both kindly and reproving. She had been a famous beauty in her youth, and she had nets of wrinkles in the corners of her eyes and a double chin. There was a look of diffidence and a touch of grief in her face, the wry look of a mother none of whose hopes has been fulfilled. Turning to me, she said, "What's happened to your certificate? Normally when

people get a certificate they use it. How can you just lose something as important as that? What happened to the woman you
married?"

"Married?" my father asked, stupefied.

"No, Father. It was just a formality. Required by the Gentiles.
So that I could take her with me."

"Be careful about such things. You might be committing a
crime."

"It's all right, Father. Everything's fine. The young woman
simply changed her mind." I winked at Shayndele, hoping she
would understand that I didn't want us to talk about this in front
of my father.

But Shayndele was relentless and shook her bewigged head.
"Why did she change her mind?"

"It's a long story."

"Evidently it wasn't fated to happen," she said. "What if you
took my daughter Lola? She has accomplished nothing hanging
about here in Warsaw. She's trying to find a job, but there are
no jobs to be had. She is an educated, well-behaved girl. She
didn't get her diploma, but what good's a diploma? If she were
a Gentile, she'd have a job in a government office or some such
place. If Gentiles can barely hold a pen, they're considered nobility, but Jews can't get anywhere. If she were to go to Palestine,
that would be a load off my mind. They say that it's easy to get
married there. A young woman must marry."

"With God's help, she'll find her bridegroom," my father said.

"Amen. But meanwhile it's hard. If only the apartment were
bigger," Shayndele said, altering her tone. "But we're crowded
together here like poultry in a coop."

"I'll leave today," my father said.

"I didn't mean you. You're family. But it's hard for you too.
You ought to do your Torah study at a real table, and not on
that wobbly little thing."

"Torah can be studied anywhere."

"I know, I know. I come from a family where Torah was

studied. But it has to be available. My father, may he rest in peace, had a roomful of books. He used to sit at a table and drink tea from a samovar. When Father was studying, we children had to be quiet. My mother, may she rest in peace, used to say, 'Hush, children. Your father's studying.' In those days Torah really was, as they say, the best merchandise. But who cares about Torah nowadays? A dandy with a curled mustache gets a fine dowry, while no one wants a scholar. Bench pressers, they call them. Who is willing nowadays to provide room and board for a scholarly son-in-law? That war of ours has turned everything topsy-turvy."

"Still there are Jews studying Torah," my father said. "Occasionally I go to Reishe, to Torna, and the synagogues are full. When the word 'Torah' is sounded on a holiday in Belz, the synagogue is so packed that you can't fit so much as a pin inside it. Jews, thank the Lord, have remained Jews."

"That may be true in the small towns, but here the touch of the Gentile is on everything."

Aharon's wife, Ida, was not at home—she had gone to her work in the hospital. Little Gershon—or Grisha, as his mother still called him—was asleep on a cot in the bedroom.

My father tugged at his beard and asked me, "What do you do? How do you make a living?"

I did not reply at once. "It's not easy."

"You're a teacher, eh?"

"Yes, more or less."

"What do you teach? Writing?"

"Yes. Writing, reading."

"There's nothing to be gained by teaching, Dovid. Of course knowledge is nice, but you can't make a living from it. A young man your age ought to get married and settle on a way to make a living."

"Who would marry someone like me?"

"Ah, conduct yourself like a Jew and there'll be plenty of interested parties. I live in a small town, but there are some prosperous folk there who are interested in making good marriages. They'll give you a dowry and support you as well. If you don't want to become a rabbi, you can open a store of some kind. Things haven't changed so much."

"No, Father, you're wrong. The world *has* changed. The Poles don't want us. We're thorns in their sides. They're doing what they can to drive us out."

"It's always been that way. But God won't permit it to happen."

"Father, I don't mean to make you unhappy, but the truth is, I don't want to be a merchant, and I don't want to be supported by a father-in-law. I'm no longer that kind of man."

"What kind of man are you? You've cut off your beard, but I don't see that you've become rich. Your brother has told me everything. You're both of you poor; neither of you has a place to live. Here I am, and I have no place to stay. There's no place for me here, the apartment's too small. Your mother (God protect us) is not well. It occurred to me that maybe a rabbi was needed on Krochmalna Street. I could move back there. There are still Jews there who remember me."

"It's impossible to find an apartment. Even for a tiny place, you have to pay key money."

"They don't have many books in my little town. They have the six volumes of the Talmud and some other books, but not enough. I want to write on Rabbi Alkazi's *Rights of the Firstborn* and the books I need can be found only in large towns. It is written that 'a workman must have his tools.' "

"I don't think you'll be able to find an apartment here. It costs money to move to Warsaw."

"I could live alone for a while. Later I'd send for your mother and your brother Moishe. He, God be praised, is studying. He is a fervent follower of the Rebbe of Belz. He's a teacher and a God-fearing man."

"Why isn't he getting married?"

"He's too young and he's waiting for you to go first."

"He ought not to wait for me. We're going down different paths."

"In God's own time, he'll marry. It's true that even in the small towns the world has changed. Young women want a bread-winner and who knows what else. You, for your part, are too enlightened, while he is too much the studyhouse scholar. How long is our life? We've been sent into this world to study Torah and to perform good deeds. That's the goal of creation. Of course, one needs to eat and to have clothing, and one can manage that one way or another. What did our Father Jacob ask for? 'Bread to eat, and clothes to wear.' The world asks, Why is it written 'bread to eat'? Everyone knows that bread is to be eaten and clothes are to be worn. Then why is it written, 'to wear'? The reply is 'Bread *enough* to eat. But not a superfluity.' One of the great Talmudists is quoted as saying, 'While the soul is on earth, it needs the body, but the body must not be indulged, lest it think it is the one that is important.' "

"Yes, Father. But people nowadays lack faith."

"What do they believe in? In this world. In that case, why do they need these wars?"

Shayndele poked her head in and said, "I've made tea."

4

WE sat at the table drinking tea and eating *kichl*. Reb Laizer Tsinamon was saying, "The gross are inheriting the earth." Turning to my father, he said, "You live off there in your little town among your books. You have no notion what's going on here. How could you know? But if you're in business, you see it. It's the ignoramus everywhere who has the power. Prosperity can result from war, but in wartime it's usually the clodhopper who's on horseback. They made a soldier of my Max, and how could he prevent it? Mutilate himself? Things aren't the way they once were. Besides, the Poles conscript you no matter what condition you're in. They're on to all the tricks. I went with Max to the conscription office. It was like turning a lamb loose among wolves. And I'm not talking about the Gentiles only. Our own people too. While they wait for the doctors to examine them naked, they play a sort of game. One man bends over, puts his head against the wall, while the others slap at—excuse my saying it—they slap at his you-know-what. And if he guesses who's hitting him, that fellow has to take his place. What sort of a game is that? What kind of sense does it make? Crude stuff. But for raw youngsters it's something to do. They wanted my Max to play the game, but he refused. So they taunted him and would have beaten him, if the doctor hadn't returned."

He continued to ramble on. "On Krochmalna Street, where you used to be a rabbi, they've all become Communists. They say quite openly that if they achieve power, they'll kill all the cultivated Jews. Your son—my son-in-law—has just come from Russia. Ask him, he'll tell you. Here in the little towns where there are Bolsheviks, the blockheads have formed mobs to beat those Jews who are bourgeois. They've dragged householders off to Russia and who knows where else. They plucked out a rabbi's beard. In Russia itself things are dark indeed—human beings have no worth at all. The Gentiles launch pogroms, and the Jewish Communists torment religious Jews. They invade synagogues and steal the books to use as waste paper. They create all sorts of havoc. They've mounted up in their man-made heaven, where they've discovered there is no God. So what's to become of us all, eh? If God means to send the Messiah, what's taking him so long?"

My father gnawed at his lip as Reb Tsinamon talked. He pulled a gray hair from his beard and studied it. He felt the glass of tea to see whether it was still warm, then pushed it a little to one side. He took his skullcap from his head and fanned himself with it. "If we are worthy of his coming, he will come."

"Right you are. But this generation won't be worthy," Reb Tsinamon concluded.

"Who knows, perhaps it will be utterly guilty," said my father, as if he were both asking and answering a question.

"What do you mean? Surely Jews like you believe in the Messiah's coming."

My father smiled. A flush came to his cheeks as he said, "How can we know the ways of the Lord? It is written, 'Since He is the Author of all, then all things are good.' "

Reb Tsinamon said he had to leave. My father and I went back to the alcove and he smiled as he looked at me, as if he wanted to ask for a favor but was afraid to. He said, "Dovid, would you like to study a page of Gemara with me?"

"Now? Here?"

"Why not? I have a Gemara in my prayer-shawl sack. Come, let's study a page."

"What's the point? Oh, all right."

My father opened the Gemara to the section on laws and customs governing prayer, the use of *tefillin*, the reading of blessings, and to various exempla in the Talmud. He particularly liked the story of Rabbi Yossi, who went to pray among ruins and heard a humming like a dove's: "Woe to the father who has driven his children away, and woe to the children who have strayed from their father's table." And the story of King David, who hung his lyre facing north, and when the wind blew, the sound of the lyre woke him and he carried on a conversation with God, in which he compared himself with the kings of the east and the west.

Since we were reading from a single volume, I had to move close to my father. His beard touched my face. I smelled his cheap tobacco, his snuff, and some other odor that was at once familiar and long forgotten. He had put a little pillow on his chair to sit on. He bent his head over the page. How well I knew all this—the Gemara, Rashi, Tosaphot. I recognized every word, every letter. Again Rashi asked the ancient question: "Why do the Jews in France recite their evening prayers and the 'Hear, O Israel' while it is still daylight?"

I did not need to listen for an answer. I knew it all by heart. I knew that this Mishnah had been studied hundreds of years ago, five hundred years, a thousand years, fifteen hundred years, and so on. Jews have been pleading, "Hear, O Israel . . ." for countless thousands of years, while the Lord continued to do what He liked. He guided the stars in the sky and devoted Himself to comets, planets, protons, electrons. He was a physicist, a chemist, an astronomer.

My father began to read more loudly; then he sang the text, giving it the ancient melody. I was embarrassed, thinking the Tsinamons would hear: "Father, not so loud."

"What's the matter? Does the Torah embarrass you?"

Dusk fell and my father said, "Can you take me to a synagogue? It's at 40 Shlishke. I'll find my own way back." He took his stick and put on his hat. It seemed to me that he shuffled rather than walked. He tapped his stick. The children in the courtyard looked at us with derision. A Gentile boy made a face, stuck out his tongue, and yelled, "Kike!" Nothing had changed. We were still objects of "shame and contempt." I indulged myself in fantasies of power—inventing an airplane that traveled at the speed of light. Somehow I acquired an explosive that could uproot mountains, overturn seas, and incinerate cities, countries, the entire globe. I punished all the enemies of the Jews. Using my explosive, I drove the English out of Palestine. The people of the Diaspora could now return, bringing an end to their suffering. Since God had not seen fit to send the Messiah, I would redeem the tormented people of Israel. As for that little Gentile boy, I would teach him a lesson he would remember the rest of his days.

My father said, "I have missed Warsaw. It's a Jewish city."

I finally got him to a synagogue. There he held on to my arm and said, "Don't go. Stay and say the early evening prayers with me."

"Father, I don't have time."

"Gentile! Recite the evening prayers."

I began to recite Ashre. What could I do when my father had bidden me stay? He said, "You're not wearing a waistband, eh?"

I stood beside him as I recited the Eighteen Benedictions. He leaned against the wall and sighed. I heard him strike his bosom as he recited the penitential prayers. Was it possible that he never had doubts at all? I wondered. I looked around. The synagogue lights had not yet been turned on, but there was a glimmer of light from what was left of the candles in a six-branched candelabrum. Jews were swaying back and forth. Here and there a young man raised a fist toward heaven. Nations had fallen, systems had altered, plagues had come and gone, but here everything was as it had always been. It was almost beyond belief. Where did they get their sense of certainty?

The sun had gone down and there was now a purple glow among the shadows. Little by little, Jews were leaving the synagogue. Only the prayer leader was left, and he waited for my father to finish reciting the Eighteen Benedictions. Evidently they knew my father here and would help him get back.

I left after the early evening prayers and walked the streets. Night had fallen and lights were shining on the sidewalks. Mannequins in the store windows were dressed in the latest fashions. The moon swam across the sky. The stars seemed to ignite over the tin rooftops. What was to be done now? What was there for me to begin?

Like Minna, I seemed to have come to the brink of an abyss or been driven into a dead end. I could not bring myself to have faith either in God or in the world. I passed a movie theater before which hung a poster of Charlie Chaplin. How appropriate was this image representing God on earth, since it stood for worldly culture, success, and progress. For God's sake and for His ilk, it seemed one had to build barricades and kill people or be destroyed oneself. I could not decide whether to laugh or cry. I knew I had to escape, but where could I run?

I turned into Leszno Street, and my feet, of their own accord, carried me to the house where Bella and Edusha lived. I unlocked the door, but the apartment was dark. Neither woman was at home. I struck a match and saw my backpack in the hallway. I lighted the gas jet and everything was suddenly clear: I had been evicted from my little room. My cot had been removed to make room for Bella's bed.

I had no right to be offended. I had been very well and even generously treated in this house, but there was a lesson here. Some part of me was glad that I would not have to say goodbye. I took my backpack, turned out the lamp, and started down the stairs. I moved with a curious slowness—as if I were an old man or a cripple. *Adieu*, Bella. *Adieu*, Edusha, I thought. I won't forget you to my dying day.

Spinoza says that substance and its endless attributes require that our moduses should encounter each other for a while. I could not help thinking that, on the other hand, "a while" itself is only another form of modus.

I started off for Minna's house. I still had the money she had given me for a month's rent. But after a moment or two I stopped. I couldn't possibly move into the apartment where I had a fictive wife, to whom I had given a fictive divorce, and where my fictive in-laws lived. I myself was nothing more than a fictive writer. No, I was finished with Warsaw.

I started off in the direction of the Danzig train station. There was enough money to buy a ticket to Byaledrevne, and I knew the train left late at night. The noises of the city sounded all around me; I felt an inner stillness I had never experienced before. "Pardon me, Minna," I murmured to myself. "Pardon me, Aharon. Pardon me, Father. There's no way I can help any of you."

I grew tired of walking and stopped. I looked into a hardware-store window in which pliers, knives, scissors, screws, and faucets were displayed. At a gate, I bought a roll. One had to eat. In this matter, surely, there was no free will.

As I gnawed on the roll, I came to a stop once more, this

time before a sausage shop. I stared at the sausages hanging there and spoke to them silently:

"You were once alive, you suffered, but you're beyond your sorrows now. There's no trace of your writhing or suffering anywhere. Is there a memorial tablet somewhere in the cosmos on which it is written that a cow named Kvyatule allowed herself to be milked for eleven years? Then in the twelfth year, when her udder had shrunk, she was led to a slaughterhouse, where a blessing was recited over her and her throat was cut."

My reverie continued. Was anyone ever compensated for their final sorrows? Is there a paradise for the slaughtered cattle and chickens and pigs, for frogs that have been trodden underfoot, for fish that have been hooked and pulled from the sea, for the Jews whom Petlyura tortured, whom the Bolsheviks shot, for the sixty thousand soldiers who shed their blood at Verdun? Even as I stood there, mulling these matters over, millions of people and animals were dying. Many men and women were trapped in prisons, in hospitals, on open streets, in cellars, in barracks. Good for you, Father, that you believe! It may even be that you're right.

I went to the train station and got on the line for tickets. It was a crowded line but—since time did not exist—what difference did it make how long I waited?

Translator's Postscript

The Yiddish version of *The Certificate* was serialized weekly in the pages of the *Forward* in 1967, when Isaac Bashevis Singer was sixty-three years old, but it may have been written much earlier. It is impossible to shake the feeling that one is reading a very young man's book. It is certainly the most playful of Singer's long fictions. It is an alert, ironic, and, I think, youthful imagination that has David Bendiger standing before a sausage shop, apostrophizing the sausage that was once a cow named Kvyatule, almost in the same breath in which he lumps together his grief for the deaths of slaughtered cattle, chickens, pigs, frogs, and the sixty thousand soldiers who died at Verdun. Or when he mulls over Kant's *Prolegomena* as, in his stockinged feet, he climbs the stairs to the shoemaker's alcove to wait while his shoes are being resoled. Or his musing as he watches the shoemaker at work:

> Not long ago I had read that each atom was a sort of solar system. I, David, the rabbi's son, was sitting in the midst of eternity, turning with the earth on its axis, which in turn was circling the sun. I myself was an entire cosmos. Yet I also felt very fearful: I was a cosmos that had nowhere to spend the night.

That freshness of vision extends to the wide-eyed way in which David Bendiger encounters the not yet fully coherent twentieth century: to the intrusions into his life of the telephone, or of automobiles bearing down on him; to his sense of himself as an unripe writer timidly adrift on the sea of literature, or as a lover puzzled by how short and how ambiguous the journey is that carries him from innocence to experience as he becomes involved with not one but three women.

The world Singer refracts for us through the eyes of the not-quite-nineteen-year-old David is a construct of bright scenes around a somber center, all of it framed by the tumultuous recent history of Europe. David feels like an old man because he has "lived through epochs" that include the Russo-Japanese War, the war that we call World War I, the February Revolution, the October Revolution, and the Polish-Bolshevik War. Now it is 1922 and the Europe he knows is in a welter of political, social, psychological, and spiritual upheaval as Communism, Fascism, Zionism, feminism, atheism, and received religion compete for attention and loyalty. David, Talmud-trained but secularized, chooses to have no loyalties except to his own sensibility, which, because he is so young, is constantly at the mercy of his appetites. These include—alternately and with almost equal force—a passion for women, for philosophy, for Jewish religious speculation, and for Walter Mitty–like fantasies.

So much for the fictitious David Bendiger. *The Certificate*, however, is something more than fiction. Its basic story is retold in Singer's autobiographical *A Young Man in Search of Love* (1978). There we learn that his brother Israel Joshua Singer helped him get a certificate of immigration to Palestine from the Palestine Bureau and that Isaac did indeed get involved in a plan for the sort of fictive marriage that he describes in *The Certificate*. This story resembles the novel in some ways, except that the year of the events is 1926 instead of 1922, the young woman with whom Singer would have made a fictive marriage is Stefa, not Minna, and the name of her fiancé is Mark, not Zbigniew. Stefa, like Minna, came "from an affluent home and was deeply in love with her fiancé." She too is a modern, educated young woman who smokes cigarettes and has advanced views—but the real-life Stefa, unlike Minna, was three months pregnant at the time she and Singer connived to outwit the British Mandate in Palestine.

There are poignancies in *The Certificate* as well as fun. Not least among them is the windowless room in which David lives in Bella and Edusha's home. There is the charged but unachieved Sabbath lovemaking between David and Sonya in the shuttered ladies' clothing shop, and the love scene between David and Edusha, when she turns to him for consolation after Hertz Lipmann's arrest. There is the fictive marriage between David and Minna, during which the poles of the wedding canopy are held by two porters, a beggar and a newspaper vendor. And there is David's shy and frightened first visit to the Writers' Club, which becomes possible only because his older brother takes him there. Finally there is the scene between David and his Orthodox father, as the passionate believer and his passionately skeptical son rock together over a volume of the Gemara.

At the somber center of it all, of course, is the story of Minna Ahronson's squandered life, which reminds us that, however youthful and whimsical Singer was when he wrote *The Certificate*, he already knew—as he would tell us later—that "the real writer's gold mine is the outside world, its constant changes, its bizarre complications, the various human characters, man's passions, follies, errors, hopes, disappointments, especially in love." Especially in love.

LEONARD WOLF